Whatever He Wants

By

Eve Vaughn

Dedication

I'd like to thank my readers for their continued support of my work. Writing has always been my passion and I appreciate the emails, shout outs and awesome reviews that mean the world to me. You guys give me the motivation to keep going.

To Nia for keeping me on track making sure I don't slack off. Thanks girl!!

Deidra, thank you so much for your encouragement and making me laugh.

And most importantly, to my partner, lover, best friend and husband. I love you. Thanks for putting up with the late nights, the crazy mood swings and helping me make this story happen.

This is a work of fiction. Names, characters, places, and incidents are products of the author's imagination or are used fictitiously and are not to be construed as real. Any resemblance to actual events, locales, organizations, or persons living or dead is entirely coincidental.

Book publication August 2014

A broken spirit…

Having suffered through an emotionally abusive childhood, self-doubt constantly plagued the shy and reserved Noelle Greene. When she finds herself at a crossroads in her life, entering into a relationship is the last thing on her mind…until she meets James. She soon finds herself in over her head when James makes an offer not of love, but of convenience.

A fractured soul…

James Rothschild has one goal in life: to be powerful enough to overshadow his shameful past. In order to achieve his goal he clawed his way to the top of the business world, associated with all the right people, and dated women with impeccable pedigrees. When he meets Noelle, she's just what he's looking for...in a mistress.

Noelle is consumed by James' commanding presence, and immediately falls for him. Though she's willing to give him whatever he wants, will James realize Noelle is exactly what he needs before it's too late?

Chapter One

"Come out with us tonight, girl. You can't stay holed up in your ivory tower all the time."

Noelle ignored her cousin's sarcasm. Simone meant well but she simply didn't understand how things were. She wouldn't have minded hanging out but things were complicated right now. James expected her to be here when—or if he arrived. And the couple of times she hadn't been, he'd made his displeasure known. He hadn't been around lately but he never told her of his comings and goings. It was a pattern they'd fallen into, he'd show up when he felt like it and she'd be at the penthouse, eagerly waiting. As pathetic as it was, she lived for those moments when they were together. "I don't think it's a good idea. James—"

"Can bite the big one." The irritation in Simone's voice was clear. "You're a grown-ass woman, why do you need to ask his permission to hang out with your cousin?"

Noelle tensed upon hearing such hostility directed toward her lover. "I don't have to ask his permission for anything. And I go out occasionally. Did it occur to you that I just don't want to go out tonight?"

Simone snorted. "Do you hear yourself? Occasionally? You're not a dog to be let out. Can't you see this thing you're involved in isn't healthy? You deserve so much better, girl."

Noelle squeezed her eyes shut. Hearing criticism of any kind was a tough pill to swallow but when it involved her relationship with James it hurt like hell. This wasn't the first time Simone spoke disparagingly about James, but tonight the cut seemed a bit deeper. It came on the heels of seeing James in the society section of the newspaper with the stunning redhead Noelle had met previously. The article focused on their newly announced engagement.

Noelle tried to tell herself it didn't matter. After all, he'd never offered her anything more than what she had: a luxurious penthouse, a closet full of expensive clothes, jewelry, access to his black card and credit accounts at all the top retail stores in the city. Some would say she was no better than a highly paid whore but in her mind there was a huge difference. She didn't stay for the gifts. She stayed for the man and she desperately wanted James to see that.

Noelle took a deep breath. She didn't want to exchange angry words with her cousin who had always had her back. "Look Simone, I know you don't like him and that's your prerogative not to but it's my decision to be with him and I wish you'd respect that."

"Whether I like him or not has nothing to do with it. How he treats you is quite another. I don't like that shadowed look in your eyes when he hasn't bothered to visit you in days, or the way you act like it's Christmas when he does. He treats you like a possession, so no I don't like him but I like even less what he's doing to you."

"You're basing that on the two times you've encountered him? That's not exactly fair is it?"

"I have eyes, Noelle. It doesn't take more than once to see the dynamic between the two of you. I'm the only family you have in the area but he acted as though you were committing a crime for inviting me over. If a man really cares about you, they'd have a vested interest in getting to know your friends and family."

"He had a long day."

"There you go making excuses for him. Stop. I know when I'm not welcome somewhere and he made me feel very unwelcome. I was more disappointed when you didn't say anything about it."

James had never come right out and said she wasn't allowed visitors but he did mention Noelle was to be available whenever her needed her to be to be. Noelle hadn't given it much thought then but the memory made her face flame with embarrassment.

"I'm sorry you felt unwelcome."

"I don't need you to apologize; I just want you to see what you have with James isn't good for you."

"Well, it's my life to sink or swim with isn't it? And as far as kept women go, I'm not doing so bad right?" Noelle had attempted to inject as much nonchalance into her voice as possible but knew she'd failed miserably.

"I hate when you put yourself down like that. You're still the sweet little Noelle I know and love. But that bastard—"

"He's not a bastard."

"I call it like I see it. He keeps you under lock and key, yet he only sees you when it's convenient for him. He treats you like dirt."

"No he doesn't."

Simone sighed loudly into the receiver. "Then explain to me why you're scared to come out tonight and have a good time. I know you Noelle; those fancy clothes and expensive baubles don't mean a damn thing to you. Hell, every time I've admired something you're wearing you nearly bust your ass trying to give it to me. What is it about this guy that has you so sprung? It's like he's a puppet master and you're allowing him to pull your strings."

Noelle flinched. She didn't like having her relationship so thoroughly dissected, especially when just about every arrow hit its mark. "That's not true. James and I just have an understanding."

"Does this understanding include him dating the right kind of woman in public and keeping his dirty little secret behind closed doors?"

Tears stung the backs of Noelle's eyes as her stomach twisted in knots. "You don't understand."

"Then make me understand. Make me comprehend what you see in this guy? Sure he's gorgeous and rich, but how great can he be when he won't even be seen with you in public. Right now, you're just his side piece but you're worthy of being put first."

Noelle hastily wiped away a stray tear that escaped the corner of her eye. "It's not that simple," she whispered. Even as she argued, she knew what her cousin said was true.

"Yes it is. He's using you as a convenient lay while he dates someone he deems acceptable for all the world to see. I know it sounds harsh but I'm telling you this because I love you and I'm tired of seeing you hurt over this prick. What about your dreams? I know the hell you went through with my mom and brothers and those little digs they made and how they treated you like you were less than the phenomenal person you are. Just because they didn't think you were good enough to be anything other than some hypocritical deacon's wife doesn't mean you shouldn't aspire to be better for yourself."

"Have you thought that James makes me happy? Look, at least he's not that disgusting old pervert Aunt Frieda tried to pawn me off on."

"And I'm proud of you for walking away from that hot mess of an engagement but you're still chained to some man who expects your world to revolve around him. But truthfully, this thing you're involved in now is worse. At least that little troll was willing to give you his name. Can you say the same for James?"

Noelle gripped the phone tightly until her knuckles changed color. She was silent for several moments before she was calm enough to answer her cousin's accusations. "You only know what you've observed. You don't know everything about us."

"Maybe not, but I know you're unhappy and any man who makes you unhappy isn't worth it, hon."

Another bitter tear slid down Noelle's face.

"Nothing to say? What about your art? And the art school you abandoned because this guy decided you were worthy to fuck?"

"I didn't give up art school for him. You know I was already having issues there. And I still sketch from time to time."

"Sketching occasionally is not what your talent was meant for. You have a gift and it's a shame you're letting it go to waste."

Noelle was sure her cousin meant well but she'd heard enough. "Are you through raking me over the coals? Because, I think I still have a little bit of pride left before you completely destroy it."

Simone didn't answer for several moments but finally she said, "I'm tired of tiptoeing around the issue. This is something you need to hear and now that it's been said what you do with it is up to you. So I guess going out tonight is a no?"

Noelle allowed Simone's words to marinate for a moment and then her mind drifted to that picture she'd seen of James and the redhead. "No. I mean, I'll go out with you tonight. Where should we meet?"

"Seriously?"

"Yeah. What time?"

"Oh, girl, you'll have so much fun! We're supposed to be meeting for drinks down on Hargrove Avenue at Dominic's and afterwards dancing at a new club we want to check out."

"Sounds like fun. I'll meet you there."

They chatted for a few more minutes before hanging up. For the first time in weeks, Noelle felt invigorated. Screw James. Let him have his perfect trophy wife if he wanted. Tonight she planned on having fun and getting drunk and there was nothing he could do about it.

Two hours later decked out in a tight pair of designer jeans, a black silk top that hung off one shoulder to reveal a generous expanse of dark chocolate skin and a pair of high heeled boots, Noelle was ready to go. She wore her hair loose, letting the curls flow around her shoulders. She made a note to herself to make a hair appointment for a weave tightening. Perhaps she'd go shorter next time but immediately thought better of it. James liked long hair, or she assumed he did. All men liked long hair. After inspecting herself in the mirror, she was pleased with her appearance. Not bad for a girl from a small backwoods town in Virginia.

Just as her hand touched the doorknob, the keyhole turned and seconds later, James pushed his way through the door. He never entered a room, he moved into it purposely.

Noelle backed up to avoid being knocked over.

He halted in front of her, his wing-tipped black brows rising in apparent surprise. Slate gray eyes roamed over her from head to toe not seeming to miss a single detail. Those full lips that no white boy had any business possessing thinned to a tight line. He didn't speak. He didn't need to. The question was asked with his expression and it demanded an answer.

Despite standing in four inch heel boots Noelle still had to crane her neck to meet his gaze. "I uh…I was just going to meet my cousin and some of her friends for drinks."

Still, he didn't speak. Noelle squirmed beneath his stare.

She ran her tongue across her gloss covered lips nervously. "Well, I wasn't expecting you, so I didn't think it would be such a big deal to go out. I'm stuck in the penthouse most of the time and I—"

"Call Simone and cancel your plans." He strode past her as if that was the end of the conversation.

Normally when he made a request of her, she complied without question, but coupled with the announcement in the society page and her cousin's words, Noelle bristled inside at his dismissive statement. "No."

He continued to the bar as if she hadn't spoken. "Take off your clothes, Noelle."

"Did you hear what I just said? I'm going out with my cousin. It would have been nice if you'd called ahead."

He stopped only when he stood behind the bar. Just as casually as he pleased, James pulled out a bottle of aged scotch and a glass. He poured himself a generous amount and took a gulp and then slowly lowered his glass. "I heard what you said, now take off your clothes."

"You can't order me around like this." She wanted to stomp her foot, but realized how childish that would be.

"Five seconds, Noelle, or I come over there and do it for you. And if I have to come over there, I'm going to paddle that delectable ass until you can't sit for a week."

Despite his autocratic tone, she couldn't help but tingle all over at the thought of him administering a spanking. No matter how intriguing the idea was Noelle wouldn't let him walk all over her—not this time. "James!"

"One." He took another sip of his drink.

"You're being unreasonable."

"Two." Another sip, this time followed by a lascivious lick of his lips.

"I'm a grown woman and you have no right to treat me this way."

"Three." He placed his glass down on the bar.

"Stop this."

"Four."

Noelle closed her eyes against his scrutiny knowing she'd give in to him. She felt her nipples tighten and panties dampen when the sound of his dulcet voice caressed her ears. Still her last vestige of pride wouldn't let her completely surrender just yet.

"Five." He moved so swiftly he was in front of her within two heartbeats. Giving her no time to protest, he dipped just enough to dig his shoulder into her midsection and lift her in the air in a fireman's carry.

She squirmed as he took the steps two at a time, earning her a sharp smack on her bottom. She howled in shock and anger. "Put me down now, James!"

"I think it's time for a little reminder of who you belong to."

Noelle was too stunned to react at first but the next swat on her ass galvanized her into action. She wiggled to loosen the tight grip he had on her. She pounded on his back with her fist. "Put me down!"

The next time his hand met her bottom, there was much more force behind it. And then another even harder swat followed. Tears sprang to her eyes. "James," she cried out in surprise.

He remained silent, taking Noelle to the bedroom and dropping her on the bed none too gently. Without a word, he loosened his tie and shrugged out of his tailored suit jacket. As he undressed, his steely gaze never left her.

James held her captive in his gray stare as he did so many times. She wanted to get off the bed and leave the room but she couldn't move or barely breathe as he discarded his shirt revealing a muscular chest and tight abs. He quickly rid himself of his pants and boxers to reveal his nude form. He was tall, broad-shouldered and lean, not overly muscular but tight and tone. The definition of his arms and legs along with the flat stomach made it evident he was no slouch in the gym.

Unable to help herself, Noelle allowed her gaze to drift to his cock which hung hard and heavy. As he advanced toward the bed, Noelle came out of her temporary paralysis and scrambled across the bed. James, with lightning reflexes grabbed her by the ankle and pulled her toward him.

"Stop, James!" She kicked out at him in defiance. For once she didn't want him to have it his way so easily. Seeing him in the newspaper snuggled up so cozily with some society dame tore at her insides. The terms had been laid out for her when they began their arrangement and there were several times when James had reminded Noelle of them. It increased her indignation nonetheless.

Noelle realized she'd only been holding on to an illusion of what she'd wanted them to have. There were times when James had been sweet and tender which she held close to her heart. Those were the moments she could forget his coldness. She could pretend he wasn't simply using her to as an object to assuage his animalistic needs.

Right now, his expression was something altogether different. It was feral and almost scary. Something was off tonight but Noelle didn't care to figure out what it was. She'd reached her breaking point.

James pulled back and stared at her as if she'd completely lost her mind. "Are you telling me no?" His tone was so eerily calm it sent a chill down her spine.

She nervously moistened her lips with the tip of her tongue as the gnawing feeling grew in the pit of her stomach. Something she couldn't quite put her finger on was happening here and somehow she knew no matter what her response was, things would never be the same between them.

"I'm not an object to be used at your convenience. I'm a person with feelings," she answered with a wobbly voice. This was the most she'd ever spoken back to him and despite his expression darkening with each word she continued. "Just because you're important in your world doesn't mean you can treat me any way you feel like. I had plans to go out with my cousin and had you asked nicely, I would have gladly changed them for you but you come in here without so much as a hello and toss me around like a ragdoll. Well, I'm going out and there's nothing you can do about it." Filled with bravado, she slid off the bed while managing not to look at him in all his naked glory.

Noelle was playing with fire but there was no turning back now. Slowly she inched around him and eased away. She half expected him to follow her, force her to stay but when he made no move she hesitated. "Well, okay I'll see you later."

Still he didn't move. She continued to exit the bedroom wary of being followed. This was way too easy. James wasn't usually one to take no for an answer.

As Noelle was about to cross the threshold of the doorway, he finally spoke. "Before you leave, mind answering some questions for me?"

Chapter Two

Instinct told her to keep going and not look back but there was something in his voice that made her hesitate. "What?" She turned around with an impatient sigh.

To her surprise he was only inches away from her. It was unnerving how a man his size could move with such stealth. "Pardon me for not being up on the latest fashion but those boots you're wearing, what are they?"

She furrowed her brow in confusion, wondering what he was getting at with such an odd question. Noelle bit the inside of her bottom lip before answering. "They're YSL."

"Yves St. Laurent? Correct?"

She nodded, still not sure why he wanted to know about her boots of all things.

"And these jeans?" He slipped closer until she could feel his breath on her face. He ran his hand along her thigh. "I noticed the fancy design on your bottom. I see a lot of the young socialites wear them. Who designed them?"

"James—"she began but was cut off when he placed his index finger over her lips.

"Just answer the question, Noelle. "

"Roberto Cavalli but I don't see what—"

"And how about the top? Pure silk isn't it?"

Noelle was sure he had a point but it was taking him way too long to get to it. "Does it really matter? Look, I've got to go. Simone is waiting for me." Before she could take a step, James gripped her forearms and twisted her around until her back was flush with his chest. James then plucked out the tag from the back of her shirt.

"Dolce and Gabbana," he read. "Nice." James spanned her neck with his large hand. "And this gold chain, how much do you think this cost?"

"I don't know," she whispered, her nerves frazzled from his touch. He pressed his hardness against her ass. She didn't want to respond to him as she so often did but her traitorous body let her down yet again.

"Of course you don't, my dear. But I do. I know exactly what everything you're wearing costs down to the lace panties." He leaned over brushing his lips against the shell of her ear. "Guess how I know."

It finally dawned on her what he was getting at and Noelle didn't want to hear another word of it. "James I'm in no mood for these games." She attempted to break free from his hold but the hand that had only been resting against her collarbone now tightened around her neck. His grip barely allowed her to breathe. "James…" she choked.

"Exactly. James. I paid for it all, signed the bills myself just as I did for that walk-in closet of clothes you couldn't pronounce when you met me or the hundreds of shoes, the jewelry in the wall safe, the lines of credit, this penthouse and the Mercedes. All yours as long as you continue to grant me the access of your delectable body whenever I want and however I want."

Unshed tears burned her eyes at his cruel reminder of the lifestyle he'd set her up in. "I never asked for any of this," she whispered.

"But you agreed to the deal from the very beginning, did you not?" He ran his tongue along the curve of her ear and her knees nearly gave out on her. She wished she didn't respond so easily to him. Her nipples pebbled against her blouse and her pussy clenched spontaneously.

"I....I never agreed to be treated like this," Noelle cried, trying again to turn around but was unsuccessful again.

His hand tightened around her throat robbing her of air and then slowly loosening yet not quite releasing her. "Oh? The bargain, if I may remind you sweetheart, is for you to be available to service my needs when and however I want and in return you'll be handsomely compensated. You're not by chance reneging on our deal are you? After all, you've never had any problem spending my money. You'd like to pretend you don't enjoy the lifestyle but you love every bit of it. So what do you call a woman who lives rent free in an exclusive neighborhood, has access to all the money her greedy little heart desires and receives other financial perks simply for the use of her body? I know a lot of women like to pretty the word up and call themselves mistresses or girlfriends but let's be honest and call it what it is. You're a—"

"Don't say it!" she cut him off knowing how much it would kill her to hear him call her the word she feared most regardless if it was true.

"Okay, I'll allow you your pretense but make no mistake about our arrangement, as long as you enjoy the benefits I provide, I expect a return on my investment. Everything in this penthouse belongs to me including you and I say you're not going a goddamn place unless I say so. Do we understand each other?"

The tears she had fought to hold back slid down her cheeks. She wanted to argue and scream at him but he didn't say anything that wasn't true. The last little bit of pride she had was hanging by a thread and Noelle realized as much as it would kill her to do so, she had to leave him if she wanted to hold on to it.

"Let me go," she bit out, her voice shaky with emotion.

James whirled her around to face him and pushed her against the wall. He placed his hands on either side of her head and leaned over until their noses touched. His handsome face was screwed up in a mask of pure determination and another emotion she couldn't quite place. His lips curled into a sneer. "You protest like you don't want me to fuck you but you're already trembling. Your body gives you away every single time, baby. I bet you're so wet right now your panties are soaked." To test his theory he slipped his hand inside her waistband and cupped her hot sex.

Noelle cried out when he touched her, ashamed of herself for liking it more than she should. He slid his finger along her damp slit before pulling his hand out of her pants. "Oh yeah. You want to be fucked so bad you can't even look me in the eye and deny it. Those pretty lips might say one thing but your body says another." James ran his dew-drenched fingers across her bottom lip, flaunting the evidence of her desire. "Lick it," he commanded.

She shook her head, denying him his request.

"Do it, Noelle. It's easy. See?" He dipped his head and swiped her bottom lip with his tongue. James then ran his wet finger over her mouth again. "Your turn."

Noelle met his intense stare which for reasons she couldn't explain seemed detached. On most days James was never an overly emotional guy but tonight something was definitely off. She couldn't reconcile this stranger from the one she'd had such a pleasant time with only a few short weeks ago. That charming man who'd held her and comforted her when she was in need seemed hell-bent on humiliating her in every way possible. "Why are you being like this?"

He raised a dark brow. "Being like what?"

"Last time…you helped me…"

"I may be a bastard according to most, but I don't always act like one. You needed help. I gave it to you. Don't mistake anything I do for more than what it is. Now stop stalling and do it," he barked.

Noelle jumped in surprise but finally obeyed his order. She ran her tongue across her bottom lip, tasting the juice of her arousal.

He smiled though it didn't quite reach his eyes. "Good girl. That wasn't so hard now was it? Now tell me how badly you want this cock." He gripped her hand and guided it to his rock hard shaft.

Noelle shook her head from side to side. "Not like this James," she whispered even though her mind screamed the words.

James squeezed her hand around his cock. "Yes like this. You're here to take care of my needs and I need you now." He moved to kiss her but just as their lips were about to meet Noelle turned her head away. He growled at her defiance. The next thing she knew he grabbed a handful of her hair and yanked her head back so hard she let out a yelp of surprise and pain.

"Don't turn away from me again, especially when we both know how hot you are to have my dick buried balls deep in your pretty little pussy", he taunted before crushing her lips beneath his. He pushed his tongue deep into her mouth, devouring and stealing her breath away. His cock pressed against her hard and ready.

Keeping a tight grip in her hair James lifted his head and grazed his teeth against her neck then bit into her vulnerable flesh. His lips smothered hers again, drowning out her cries.

Noelle brought her hands up to push him away but something happened to her the second she touched his heated flesh. A delicious wave of electricity licked its way along every single nerve ending in her body. Her pussy tingled and she desperately wanted him thrusting deep inside of her. Her mind and her body were at odds. One screamed stop, the other screamed don't ever stop.

James grabbed a handful of her shirt and ripped it down the front. "You're mine. You belong to me. All of you." He released the grip on her hair, giving Noelle only a moment's relief before hauling her in his arms and carrying her the short distance to the bed.

He dropped her in the center none too gently. The temporary disconnect of their bodies gave her passion-hazed brain a moment of clarity. "James, please. Can't we talk about this?" She tried to sit up but James was on her before she could slide off the bed. When he straddled her, Noelle attempted to push him away, but he captured her wrists in his strong grip.

"If the conversation doesn't involve my cock in your cunt, there's nothing to discuss. I already told you, you're mine and I will have you when I want and how I want." In an effortless demonstration of his strength, he took both wrists in one hand and held them over her head. He wasted no time ripping her bra down the front, ruining it.

Noelle's face burned with humiliation even though her insides flamed even hotter. She pressed her thighs tightly together embarrassed at how badly she wanted him inside of her despite his offhand treatment and the blatant disregard for her feelings.

He captured one of her now exposed nipples between his lips sucking so fiercely he pushed her to the edge of pleasure and pain. He licked and laved the area and bit into her tender flesh digging in deep enough to break skin, to hurt her—to mark her.

"Please," Noelle cried out not sure if she was begging for him to stop or continue.

He raised his head long enough to give her a sardonic grin. "Please what?"

Noelle shook her head from side to side unable to get the words past her lips. That knowing smile was her undoing. She turned her head away unable to meet his gaze, ashamed of her own weakness.

He chuckled, almost manically. "That's right. You want it so bad you can't speak." He returned his attention to her breasts, rotating between each one and leaving his mark on both before moving lower.

Releasing her wrists, his hands flew to her jeans. Noelle's mind was in a haze as he made short order of divesting her of her boots, jeans and panties. It occurred to her while he roughly removed the remainder of her clothing she should fight back but he'd primed her for his touch making it damn near impossible to protest.

"Clasp your hands together, place them over your head and don't move."

"James—"

"Do it!" he barked.

She did as he commanded trembling in anticipation and anxiety. He'd been forceful with her before but not quite like this. She was, however, too caught up in her own warring emotions to analyze it.

James gripped one of her thighs digging so deep his nails pinched her. He parted the damp folds of her pussy and ran his thumb over her clit causing Noelle to quiver uncontrollably. "Look at all this sweet honey dripping from this juicy cunt just for me. You can't wait to be fucked can you?" He shoved his index and middle finger inside of her without his usual finesse creating a delicious friction. "Tell me how bad you want me."

Noelle bit the inside of her lip aching for him to take her but clinging to her last bit of pride.

James's intense gray gaze bored into her. "Tell me," he whispered, silkily letting up on the pressure just a bit to stroke her just right and managing to hit every single erogenous zone inside of her.

"Don't make me," she whispered all while she continued to respond to him slamming his fingers in and out of her.

He pulled his wet fingers out of her pussy and pinched her clit applying more pressure than she was used to. "Say it, Noelle."

It hurt a bit but it was the kind of pain that felt so good. "Yes," she whispered.

He pinched harder. "Louder."

"Yes! Fuck me James!"

His eyes flashed with a spark of possessiveness that sent a quiver racing along her spine. "Since you ask so nicely..." He guided his cock to her entrance and slammed into her so deep the air was robbed from her lungs.

His thrusts were hard and angry as if he was proving to her the very thing she tried to deny. She was nothing more than his whore. "Look at me when I fuck you, Noelle. I want you to know exactly who you belong to you. I want you to look into my eyes when you come."

When she refused, he gripped her chin and forcefully turned her head. "I said look at me!" he ordered through gritted teeth. "I'm the one in control. I have the power!"

A moment of fear washed over her as she thought that perhaps his last few words weren't directed at her but maybe someone else. As she'd previously suspected, something much deeper was going on here than her defying him. Sure James could be cold, sometimes borderline cruel but never like this. Something happened earlier to cause him to act out in a way that was not only hurting her but him as well.

Compelled to make some kind of connection to him, Noelle reached out to touch his face but he pushed her hand away. He wrapped his fingers around her throat and squeezed as he pushed deeper and harder. "I said to keep your hands above your head," he started coldly.

"James, "she gasped out for air but he continued to fuck her relentlessly.

Noelle grew light-headed as she got closer to her peak. With each thrust, he'd press his thumb against her windpipe and then ease up. "Mine,' he'd growl over and over again. While he moved in and out, she could feel the distance between them grow despite her body getting closer to its climax.

When she reached one of the most explosive orgasms she'd ever experienced, she'd come to two realizations: their relationship had reached the point of no return and the thread her pride had been hanging on was completely severed.

Chapter Three

One year earlier…

Noelle's head pounded and her body ached with tension after she walked out of class, disappointed and more than a little frustrated. There wasn't much she could brag about but her art was one thing she could at least say she was good at. Now, she wasn't so sure. Her professor seemed to have it out for her. No matter how hard she worked on a project, he always found something wrong with it. To make matters worse, it seemed as if he'd go out of his way to humiliate her in front of the rest of the class, holding her work up for scrutiny and ridicule.

At the end of his classes she felt two inches tall. Today was no exception. Perhaps her Aunt was right. She would never be good at anything and she had no business coming to the city to pursue the pipe dream of making a living from her art.

On the bus ride home, she sat in the back with her head against the window trying to hold back tears. By the time the bus came to Noelle's stop, her head felt as if it was literally being hit with a pickaxe over and over again. The pain was nearly unbearable and her vision blurred. In times of stress, she got terrible migraines that caused her nausea and vomiting. Her stomach twisted in knots and it took a considerable amount of effort to walk to the apartment she shared with her cousin.

Noelle practically crawled up the stairs to get to her door and unlock it. Somehow she made it to her bedroom. Once there, she closed the curtains not allowing any light to come in and she fell across the bed. She didn't remember passing out but she must have because the next thing she remembered was feeling something cool and damp being placed across her forehead. She also experienced the sensation of being elevated and pills being pushed past her lips followed by a glass of water.

"Come on hon, take a sip to wash the medicine down. They'll make you feel better." Her cousin's soothing voice broke through her haze.

Noelle winced as she drank just enough to wash the pills down. "Thank you," she whispered.

"No problem. You call me if you need anything, okay?"

Noelle twisted her lips in what she hoped was a smile. After being gently positioned against her pillow, she fell into a deep dreamless sleep. When she woke up again her head felt significantly better. Glancing at the digital clock on her nightstand, she saw she'd been out for at least four hours.

She found Simone standing over the stove, cooking dinner. "Something smells good," Noelle complimented, going to the refrigerator to get some orange juice.

"Thanks. I'd thought I'd try a stir fry tonight. How's your head?"

"Much better, thanks. Did I imagine it or were you home earlier than usual today."

"Yes. There was a bit of an incident at the store so I came home early. I saw the apartment door was open and knew something was the matter. What's going on? You only get sick like that when something's bothering you."

Noelle poured herself a glass of juice and placed the container back in the fridge. She took a seat at the kitchen table. "Professor McGregor hates me and hates my work. I've tried really hard to please him but nothing ever seems to make him happy. And he goes out of his way to make an example out of my work in front of the class. Aunt Frieda was right. I have no business going to art school. Art is the only talent I have and now I have a professor basically telling me I'm not good at it."

Simone turned around with compressed lips and her hands on her hips. "Girl, not this shit again. My mother doesn't know everything even though she thinks she does. And since she married Pastor Walter, her head is even further up her butt than it was before. You have to stop doubting yourself. What does that stupid professor know anyway? If he was so great, why isn't he making a living as an artist? You know what they say… those who can't teach.'"

Noelle appreciated Simone taking up for her but it was hard to believe in herself when she had been told most of her life, she wouldn't amount to much of anything. "Professor McGregor has a doctorate in art studies and he's written several books that are respected in the art community. And he seems to think I suck. At this point, I'm inclined to agree with him. If I can't make it in his class, maybe I should start focusing on something else."

Simone held up her hand. "Stop it. I hate hearing you so down on yourself all the time. It makes me sad because you have this gift and there's so much going for you but you just don't see it. You've been away from my mom's influence for three years. It's time to stop believing all that bullshit she fed you."

"It's easy for you to say. You're pretty, smart and outgoing. I'm--"

"Noelle, whatever you're about to say, I don't want to hear it. There's only so many times I can tell you how wonderful you are but unless you believe it, I'm wasting my breath. Obviously, your professor is a prick. He's probably jealous of your talent. If you feel he's not giving you a fair chance, then transfer classes or take the class next semester. If you're not going to do anything about it, stop whining."

Simone turned her back to Noelle, clearly irritated with the conversation. She hadn't meant to annoy her cousin.

Simone was only other person who'd ever championed her besides her mother.

Noelle didn't remember her father since he'd passed away when she was a baby, but her mother had been her everything. They didn't have much in the way of material things but what was lacking in the financial area was more than made up for in the abundance of love her mother had showered on her. Dorothy Bea, her mother, had been so achingly beautiful people would give her give her second, third and often fourth looks as she'd walk by. Noelle's favorite memories or her mother was when they baked together. Her mother would come up with the most amazing concoctions. She worked in a grocery store bakery and had dreams of opening her own bakery.

Those dreams came to a screeching halt when Dorothy Bea died. Noelle was devastated. She'd lost her rock and her best friend. She'd always been shy and found it hard to make friends because of a stutter which was particularly bad when she was nervous or agitated. With the loss of her mother, her speech impediment grew worse. She was teased for it to the point she talked as little as possible.

It didn't help matters that she was taken in by an aunt who made it a point to let her know she was only doing her Christian duty than any sense of loving feelings toward her niece. Her Aunt Frieda had not been openly cruel or laid a hand on Noelle. But she had a subtle way of making Noelle feel as though she were a burden and less than worthy of any kind of love. Ten years of subtle barbs inferring she was stupid, unattractive, and just generally a waste of breath had worn down her self-esteem to the point where she barely had any. She'd only had her art but now she wasn't sure she had that.

Noelle wanted to say something that would stop her cousin from being mad at her but she was at a loss for words.

She looked down at the table and twiddled her thumbs for lack of anything better to do.

It was Simone who finally broke the awkward silence when she walked over, pulled out a chair and plopped down with a heavy sigh. "You know I love you don't you hon?" Simone took Noelle's hand and gave it a gentle squeeze.

"Yes," Noelle whispered in reply without looking up.

"You're more than a cousin to me, you're my little sister." Simone continued to rub her hand.

This brought a smile to Noelle's lips. Simone had taken Noelle under her wing when she'd moved into her aunt's house and had always been kind. She'd made those first few years in the house almost bearable. And now in adulthood, they were closer than ever. "Yes, I know. I'm sorry for annoying you. I don't mean to."

"You have nothing to apologize for. I shouldn't have snapped at you. Blame it on my bad day." Simone got a faraway look in her eyes but just as quickly as it appeared it disappeared.

For the first time since she entered the room, Noelle noticed something was the matter with her cousin. It was her turn to give an encouraging squeeze. "Simone is everything okay?"

Simone's smile didn't quite reach her eyes. "I'm fine."

"No you're not. I think I know you well enough to notice something is really bothering you. Did the work situation really get to you?"

Simone pulled her hand away and rubbed her temples. "I'm ready to leave my job. The powers that be are taking the store in a direction I'm not happy with and it's no longer employee friendly. I want to start my own boutique to showcase my designs. I think all the chaos at work lately is some kind of sign I should go for my dream now rather than later. I have a pretty nice nest egg set up and if I can get a business loan that would take care of the rest."

"That's wonderful, Simone. If anyone can make it happen, you can. You've always dreamed of owning your own clothing store."

Simone smiled. "Yes and I think it's time to make that dream come true. It's going to take a lot of hard work and time but if it's not worth working for, it's not worth having right?"

"Everything you've put your mind to, you've been able to accomplish. I don't know how much help I'd be but if you need me in any capacity, I'm here for you."

"I'll hold you to that. But for now, how about setting the table so we can eat? Oh, and by the way, I won a one month free trial to this really upscale gym. I was thinking of checking it out tonight. Apparently all the rich people go there. What better place to start networking?"

"Sounds like a plan."

"I'm allowed to bring a friend. How about it?"

Noelle who had never stepped foot in a gym in her life knew she'd probably make a fool of herself. "Uh, I'm an uncoordinated mess. I'll pass. Why don't you take Tanisha? She'd like rubbing elbows with rich people. And she's in much better shape than I am. I'm sure she'd appreciate it more than I would."

"I'd rather go with you. Come on, a good workout will help clear your head. And who knows? You might meet some rich hunk who'll sweep you off your feet."

Noelle rolled her eyes knowing there was absolutely no chance of that happening.

Chapter Four

"I find it perplexing why you're calling me when I've made it clear our arrangement is over. How did you get my personal number anyway?" A vein throbbed in James' forehead and he could feel his blood pressure rising. He had enough stress from his job without dealing with an ex-mistress who refused to take no for an answer. Megan was beautiful, charming, witty and so sophisticated. But among those attributes was the flaw of not realizing when things were over.

"Stella gave me the number. Don't be mad at me Jaime. I needed to talk to you. You can't leave things the way they are. How about you come over for a nightcap and I'll—"

"And you'll what? Be waiting for me naked and ready when I arrive?"

"Of course." Her voice dripped with the smug arrogance of someone who was used to getting her way. "I know how to give it to you just the way you like."

"Would you do anything I wanted?"

"Anything, darling."

"Promise?"

"Cross my heart."

"Be out of the penthouse by the end of the month and do not call this number again, or you can forget about the bonus." James ended the call without waiting for a response and immediately phoned his executive assistant.

"Yes, James?" Paul Winters answered on the second ring.

"Cancel Ms. Matthew's cell phone account as well as any memberships she has. I'd also like you to personally see to it that all of her belongings have been removed from the penthouse. And I'd like for you to relay to Stella my number is not to be given out unless I say."

"I'm on it."

"I'll be at the gym for the next hour in which time this phone will be off. I'll need you to have those documents on the Garrison Group on my desk first thing in the morning. And I trust we won't have any more slip-ups with Stella."

"Will do."

He hung up the phone and put it on sleep mode. Though it was left unsaid he knew Paul would let his secretary know if she overstepped her boundaries again, she'd be out of a job. James ran a multibillion dollar corporation where one bad decision could lose him millions and lay off thousands. He worked hard, giving his one hundred and ten percent and he expected no less from those he employed.

Despite the daily pressure, there were two things that eased his stress and that was sex or a good workout, both if he could squeeze it in. However, now that he was in between lovers, he'd have to settle for sweating it out in the gym.

After changing and locking away his valuables, James headed for the treadmill. He usually warmed up with a four mile run before hitting the weights.

James popped his earbuds in and turned his MP3 player up loud enough to drown out all other sound. He started at a moderate jog and steadily picked up the pace to a full out run. With the cardio machines being located on the second floor, he could see the other patrons working out below him. He rarely paid attention to them but one woman caught his eye when she tripped over a dumbbell and face-planted. For a second she lay on the ground, unmoving and he debated cutting his run short to see if she was okay. The decision was taken from him as several people including some staff members rushed over to check on her.

She looked more than a little dazed as she was helped to her feet. He felt sympathy for the unfortunate woman but quickly pushed her out of his mind as he focused on his run. Afterwards he stretched and headed downstairs to tackle the weights. On his way to the free weights something slammed into his back.

"I'm so sorry," a frantic voice cried from behind him.

It wasn't the first time a woman "accidentally" bumped into him although not this much force was usually applied. More than a little annoyed, he turned around to see who his assailant was and came face to face with the woman he'd spied earlier. He planned on telling her to watch where she was going but stopped at the sight of her stricken face. This was no ruse to gain his attention. Judging from the tumble she'd taken earlier, the woman was nothing more than a klutz.

"I wasn't watching where I was going. I'm really sorry," she apologized again. "Are you okay?"

There was something about this woman that kept James rooted to the spot when he would have dismissed her by now. She was by no means a conventional beauty. At most, she was passably pretty but her face was arresting nonetheless. Possessing large, doe-like dark brown eyes crowned with long curly lashes, the mystery woman gave off an air of innocence. She was of average height, yet even beneath her bulky sweat suit he noticed her curves. She held an air of mystery—hidden depths that challenged him to slowly peel away each layer and discover the treasure beneath the innocent demeanor.

Her hair was pulled back in a short messy ponytail accentuating a heart-shaped face and an expanse of dark cocoa brown skin. Her nose was wide but still feminine and her lips were overly generous, but James couldn't stop staring. The sudden urge to lean forward and sample her inviting mouth, hit James all at once and caught him off guard.

He'd ended his arrangement with Megan two weeks ago and hadn't had sex since. It was the only explanation he could think of for reacting to a woman who in most circumstances wouldn't garner a second glance from him. But still, he couldn't bring himself to walk away. The lady in question was the one to speak first. "Well, uh, again, I'm sorry," she said as she slowly edged away from him, cheeks stained maroon from her apparent embarrassment.

"Your name," he demanded.

She looked around as if to see if anyone else witnessed their exchange. "Noelle. Noelle Greene."

His lips twitched involuntarily at the wobbliness of her voice. He made her nervous. It had been a long time since he'd been in the presence of a female who didn't have a contrived reaction to his presence. James held his hand out to her, "James Rothschild."

She looked at his outstretched hand before taking his in a surprisingly firm grip. "Nice to meet you. Your eyes are amazing."

He raised a brow. "Excuse me?"

She yanked her hand away and slapped it against her forehead. "I'm sorry. That was awkward, wasn't it? It's the artist in me. I notice things like that." She looked at her feet while she spoke to him. "I've taken up enough of your time. Enjoy the rest of your workout." She backed away but James was reluctant to see her go.

"Noelle, do you have plans after the gym? Perhaps, you'd like to catch a quick bite to eat?"

She raised her head and pointed to her chest. "Me?"

This time he really smiled. False modesty was a huge turn off to him but this was no act. There was something strangely endearing about Noelle Greene. "Yes you. I usually grab a quick bite after the gym, nothing too heavy. There's a deli down the street that makes sandwiches and wraps. My treat."

Noelle furrowed her brows together and looked over her shoulder. "I ate before I came and I'm here with my cousin. Thanks for the invite but I can't."

Her rejection caught him off guard. James prided himself on being able to get a good read on people and he could tell from her body language, his attraction was one-sided.

"You can't what?" A woman whom James assumed was Noelle's cousin joined them. She was tall and slender but unlike Noelle her workout clothes hugged all her curves. This woman fit more into the classically beautiful category, more his type but the shy Miss Greene intrigued him.

"I was inviting Noelle for a bite to eat afterwards but I've been informed she's eaten."

"She barely touched her food. I'm sure she'd love to have a meal with you." The woman smiled brightly.

Noelle slid closer to her cousin. "Simone, we came together."

"I'm a big girl. I can find my own way home. Besides, Mr....?" Simone smiled up at him.

"James Rothschild," he offered.

"I'm sure Mr. Rothschild will see you home. He looks like a nice enough guy and he's a hunk. Besides, it's not like he'll try anything funny since I can now describe him to the police." Simone paused with a frown. "I've heard that name somewhere." She looked up at James expectantly but he had no intention of volunteering anymore information.

James smiled at Noelle. "Your cousin thinks I'm harmless."

"She'd love to go. As a matter of fact, I was just coming over to tell her I was ready to head home, so why don't you two go ahead. I'll catch you back at the apartment Noelle." She gave her cousin a wink before walking off leaving Noelle with her mouth wide open.

He hadn't meant to put her on the spot and he wouldn't if she truly didn't want his company. "Look, Noelle, if you're uncomfortable you don't have to come out with me."

She shook her head vehemently. "It's not that, it's just…"

"Noelle, it's perfectly okay. I'll tell you what. I'm going to finish my workout, shower and change. I should be ready in about forty minutes. If you'd like to go with me to the deli, we'll meet at the front of the gym. Otherwise, no hard feelings. Fair enough?"

Noelle silently nodded. James gave her a tight smile before heading off to finish his workout. Once he was away from her he wasn't sure what had possessed him to ask her out in the first place. Perhaps his libido was out of control. But why her? There were a number of women who would jump at the opportunity to share his bed. Since making his first million, women came easy to him.

As he hit the weights, he reexamined his motives. Perhaps it was the novelty of her apparently not knowing who he was. Her cousin had recognized his name but didn't know where she'd heard it from. She'd find out eventually but by then it wouldn't matter. He'd get what he wanted from Noelle and never spare her another thought.

Noelle remained rooted to the spot minutes after James walked away. Men like James Rothschild didn't ask out awkward, dumpy women like her. That only happened in movies and the romance novels she used to read as a teenager. What could he possibly want from her when he was by far one of the most attractive men she'd ever seen?

The artist in her noted every line and intricate detail of his face, from the square jaw to the dark sinister brows slashing over intense, slate-gray colored eyes. His nose was prominent and slightly askew as if it had been broken at some point and not set properly, but it suited him. The slight imperfection humanized him, adding character to arrestingly handsome features.

James looked to be around six foot two or three because he had towered over her five foot five frame. His body was muscular but tone—a boxer's build. She glanced in the direction he'd headed and saw him by the weights lifting way more than she could dream of attempting. The sheer power of his movements sent a shiver through her body. A woman would never be the same after being with a man like James. He frightened and fascinated her and Noelle wasn't sure which emotion was winning.

"He's something else, isn't he?" Simone's voice brought her out of her silent perusal.

Noelle jumped. "I thought you'd left."

"Not yet. I just wanted to stick around long enough to make sure you follow through on this date."

Her cousin meant well, of that Noelle was sure, but it was no less embarrassing to be offered up like some prized pig at a county fair. "I could have done without your intervention."

"Oh, I beg to differ little cuz. If I hadn't walked over when I did, you would have allowed that Grade-A prime hunk to walk away. Someone that fine doesn't come along often. Did you check out his body? If he didn't have eyes only for you, I would have given him *my* number."

"How do you know he isn't some kind of serial killer? You said you recognized his name, maybe you saw it on the news because he killed a bunch of random women."

"Girl, if the police were looking for him, I doubt he'd be here. No, I heard his name somewhere else. I could have read it online or in a magazine. I'm not sure but I'll do a web search when I get home. Why, do you think there's something wrong with him?"

Noelle was uncomfortable having this conversation in a gym full of people. "Can we go outside? I need air."

"Are you okay?" Simone eyed her with concern.

"Yeah, but I'd rather not talk here, okay?"

"Sure. Let's go." When they were outside, Simone didn't wait for Noelle to gather her thoughts. "Okay, spill it."

Noelle leaned against the brick building for support. "I just don't get it. What does that guy want with me?"

"Uh, he obviously wants to have dinner with you. I've been telling you to get out more and here's your opportunity."

"That's not what I meant and you know it." Noelle balled her fists at her sides in frustration. All the old taunts from her Aunt and cousins came back to her, bringing Noelle's insecurities front and center. She had limited dating experience and even less confidence in dealing with the opposite sex.

Not a day went by when Noelle wasn't told she was ugly, her hair was too nappy, her lips were too big, she was too dark and she was stupid, all by either her Aunt or her twin cousins, Derrick and Damon. Uncle Ebenezer simply ignored her most times except when they were at Church where he was Pastor.

Simone defended her as best she could but when Noelle realized her cousin suffered for standing up for her, she learned not to let anyone see her cry. She wouldn't talk or complain about it. Noelle absorbed it like a sponge until she began to believe it. By the time Simone left home, Noelle had no one and the psychological beat down continued to the point where she couldn't stand looking in the mirror.

It had been three years since she'd moved out of that house but the scars were still fresh. She'd shied away from any type of relationship since Walter, despite Simone's attempts to set her up. The few times she'd been persuaded to go out on a blind date they ended in disaster. Nothing was worse than seeing the disappointment in a man's eyes when they first laid eyes on her. And now this really together guy, who looked like a Greek god, was asking her out? Something had to be up.

"Then tell me what you mean, hon." Simone gently prompted.

"I used to have a crush on the captain of the basketball team. His name was Antoine, really good looking and very popular with the all the girls and female teachers alike. I knew I never had much of a chance with him but he started paying attention to me and I lapped it up, of course. He asked me to the fall harvest dance. Aunt Frieda said I could go because she was having company that night and didn't want me around. We agreed to meet at the dance. Even Derrick and Damon were being nice to me. They offered to drive me there with them since they were going to the dance anyway. I guess I should have known something was up then because those two were never nice to me. I was just so excited a boy liked me I didn't stop to analyze the situation. Anyway, when I got to the dance, I saw Antoine dancing with Ramona Fields, one of the popular girls."

"Up until that point, Ramona and I never said a word to each other but when they'd finished dancing, I walked over to Antoine to let him know I was there. I barely said hello when Ramona ripped me a new one. She made fun of my outfit, called me just about everything but a child of God. I was so humiliated. Antoine stood laughing and he told me it was just a joke and he didn't think I'd show up."

It happened years ago but the memory haunted her like it was yesterday. She tilted her head back to keep the tears from spilling. "Apparently most of the people at the dance were in on the joke except me. Derrick and Damon, of course, knew about it which is why they were so eager to take me to the dance. I was so mortified I left the dance and walked home. After that, I knew better. Even that worm Walter had an ulterior motive for wanting to be with me. So why is James interested in me?" The memory of that humiliation still burned to this day. She wiped a stray tear that slipped from the corner of her eye.

"Oh, sweetie, those kids were a bunch of assholes. You've got to know that. As for my brothers...well you know they're not worth the effort it took to bring them into the world." Simone closed the space between the two of them and captured Noelle's face between her hands. "I know you had it hard living with my mother, Ebenezer and the twin terrors but they can't hurt you anymore. And those jackass kids who pranked you can all go to hell. If you buy into the bullshit they tried to sell you, then they won. Don't give them that victory, babe." She leaned forward and placed a kiss on Noelle's forehead.

Simone's heart was in the right place but some things were easier said than done. "Thanks, Simone."

"You're welcome. Now stop thinking about a bunch of rotten kids from high school. I'm sure James is nothing like them. He doesn't strike me as the kind of man to play those types of games. Obviously he sees in you what I've been saying all along but you'll never know for sure unless you give him a chance. Why not just go out with him for that meal and if it doesn't work out then at least you won't have to wonder what if."

"But he's so good looking—"

"And so are you."

Noelle could see her cousin wasn't going to give up until she acquiesced. She took a deep breath and nodded. "Okay. I'll give it a shot."

Chapter Five

James half-expected Noelle to be gone by the time he'd finished in the gym but there she was in the lobby with her hands folded in her lap. When she spotted him walking towards her, her full lips curved into a shy smile. The more he looked at her he could see she was more than passably pretty. She was actually quite lovely. Noelle's was a subtle beauty that didn't hit you all at once, but snuck up on you and slowly stole your breath away.

She stood up and smoothed her clothing down. "I didn't bring a change of clothing. But I didn't really do much working out after my tumble so I hope what I'm wearing is okay."

He took in the baggy sweats and smirked. His women usually dressed to the nines in the latest brand name designs. Megan wouldn't have been caught dead in an outfit like Noelle's but he liked how she wasn't trying to impress him. "You look just fine. We're just going to a deli unless you had something else in mind."

"Oh no, the deli is fine."

"Good." He held the front door open for her. "Shall we?"

He noticed her plump backside as she walked by him. What he found most intriguing about her outfit was imagining what was underneath it. Noelle didn't strike him as the type to reveal her secrets so easily but he'd learned from an early age, everything had a price. As did everyone.

"The deli is a few blocks away. We can take a walk or I can drive us. You decide."

"It's a nice night. I think I'd like to walk," she answered without making eye contact.

"Walking it is. Mind waiting here a sec while I put my gym bag in my car?"

"No. Go ahead." This time she did look up at him but just as quickly, she turned away. He'd definitely address that when he returned. James took his time walking to his car as he still tried to sort out his attraction for Noelle. A little voice told him she wasn't the type to accept the kind of relationship he was willing to offer but then again he hadn't gotten to where he was by taking no for an answer.

Noelle was propped against the building humming a soft tune to herself when he returned. "All ready?" he asked.

"Yes." As they started toward their destination she whispered, "thank you."

"What are you thanking me for exactly?"

"Thank you for asking me out. Simone says I should get out more but I'm not really good at this dating thing."

"An attractive woman like yourself? I find that hard to believe."

She smoothed the flyaway hairs that escaped her short ponytail in a self conscious gesture. "You're teasing me."

"I don't tease…outside of the bedroom."

Her step faltered. "The bedroom?"

Either she had little experience with men or she was a hell of an actress. Everything pointed to the former which told him he should tread lightly with her. "What I meant," he hurried to cover his faux pas, "is I don't lie about things like that. Flattery has its uses of course but it's often mired in deceit. I promise, I will never be anything but honest with you."

She stopped walking for a moment to give him a searching look. A long awkward silence fell between them before that sweet smile touched her lips again. "You're a nice guy."' They started walking again.

He chuckled with a shake of his head. "I don't think anyone has ever called me that before."

"You didn't yell at me for bumping into you. Speaking as someone who's taken many spills in her lifetime, sometimes into other people, your reaction was on the tamer side."

"I'll admit you did look like you hurt yourself when you tripped and fell on your face."

She winced. "You saw that? That was pretty embarrassing. My shoelace came undone and I tripped over it. The next thing I know, I'm eating the floor. I'm just thankful no one laughed at me."

"You could have been seriously injured. There was nothing funny about it."

"Well, not everyone is nice."

"You don't have to sell me on that one."

She raised a brow. "I doubt anyone has been mean to you but you say that like they might have."

She'd probably cringe if he told her just how unkind people could be. But he had no plans to open up on that matter especially when he wasn't sure they'd see each other after tonight. "Don't we all have our stories to tell?"

"So what's yours?"

Talking about himself was James' least favorite subject, so he deflected. "My story isn't a new one. I'm more interested in hearing yours."

She shrugged. "There's not much to tell."

"Let's start with vital statistics then."

"Well, I just turned twenty-three a few months ago. I live with Simone, who you've met. I'm from a small southern town no one has heard of outside of it. Er…what else did you want to know?"

"Where do you work or are you in school?"

"I've been in art school for the past couple of years. But I'm thinking about taking a break from it. Before I went to school, I worked with Simone at the boutique she manages"

"Why are you thinking of taking a break? Art is a very specialized subject so I imagine you'd need talent to even get into that type of program."

"I've discovered I may not be as great as I thought." He could hear the sadness in her voice and he had this sudden need to reach out and comfort her. It caught him off guard at how easily Noelle had gotten under his skin in such a short period.

James shoved his hands in his pocket to fight the urge to throw an arm around her. "I'm sure you'll find something else to your liking. You're still young."

"I guess."

"You don't sound enthusiastic, Noelle."

"What's to get excited about? The one thing I believed I was good at, I wasn't. I think people should have a passion for what they do so going forward whatever I settle for would just be a job. No more."

"In my opinion, you could have the talent of Van Gogh but if you lack the drive and, as you put it, the passion to make it a success, then you'll fail. I'm sure you're talented but just because you're good at something it doesn't necessarily mean you should pursue it. I used to play baseball in school and I wasn't bad. I was all-city actually, but I couldn't see myself becoming a professional ball player. I liked it, but I didn't live and breathe it the way some guys do."

"I never thought of it that way. Now I'm worried if I'll ever find the thing that'll give me that spark."

"Give it some time. When you least expect it, a switch will flip on."

"Thanks, James. I'm sure a guy like you has always known what they wanted in life."

He balled his fists and shoved them deeper into his pockets. She had no idea. "You could say that," he said not wanting to give more away than he already had.

"How about you, James? Do you enjoy what you do?"

"Let's just say it's enabled me to accomplish a lot of my goals."

"Very evasive answer," she noted.

He was saved from responding as they came upon the deli. "Here we are."

The place was small and was rarely packed which is what he liked about it. Most people got their orders to go as did he but tonight they would dine in.

"Order whatever you like. The wraps are excellent and they have great salads. The club sandwiches are a favorite of mine."

She glanced at the menu before turning to him, "Everything looks really good, but I'll go for a chicken caesar wrap."

"Great choice. I think I'll get one of those as well."

James ordered for them while Noelle found them a table. She settled on a booth by the entrance. Noelle took the seat facing the counter enabling her to observe James unobtrusively. The man exuded masculinity from every single pore of his body. He made her nervous but oddly she found it easy to talk to him without tripping over her tongue as she did with most attractive men. He aroused things within her she never dreamed of experiencing. The tingling between her legs and the hardening of her nipples were sensations she had only ever experienced reading naughty books. The feelings she experienced in his presence excited and scared her at the same time.

Noelle's only boyfriend had been a church deacon her aunt had set her up with. Looking back, there had really been no formal discussion of their relationship status. It was just assumed by everyone they were together because he was always where she was. There had been no excitement with Walter. He was twenty-five years older than Noelle and a widower with kids older than her. Aunt Frieda had been the one to promote the relationship, telling Noelle she was lucky someone was interested in her.

Besides being older with grown-up children who still lived in his home, Walter expected her to wait on him hand and foot. He took it for granted they would marry and she would basically be an unpaid housemaid, spitting out more children for him. He always found a reason to touch her though she never gave him any indication that kind of attention from him was welcome. Had Simone not intervened, Noelle would probably be married to him with a couple of babies. Just thinking about her ex made Noelle shudder with mild disgust, and thank her lucky stars she'd gotten out of that mess before it was too late.

As she studied James, she wondered what his angle was. Why was he being so nice to her? She noticed his evasiveness when she asked certain questions. Noelle could put it down to him being a private person but she sensed there was more to it. She could tell he was a man of many layers.

She wondered what it would be like if he kissed her. The very thought made the blood rush to her face. Thankfully she wasn't afforded the luxury of dwelling on that line of thought for long because James returned with their food. She smiled at him and took the tray he held out for her. "Looks good."

"It is good. Enjoy."

"Thank you for the meal."

"My pleasure." His smile was disarming. Noelle lowered her lashes, unable to withstand the potency of his stare. Something was happening she couldn't explain. To prevent herself from saying something stupid, she grabbed her wrap and stuffed it in her mouth, barely tasting it. She was sure it was as delicious as he said but it was difficult to concentrate on her food with him sitting in front of her. She ate the entire wrap so she wouldn't appear rude.

It wasn't until she was finished with the entire thing that she realized a word hadn't been exchanged. Instead of embarrassing herself by saying something awkward, she did it by stuffing her face. He probably thought she was a pig.

"I can't believe I just shoveled all that in my mouth." She groaned.

"Don't apologize for enjoying your meal. If truth be told, it's a nice change of pace to have a dinner companion who enjoys her food rather than picking at it or pretending to eat. Look, I'm done too."

James put her at ease as he asked general questions about herself. During the course of the conversation they found they both enjoyed movies, classic rock, and old school R&B. It was only when the worker behind the deli counter shouted they'd be closing up soon did they notice the time. It was nearly eleven and she figured James probably needed to get to work in the morning though he never told her what he did for a living. Noelle assumed it was something where he held a high ranking position on the sheer strength of his personality alone.

James eased himself out of the booth and helped Noelle to her feet. "So how did you and your cousin get to the gym?"

"We took the subway. We only live a few stops away."

"Then allow me to take you home."

"It's okay. I don't want you to go out of your way."

"Noelle, I won't argue with you about this. It's late, you're by yourself and I'm taking you home. End of discussion." His voice was laced with steel brokering no further argument.

Any retort Noelle may have had, died instantly. It dawned on her that James was the kind of man who was used to getting his way. "Uh, thank you. I appreciate it."

"Not a problem." They walked in silence to his car. James stopped on the passenger side of a slick black sports car. After unlocking the door, he held it open for her. She was impressed by his chivalry because no one had ever held a car door open for her before.

Noelle slid inside, practically melting against the soft leather material. She tentatively ran her fingers across the dash before quickly folding her hands in her lap.

James climbed in next to her and started the engine. Besides Noelle giving him directions to her apartment, no other conversation was exchanged. When he pulled his car to stop, Noelle hesitated for a moment not sure what to expect. She wasn't sure if this qualified as a date or not.

"Well, thanks for dinner. It was nice meeting you tonight, James."

James faced forward, his jaw clenched tightly and his grip tight on the steering wheel. From his silence, Noelle could only discern he didn't want to see her again after tonight. Maybe he found the way she ate repulsive or perhaps he thought she wasn't pretty enough to take out. Whatever the reason for his silence, she wasn't surprised he had second thoughts about her.

"Um, well, goodnight." With a slight wave she reached for the door handle to let herself out.

"Noelle, wait." His tone was soft but when she turned to look at him he was still faced forward, holding on to the steering wheel with a tight grip.

"James?" Noelle tentatively reached over and placed her hand on his arm.

"Before I let you go for the night, there's something I need to know."

"What—"The words weren't out of her mouth before he turned and gripped her by the forearms and pulled her against him. The intensity of his gray gaze sent her heart racing. Instinctively, she didn't believe he'd hurt her but something else was going on here she didn't quite understand. Noelle swiped her tongue across her bottom lip in a nervous gesture as he held her captive.

James let out a low moan and lowered his head, crushing her lips beneath his. She stiffened, shocked by his touch but only momentarily. As his kiss became more demanding, hungrier, Noelle found herself melting against the hard wall of his body.

He gripped her ponytail, tilting her head back. James took advantage of her slightly parted lips by pushing his tongue in her mouth. The taste of mint, and spices from their meal and something uniquely James, exploded on her taste buds. Noelle was drowning in his kiss as a heat slowly ebbed its way through her entire body. She'd been kissed before but Walter's wet, sloppy technique had never stirred her.

A tingling sensation seared her core and her nipples tightened. This was the feeling she'd often read about, never believing one day she'd actually experience it for herself. She gripped his arms, clinging to him, wanting more. Though Noelle was inexperienced in the art of seduction, she worked on instinct, shyly pushing her tongue forward to meet his.

"So sweet," He murmured into her mouth before taking her tongue and sucking it between his lips. While one hand still firmly gripped her hair he used, his other hand to explore her body starting with her face and trailing down her neck until he reached her breast.

Noelle whimpered in surprise as she quickly fell under his sexual spell. He rubbed the heel of his palm against her breast plucking and pulling at it. She was so hypnotized by his touch that it took her several moments to realize his hand was now beneath her sweatshirt and his fingers were inching their way inside her sports bra.

She twisted her head away from his still seeking lips, fighting for air. "James," Noelle moaned his name, excited beyond comprehension.

He pressed sultry kisses on her throat, grazing his teeth against her sensitive skin as he found his way beneath her bra, twisting one taut nipple with the ease of a skilled lover.

All Noelle could do was grip his shoulders and hold on tight on this passionate ride of lust. "James, James, James," she moaned his name over and over as each mindless sensation coursed through her being.

"I like how responsive you are, Noelle. But how wet are you for me? Shall we see?" He nuzzled her neck with his nose.

It didn't register what he meant at first until his hand left her breast and slowly eased inside the waistband of her pants. She caught his hand in a moment of sanity. She'd just met this man yet he took all kinds of liberties—liberties she allowed. She could hear Aunt Frieda's voice in her head calling her shameless.

James brushed his lips against hers. "Let me, sweet Noelle." He wasn't asking, it was a quiet command. Underneath that slate gaze, she was powerless. Noelle released his hand, giving him access to the most intimate part of her body. As he slid his fingers inside her panties, she blocked out every misgiving and willed herself to enjoy his erotic ministrations without guilt. When his thumb grazed over her slick little button, Noelle let out a cry. "Oh!" She squirmed against his fingers as one of them found its way past her labia and into her sheath.

"Damn baby, is this all for me?" he whispered leaning forward to nip her earlobe. He pushed his finger deeper inside of her with one hard thrust eliciting a moan from Noelle. With careful precision, he pulled his finger nearly out of her body and then pushed it back in. James repeated this motion for several more strokes, adding another finger as he went.

Noelle was slowly coming apart with each caress. Liquid heat surged through her body, forming in the pit of her belly and licking its way through every single nerve ending. She trembled with her need for more. She didn't know what was happening to her but she didn't want it to ever end.

"That's it baby, move with it," he commanded softly as he continued to drive her to the edge of an explosive climax.

Noelle gyrated her pelvis against his hand, unable to keep still. Each passing second, her temperature rose until an orgasm ripped through her body like an electric current. She screamed until her throat was raw. Nothing could have ever prepared her for this moment—books, movies and Walter paled in comparison to this very real passion.

She leaned forward, pressing her forehead against his to catch her breath. Her racing pulse slowly returned to normal after several seconds. James eased his fingers from her wetness. Noelle found herself in the crosshairs of his gaze as he brought those damp fingers to his lips and proceeded to lick them clean, his eyes never leaving hers. "Delicious."

An involuntary shiver shook her shoulders.

"You're a very passionate woman, Noelle. Did you know that?" He caressed the side of her face with the back of his hand.

Unable to form the words, she shook her head.

"Maybe you didn't, but I did. I live on something called instinct, Noelle, and it rarely fails me. When I saw you, I knew you were a woman of hidden depths. I can help you discover all those hidden passions." His voice never rose above a whisper but there was an undercurrent to his words, something she couldn't quite put her fingers on.

"How?" Her voice came out in hoarse croak.

"I have a proposition for you."

Chapter Six

"James, your two o'clock appointment is here. Would you like me to sit in on this meeting or send Stella in to take notes?" Paul inquired, poking his head inside James' office.

"That won't be necessary. Send Mrs. Alexander in and please cancel my three o'clock meeting and reschedule. I also need you to go over the files for the Matsuki Group and give me some input. We can meet to discuss later this afternoon," James instructed without looking up from the figures on his desk.

"I'll get right on it." Paul stepped out of the office leaving it slightly ajar for James's two o'clock to come in.

James didn't need to look up to see when his visitor entered the room, he could smell her perfume. Only when she remained by the door did he raise his head to view the stunning brunette. Her dress clung to her willowy figure like an expensive glove, and fell just at her knees to reveal the curvy expanse of long legs. Her hair, worn loose, framed her shoulders and cascaded down her back. Her full lips curved into what James saw as a self-satisfied grin.

"James, it's been a long time." She sauntered toward his desk, in a pair of six inch heels that screamed "fuck me." Her fragrance, which seemed to be heavily applied, almost choked him the closer she got to him. At one point, the scent had held fond memories for him but now it served as a reminder of a time he wished to forget. She was dressed for seduction and not for the business she claimed she'd wanted to discuss with him. James knew exactly why she'd come. He could have declined but didn't, mainly for the ego stroke of having his ex beg him for something he had no intention of giving her.

"Gillian." He inclined his head forward in acknowledgement. "Please, have a seat."

She raised a dark, sculpted brow. "No hug for an old friend?"

He placed his elbows on his large oak desk and threaded his fingers together. "I wouldn't want to ruin the effect of that outfit."

Instead of taking the seat in front of his desk, she headed to the couch and perched herself on the edge. James was sure he didn't imagine her inconspicuously running her fingers along one outstretched leg. "This old thing? It's so last season. So how have you been?" She gave him that wide-eyed stare that used to quicken his heart. Now he could see the artifice behind it.

"I can't complain, Gillian. And yourself?"

"I've been keeping busy." She paused for a moment to take in her surroundings. James could read the calculation in her baby blue eyes. "I'm quite impressed with the set-up here. You've done quite well for yourself. You're mentioned in the paper quite a bit. I always knew you'd make it here one day. I really wish we hadn't lost touch, but I didn't want to make waves with David." She lowered her lashes for a brief moment, hiding her expression but it wasn't hard for James to figure out what she was thinking. She regretted passing him over for his brother who had been in a more secure financial position at the time. Now the tables were turned, and she wanted to give him her lost little girl act. He didn't buy it for a minute.

"It's strange how we remember things differently, Gillian. You couldn't end things fast enough with me because you believed my future was uncertain. I believe those were you words, weren't they?"

Her eyes suddenly welled with tears. "I know what I said. And at the time I was under a lot of pressure from my parents. You have to understand they had certain expectations of me. I couldn't disappoint them."

James' bullshit meter was on overload. He wondered if she actually believed the lies she spewed. "So you disappointed me instead. It's okay, I'm well aware of how things are. Anyway, we both know you didn't make this appointment with me to rehash the past. What do you want, Gillian?"

Gillian caught her bottom lip between her straight white teeth. "James, can't we at least be civil? We did mean something to each other once."

"Once, as in no more."

She bowed her head with an exaggerated sigh. In a movement that would have gone unnoticed by a less observant person, she moved her hand to her thigh and raised the hem of her dress ever so slightly. "But there's no reason we can't rekindle that friendship...didn't you practically beg me to stay with you?"

Though that comment hit below the belt, he maintained his composure. "We all make mistakes."

"I'm offering you a chance to get in good with the Alexanders. Isn't that something you've always wanted?"

"Apparently, not as much as you, Gillian."

She at least had the good grace to blush, although he could barely tell beneath the artificial enhancement that lined her cheekbones. "You never used to be so cold."

"You never used to be this transparent." The little bit of patience he'd held on to was now nil. "I'm a busy man Gillian, state your business otherwise this meeting will adjourn."

She flinched, and was apparently surprised her charms were no longer his kryptonite. As if to test out his reaction, Gillian slowly ran her tongue across her lip and flipped her hair. James remained impassive, unimpressed with her attempts to arouse him. A wave of crimson colored her face briefly and she fidgeted on the sofa.

"Perhaps, you'd like to take this seat. It would be easier for you to discuss business if you're facing me rather than lounging on the sofa at the other end of the room."

"Well, I was hoping you'd join me over here," she purred.

"Gillian, you're really starting to bug me."

She huffed and puffed as she stomped over to the seat he'd offered. She plopped down without the same panache she displayed earlier. "I didn't expect you to be so hostile."

James glanced at his watch to underline her time was running out. "I don't have time to play catch-up. What the hell do you want?"

"I..." She raised her chin defiantly and narrowed her eyes. "I think you've punished us enough James. Call off your dogs."

He found it pathetic that the Alexander men would send Gillian to plead their cases when she probably knew less about running a company than the average laymen. For the first time since she'd entered his office, James found himself amused. It wasn't because she had swallowed her pride to ask him for help: it was that she had the nerve to. "To what are you referring, Gillian? I work on specifics."

Her fists balled at her sides almost as if she wanted to get up and punch him. "So we're playing that game? You're going to make me grovel?"

"I can't make you do anything although you're the one who came to me wanting something, so unless you spell it out I can't help you."

"You've changed."

"I think we've already established that."

"Do you really hate us all so much?" she whispered, placing her hand over her ample bosom. "Me especially? I'm so sorry for what I did. If what you want from me is an apology, you have it."

"That would mean a lot to me...if I still cared. Since you're skirting around the issue, I assume you're here because I've authorized the termination of AlCore's contracts with my hotels?"

"You know it is," she answered tight-lipped, not bothering to maintain eye contact.

"And the Alexanders believe I've done it out of spite."

She shrugged. "Didn't you?"

"To make such an accusation would be an acknowledgement that they had some prior connection with me or they've done something to warrant me wanting revenge. To the best of my knowledge, there is no association. You, yourself, know I have no ties to them."

She didn't look at him but her body language screamed embarrassment. In different circumstances, he might have felt sorry for her. But then all he had to do was remember their last encounter and any semblance of pity that tried to form within his heart was immediately squashed. "So you won't help us?"

"And what would be the benefit of my helping a company that's weeks away from filing bankruptcy? I'd be throwing money away if I continued doing business with AlCore, which by the way has been so grossly mismanaged in the past several years. It was only a matter of time before it faced financial ruin. Not to mention, the quality of the products have gone down. That's the gist of it. I can't continue to allow AlCore to supply my hotels with an inferior product.

Our clients deserve the best. I run a business, not a charity, my dear."

"Won't you help for David's sake?"

At the mention of that asshole, James finally reached the end of his rope. "Speaking of David, I find it odd a CEO who cares so much about the future of his company would send his wife, who I'm sure hasn't spent one day in the office, to speak on his behalf instead of coming himself."

When no answer came, he pounded his fist on his desk making Gillian jump. "Get the hell out of my office, Gillian. You're wasting my damn time."

This time she smirked. "I thought you said you no longer cared."

"I don't but neither do I like being played for a fool."

She shot daggers with her stare. "Fine, I'll leave. Bitterness doesn't suit you at all, James."

"And desperation doesn't become you, my dear."

"Just like that? You won't help us. Think about your family."

"What family, Gillian? You're barking up the wrong tree. And frankly, I find it pathetic how your husband is willing to prostitute you to save a company he doesn't have the balls to fight for himself."

Gillian rose to her feet in a huff. "Bastard. You think you're so much better than us now because of all this?" She swept her hand out. "Well, don't forget where you come from."

"I'll never forget, Gillian, and therein lies the problem. Goodbye." He returned his attention to the papers he had been studying before she'd entered his office. It was only when she marched out of his office and slammed his door behind her did he give up the pretense of working. Her barbs had hit more marks than he was willing to admit.

Though he was no longer sexually attracted to her, Gillian still reminded him of a past he wished to bury.

A soft knock broke James out of his silent musings. "Come in," he called knowing it could only be Paul, or his secretary Stella.

"Is everything okay, James?" Paul poked his head inside the office without stepping inside.

"Yes, I'm fine, but I think I'm going to need you to rearrange the remainder of my appointments today. And I'll need those packets I asked Stella for first thing in the morning. Make sure she prioritizes that."

"Will do. Can I get you some lunch? I notice you haven't eaten today."

"No, thank you."

Paul ducked away and closed the door.

James had been truthful with Gillian when he'd told her he had not deliberately set out to harm AlCore. In fact, had AlCore maintained the same high standards that had made them one of the biggest hotel and office suppliers in the industry, he would have continued their business association. He didn't get to where he was by making decisions based purely on emotion. But knowing the Alexanders were suffering, perhaps worrying about how they would keep their superfluous lifestyle, proved to him karma was indeed a bitch. And that bitch was on his side.

<><><><><>

Simone shook her head at Noelle as she paced the living room. "Are you out of your ever loving mind? Please tell me you're not considering this."

For the past few days, Noelle agonized over what happened between her and James and their subsequent conversation. Looking back, it almost seemed as if it had happened to someone else.

"I have a proposition for you."

Noelle's body continued to throb with desire from his touch. She could see his lips moving but couldn't quite make out the words. "Huh?"

"I said I have a proposition you may be interested in."

She moistened her now dry lips." Are you offering me some kind of job?"

"You can say that. As I already stated, I'll never be anything but completely honest with you. Noelle, when I first saw you I couldn't quite put my finger on why I was so drawn to you but I suspected you would be a woman of passionate depths and now my suspicions have been confirmed. I live a certain lifestyle one which requires a lot of a travel and several hours a week in my office. I don't have time for dating and I'm far beyond the age of running through a different bed partner every time the whim takes me."

Noelle never considered herself some great genius but she wasn't stupid. As he continued to talk it became clear to her exactly what he was getting at. "You want me to be some kind of regular booty call?"

He raised one dark sinister brow. "I wouldn't put it in such uncouth terms but I am looking for a steady companion who can make herself available upon demand. My schedule is erratic so I may need you in the mornings or late at night."

"And I'm just expected to drop everything for you?"

"I gather from what you've told me about art school, making yourself available to me won't be an issue. As far as your search for employment goes, there's no need. Should you agree to this arrangement, you'll be compensated for your time. I own a penthouse in the city where I'll expect you to live for the duration of our agreement."

"You mean move in with you?" she asked softly still trying to make sense of this whole thing.

"I have my own house but when I need you, I'll visit you not the other way around. You'll also be given a monthly allowance for clothing, lingerie, entertainment, beautification and any other personal effects you require. My EA will see to all your household needs."

"And all I'd have to do is sleep with you?"

"I believe we've already established that." His words were formal, a jarring contrast to his earlier tone.

"What kind of woman do you think I am?"

James didn't answer right away as he gave her a long accessing look. "You're a woman of many layers and I'd like to be the man to peel each of them away."

Though they shouldn't have, his words made her squirm in her seat. She bit the inside of her cheek to hold back a whimper.

James reached over her and opened his glove compartment. He pulled out a small white rectangular card and handed it to her. "That's my information with my secretary's number on the front. Should you decide to discuss this arrangement in further detail, contact her and you'll hear back from either me or my EA."

"I can't contact you directly?"

"I'm a busy man."

"I see." She didn't really but it was getting harder to be so close to him and keep a clear mind. It was as if she'd been dumped in the center of a bad B-movie. Things like this didn't happen in the real world and if they did not to her. "Well it's been nice James but I have to go now."

He placed his hand on her thigh to keep her immobile. "Give this some thought, Noelle."

"I've only met you tonight…I can't just agree to this without at least getting to know you better."

His eyes narrowed and he looked at her like he was inspecting a rare species of insect. Noelle shifted uncomfortably in her seat under his piercing gaze.

"Two dates."

She stroked her bottom lip with her tongue. "I don't follow."

"You're right. It's a bit forward of me to ask something like this of you on such a short acquaintance. Let's go out on two dates. At the end of the second one, I'll expect an answer. Yes or no."

Any sane woman would tell him to go to hell. But she couldn't deny the strong connection she felt between them. "You'd take me out first?"

"It's what you want isn't it?"

"But you're only taking me out on the condition of my becoming your lover?"

"You're free to say no. Think about it."

"Okay, I will. Think about it, I mean."

He offered her a tight smile in response, releasing his grip on her thigh.

"Well, I uh, guess I'll be going now. Good night."

"Take care, Noelle."

This time when she grabbed the handle to step out of the vehicle, he didn't stop her. After waving a quick good bye, she slid out of the car and slammed the door behind her. Too afraid to look behind her, she hurried inside her apartment building.

Simone paced the living room with her hands on her hips. "Are you listening to me? Noelle? Does this guy think he's Robert Redford in *Indecent Proposal*? Someone should inform him this is real life and not a movie. Call him up and tell him hell no."

Noelle hugged her knees against her chest. "You were the one who pushed me to go out with him in the first place. And the time we've spent together was nice. He's charming and I enjoy his company."

Simone stopped in her tracks and snorted. "He comes off that way because he's trying to get into your pants. So what if he's taken you out a couple times? That doesn't mean squat if he expects you to repay him with some ass when all is said and done."

"He's been a perfect gentleman when we've gone out." Noelle didn't bother mentioning how hot and heavy they'd gotten the night they'd met at the gym. As agreed, James had taken her out twice. The first time he surprised her with a limo ride around the city. As they enjoyed champagne and soft music in the back seat, he regaled her with some of the sites he'd seen in his travels. Noelle had hung on every word.

Their second date, he took her to a club off the beaten track that played the smooth R&B music they both enjoyed. They'd talked mainly about art because James knew it was something that interested her. She found he was quite knowledgeable about the subject. It was incredible to Noelle how someone so worldly would be interested in someone as gauche and inexperienced as her but James put her at ease. She felt special to have his attention.

It didn't occur to her until after their dates that despite all he'd shared with her, like what he did for a living, and places he'd been, he was still an enigma to her. Noelle figured in time he would share more of himself with her. At least that was her hope.

"I can tell by your far-off look you're contemplating this and I find it disturbing on so many levels. Why would a man who has more money than God go around asking random women to be his mistress? It doesn't make sense."

She flinched at Simone's reminder of James' status. When she'd come home that first night, her cousin had informed her James Rothschild was the head of an international chain of luxury hotels and resorts and at only thirty-four he was already a billionaire. Besides being self-made, he was known for always having a pretty socialite or celebrity on his arm, none of whom looked like Noelle.

"Simone you don't have to talk in circles. You can't believe he'd ask this of someone like me. I get it."

Simone shook her head vehemently. "Honey, no. That's not what I meant." She walked over to the couch and scooted next to Noelle. "I think the world of you. You're fabulous, girl. The problem is, you haven't figured that out yet. From what it sounds like, he's looking for his own personal sex slave."

"It isn't like that. I believe we can build something on this."

Simone crossed her arms over her chest while shaking her head. "Really? Is he offering to take you out after you become his kept woman?" Noelle had no answer. She sincerely wished she hadn't shared so many details with Simone.

When Noelle didn't respond, her cousin nodded her head in confirmation. "I didn't think so. Open your eyes honey. I can see you're already falling for this guy. What's going to happen when he discards you? And it won't be if. Guys like him treat women like a spoiled kid treats a new toy. They play with it for a little while until something shinier comes along. I don't want to see you get hurt."

What hurt was Simone's harsh judgment of the situation. Noelle had experienced real passion for the first time in her life and loathed the idea of walking away from James, at least not without finding out if there was something more between them. At first, Noelle had doubts but after a few nights of kinky dreams and waking up so horny she had to touch herself for relief, she seriously contemplated his proposal.

Noelle wanted to be in James' arms again and feel his lips against hers. She wanted to wrap her legs around his waist as he slid in and out of her while she screamed his name. And though he hadn't touched her beyond a chaste goodnight kiss on their subsequent dates, it only intensified her desire to give herself to him completely. "You only know what you've read on the Internet about him. I've actually spent time with James. He's not the cold bastard you're making him out to be."

Simone rolled her eyes and released an exasperated sigh. "Now you're being naïve. Use your head, Noelle."

Noelle stiffened at the admonishment. It was the same thing her Aunt Frieda used to say when she'd chastised Noelle for some random transgression. "Maybe I'd rather listen to my heart instead of my head. You're the one who said I should go out with him in the first place but now you're telling me to leave him alone. Is it because he looked my way instead of yours? Simone, men fall over their feet when you walk by but one guy wants to be with me and you have a problem with it?"

"He doesn't want to be with you. He wants to fuck you!" Simone snapped and then immediately covered her mouth in surprise as if she couldn't believe she'd actually said that. "Noelle—"

Noelle held up her hand. "Save it. Good to know what you really think of me."

Simone grasped Noelle's hand to keep her on the couch when she tried to get up. "You know I didn't mean it like that. I just think you're better than this."

Noelle yanked herself out of her cousin's grip and stormed out of the living room and didn't stop until she was out the door. She walked a few blocks to cool off. Simone had never been anything but kind and supportive for as long as she could remember. She shouldn't have implied her cousin was jealous but being told someone was only interested in screwing them would rub most people the wrong way. Maybe Simone was right and James really was just using her for sex, but if she didn't take this chance, she would wonder "what if" for the rest of her life. Besides, if she didn't go for it, Noelle might as well admit Aunt Frieda was right: that she was incapable of being loved.

Simone was thankfully absent when Noelle returned to the apartment. On the nightstand in her bedroom was the business card James had handed her. She picked it up and studied the name on the card. Stella Martin. Before she lost her nerve, she picked up her cell phone and quickly dialed the number.

Chapter Seven

Noelle barely managed not to pinch herself. This place was unreal with its cathedral ceiling, grand spiral staircase, a large modern kitchen with all the latest amenities and three bedrooms all with grand terraces. The square footage of the living room alone was larger than the entire apartment she'd shared with Simone. While her new living space was not ostentatiously decorated, it still screamed money. She was almost too scared to touch anything for fear of breaking something.

"This is mine?" she asked the man standing behind her.

"While you reside here it is."

Noelle stiffened as the gravity of her choice suddenly hit her. Her knees grew wobbly and she took the closest seat which was on a leather arm chair. She wrapped her arms around her body in a protective hug. "I'm not the first woman who's stayed here, am I?" she asked softly without looking in the direction of James' EA. Shortly after her call with Ms. Martin, she was contacted by Paul Atkinson. He'd been straight to the point, shooting off a handful of instructions and necessary appointments she needed to make. That had been two weeks ago.

Noelle and Simone had barely talked in that time until the movers came to remove Noelle's belongings. Simone had tearfully begged Noelle to reconsider but she'd already made up her mind. It was for the best. She'd always felt as though she was mooching off her cousin because Simone had paid the bulk of the bills.

Paul didn't answer Noelle's question right away and didn't seem as if he would. "I'm not, am I?" Noelle persisted.

The blond man who had been all business moments before seemed to soften a bit. "I'm sorry but I'm not at liberty to discuss my boss' personal life."

Noelle chuckled humorlessly. "I am his personal life."

"Be that as it may, I can't answer that question, Miss Greene."

"I understand. And please call me Noelle. Miss seems so formal."

"I don't think that would be a good idea."

"But you said I should call you Paul. It would only be fair."

"Very well." He paused to look at his smartphone. "I've done a run- through of the penthouse and everything appears to be in order. The housekeeper, Marsha, comes on Tuesdays and Thursdays. She has her own key so don't worry about letting her in. Marsha also keeps the refrigerator stocked so just leave a list for her if there's anything specific you need for her to acquire. For all your other needs, my number is programmed in your new cell phone. I've left the pass codes for the elevators and anything else you'll need them for. Any questions?"

This was the most awkward meeting ever. She felt like this was her first day on a job. "Umm, when will I see James?"

"I'm afraid I don't have an answer for you. He's a busy man. You're free to go shopping to pass the time. I've left a list of stores you now have an account with." He probably said it to placate her but it left Noelle more than a little uneasy.

"Okay." Paul was cool toward her but not rude. She suspected he was only doing his job but it bothered Noelle that he may think she was nothing more than a gold digger, only with James for his money. For reasons she couldn't explain, she didn't want this man to think badly of her. "I'm really grateful for what you're doing."

"I'm just doing my job, Miss—Noelle."

"Thank you, anyway."

Paul looked to be at a loss for words for a moment. He gave her the impression he wasn't used to being thanked in this scenario. Noelle studied him briefly. He wasn't a bad looking man, although he was no James. Actually, he was quite handsome. His dark blond hair and baby blue eyes behind wire framed glasses presented a pleasing aesthetic. He was tall and lanky but wore his expertly tailored suit well.

His mouth nearly curved to a smile. "You're welcome. If you need me for anything at all, please don't hesitate to call."

"I really appreciate that." She stood up. "Let me walk you out."

"That won't be necessary. Take care of yourself, okay?" He almost sounded as though he meant it.

"Sure." Her attempt at a smile was painful so she waved him off instead.

Once Noelle was alone in what would be her living accommodations for an indeterminate time, self-doubt assailed her. She thought she knew what she was doing when she walked into this situation, but now Noelle wondered if she'd jumped the gun. What had been forefront in her mind was how much she'd miss James' touch, yet she hadn't spoken to him in the two weeks since she'd taken him up on his offer.

Paul had handled everything; from taking her to the doctor to get tested for STDs and ensuring she was prescribed birth control. If that wasn't embarrassing enough, she was given a contract to sign which stated she was not allowed to discuss their arrangement with the media nor would she try to profit from their association once the affair ended.

It all seemed so sterile. And the worst of it was, she didn't know when James would actually visit her. The longer she sat alone in this luxurious penthouse suite the lonelier she felt. She wanted to call Simone but things between them were still slightly raw. Unable to sit for a second longer, she walked around the apartment until she came to her boxes that were spread out on the spare bedroom floor. She gravitated toward one box in particular. It was the one full of keepsakes from her mother.

Noelle opened it and looked through its contents. She pulled out a photo album and thumbed through the pages. The pictures brought a smile to her face. They reminded her of a time when she'd truly been happy. Noelle touched each artifact inside the box, feeling closer to her mother's spirit and getting comfort from them. One of the last items she found was a cookbook which held all her mother's old recipes. Aunt Frieda had tried to take it from her but it was the one thing Noelle wouldn't relent where her Aunt was concerned. It meant so much to her because she remembered helping her mother cook in the kitchen. Many of the recipes her mother had come up with herself.

A sudden bout of inspiration hit Noelle when she decided to try a few out for herself. Besides art, cooking with her mother had always provided Noelle with her greatest source of joy. She made her way to the kitchen and began searching for ingredients, and was pleased to find exactly what she needed to make several of the recipes many times over.

Noelle immersed herself in baking and was just taking her second cake out of the oven when she realized she wasn't alone. She hadn't heard anyone enter but she felt a presence. Looking up from her task, she saw James standing at the kitchen entrance looking sexier than any man had a right to.

Feeling shy in his presence, she placed the cookie sheet on the stove and placed her oven mitts on the counter. Even in a suit she was sure cost more than her entire wardrobe, there was no disguising James's broad-shouldered ruggedness. He was even more handsome than she remembered.

She moistened her now dry lips with the tip of her tongue. "Hi, I wasn't expecting you tonight."

"You should always expect me Noelle. I believed you understood that per our contract." His cool reminder was like a slap in the face. Not for the first time, she wondered what possessed her to agree to this madness. The calculated way in which this was all set up made her wonder who the real James was—this cold stranger standing before her or the charming man she'd originally met.

She squared her shoulders hoping he couldn't discern her internal conflict. "You're right." Noelle took the cookies off the sheet and placed them on a platter to keep her hands busy. "Would you like something to eat? It's getting close to dinner and I can fix us something. There's a lot of food here."

His expression was unreadable but she could sense his disapproval. "I'm glad to see you've made yourself at home but it's not necessary for you to cook my meals. I have a chef for that at my own house."

A lump formed in her throat but she managed to respond. "Duly noted."

"You're welcome to hire a chef to cook meals for you as well. Paul can make the arrangements."

"That's okay. I don't mind cooking. Actually, I like it."

"Noelle, if you're trying to impress me with you domestic skills you can stop wasting your time. I didn't want you because you can cook."

"I'm not. I'm just capable of doing certain things for myself and cooking is one of them. I offered to make you something to eat because that's the hospitable thing to do." Noelle didn't know what his problem was but she wasn't sure if she could handle walking on pins and needles around him for the remainder of the night. Maybe it was best to cut her losses now before she was in too deep. "James, I've given this some thought and I don't think I'm cut out for this kind of thing after all. I'm sorry I've wasted your time."

He stepped farther into the kitchen. "Do you mind telling me why?"

She backed away as he moved closer, unable to trust herself with him in close proximity. "It all just seems so cold and emotionless. I should have mentioned this earlier but all I could think about was..."

"What Noelle?" He continued to advance.

Noelle walked around to the other side of the island to put distance between them. "At this point, does it really matter? This is the first time I've seen you since our last date. I haven't even been afforded the courtesy of a phone call, yet I've been subjected to a humiliating medical examination to prove I've got a clean bill of health, and made to sign some contract like I can't be trusted. This hardly seems fair."

James raised both brows as though he was genuinely surprised. "Having a very generous allowance and access to any high end store along the East Coast isn't enough for you?"

"I'm not interested in the money."

He chuckled. "But you're here, so tell me again my money doesn't matter." He continued to advance and Noelle backed away until she found herself pressed against the kitchen wall, his chest flush with hers. James lowered his head until the heat of his breath grazed her face.

Noelle turned her head to the side. "It doesn't. I wanted to be here because I wanted to get to know you better."

He captured her face in his grasp and forced her to look at him. "There's no doubt the sexual attraction is strong between us, but let's not pretend the money hasn't captured your interest either. Things will go much better if we remain honest with each other. And I have a truth for you. Wanna hear it?"

Her breath caught in her throat. The scent of his cologne and raw maleness assailed her senses. Her brain was mush and she couldn't form words. Noelle wanted to argue with him and deny how wrong he was but nothing mattered in that moment. She was captive beneath his gaze—James' willing prisoner. Finally, Noelle nodded in answer to his question.

His lips curved into the most devilishly sexy smile she'd ever witnessed. Her heart fluttered in response and her pulse raced. "I was thinking about you all day, Noelle. Knowing you were here in this house, walking around with that adorably sexy lost-little-girl look. That one taste I had of you wasn't enough and it drove me so crazy, I cancelled all my afternoon appointments. I broke several traffic laws to get here. To have you." He pressed his hardness against her. "I can feel the heat from your body. You want this as badly as I do. After what we shared, there's no walking away because your body won't let you. Will it, sweet Noelle?"

Chapter Eight

James knew Noelle was his for the taking the second he touched her. He hadn't lied about thinking about her all day and couldn't go a moment longer without getting another taste of those sweet lips. He brushed his mouth against hers. "Tell me you want this."

Noelle released a low moan. "I-I do."

"Tell me you won't walk away."

She closed her eyes briefly. "I can't."

The two weeks it had taken to set things up had been pure torture for James. There was something nearly untouchable about Noelle, a pure quality that almost seemed like a sin to tarnish. But he'd steered himself from the direction of those thoughts. Growing up, he'd been denied so much and had constantly been told what he couldn't have. But he fully intended to have Noelle.

Her very presence told him that she wasn't so above the other women he'd had similar deals with. He didn't care that she was just as interested in what he could give as much as the sex. Most women operated that way in his experience. He wouldn't allow her to play the ingénue with him because she knew exactly what she was doing. After he fucked her a few times, she'd be out of his system and he could move on to the next woman.

"That's right. You can't because you want it so bad you can barely speak." He kissed her gently at first, reacquainting himself with the taste of her lips. James grasped her ponytail and yanked her head back, allowing him to deepen his kiss.

He pressed his tongue forward to explore the slick sweet cavern of her mouth. She tasted even better than he remembered, validating his reason for choosing her.

Noelle was the one to break away, turning her head to the side. She gasped for air. "James," she whispered.

He placed a hand against her breast and began to massage it. "Does this feel good?"

She let out a moan. "Yes."

"How about this?" He slid his hand down the length of her body until he reached between her thighs to cup her pussy. Even through her jeans, he could feel the incredible heat. He already knew how wet she could get and he was looking forward to seeing if he could make her even wetter by the time this night was over.

She wiggled against his hand. "James," she cried out his name again.

"Tell me what you want me to do, baby."

"Touch me."

He chuckled. "Aren't I already doing that?"

"Skin to skin."

"Your wish is my command." James pulled away, taking Noelle's hand in his and leading her out the kitchen. He already knew from Paul which bedroom she'd picked so he didn't have to ask where to take her. Once they reached their destination, James took a seat on the edge of the bed and pulled Noelle into a standing position between his thighs facing him.

"Take off your top." He wanted her to undress for him to make her a willing participant but mainly because the idea of her stripping for him made James unbelievably hard.

Noelle hesitated briefly before lifting her top. James grabbed her wrist to halt her hurried actions. "Not so fast, honey. We have all night. Do it slowly."

She gnawed her bottom lip, a movement, he realized, Noelle did when she was nervous. Slowly, she pulled up her top in an unhurried fashion revealing inch by inch of delectably chocolate skin until it was completely off.

Unable to help himself, James pressed a string of fluttering kissing against her belly. "Very nice, baby. Now the jeans. And remember—don't rush."

Noelle unbuckled her jeans, eased the denim material down her rounded hips and stepped out of them. Once she stood before him in only a bra that had seen better days and pair of serviceable cotton white panties she covered her arms over her chest. The sight of Noelle in her underwear affected James in a way so unexpected it made him pause. That air of innocence swirled around her causing doubt to creep in yet again.

Noelle seemed so vulnerable and unsure of herself. She trembled as if she was cold and her eyes were downcast. A small part of James felt as if he was about to defile her. He could squash this whole thing now and allow her to walk away as she suggested earlier but he quickly squashed that thought. If she didn't want to be here, she wouldn't have signed the contract.

Now more determined than ever to have her, he grabbed her arms and forced them to her side. "Don't cover yourself, honey. This body was made for loving."

James drank in the sight of Noelle's body and admired what he saw. Noelle had more than a little flesh than he was used to on his women but it suited her. She was breathtaking, from her breasts that appeared to be more than a handful down to a small waist that flared into shapely hips and a generous ass.

He licked his lips in anticipation. "Now the bra. I want you to lower one strap at a time and then unhook it." How he was able to keep himself from grabbing Noelle and throwing her on the bed surprised him. The control he prided himself on was quickly waning but he didn't want to take her like a rutting bull the first time they were together.

Noelle's hands trembled as she obeyed his command. When she tossed her bra to the floor, she revealed the most beautiful pair of breasts he'd ever seen. They were large and round, sitting high on her chest. Capped with blackberry hued nipples, they made his mouth water. If he lifted his head just enough, he could suck one of the tantalizing tips into his mouth. And that's exactly what he did. As he suckled one breast he kneaded the other with his free hand, molding and massaging it.

Noelle gripped his shoulders. "James, that feels so good."

He lifted his head just enough to speak. "And by the end of the night, I'll make you feel even better." Unwilling to wait for Noelle to finish her strip tease, James pulled her on the bed and rolled on top of her. He immediately latched on to her breast again, licking, sucking and nipping at the turgid tip as he reveled in the texture of her skin against his tongue. Her beautiful body, coupled with her breathy moans, drove him over the edge of reason. James had promised himself to go slow with her tonight but now he wasn't sure he could.

Noelle threaded her fingers through his hair and held his head against her chest. He bit down on her nipple, eliciting a cry of surprise from her and he quickly soothed her injured flesh with his tongue. He turned his attention to her other breast, giving it the same treatment until she writhed and wiggled beneath him. "I need you, James."

"Patience," he whispered, although James wasn't sure if he'd be able to follow his own advice. Soon, playing with her breasts wasn't enough for him. He wanted to taste her pussy. In an attempt to not appear eager, he rained a trail of kisses down the center of her body until he made it to the juncture of her thighs. Using his teeth, he grabbed the edge of her panties and pulled them down her legs. Once they were at her feet he tugged them off completely. "Open your legs for me honey. I want to see all of you."

James didn't wait for Noelle to comply. Instead, he pushed her knees apart and settled between her dark thighs. While she wasn't shaved as he was used to, her bikini area was neatly groomed. Her scent was intoxicating with just a hint of womanly musk and sweetness that was unique to her. He bumped his nose against her slit, inhaling her aroma. James slid his middle finger along her dew-glistened slit.

Noelle bucked her hips, silently begging him for more. He couldn't help the smile that spread his lips. Her reactions were so delightfully honest. The body never lied. He parted her slick labia to examine the juicy pink center. "You have a pretty pussy. Did you know that baby?" He looked up long enough to see Noelle shake her head. "Well you do and I'm going to eat it and then I'm going to fuck it. What do you think about that Noelle? Are you going to let me suck and fuck this pretty little cunt?"

Her mouth opened but no words came out. James was determined to have her begging for it before he continued. He pressed his thumb against her clit and watched her tremble. "Tell me to eat your pussy, Noelle."

"P-please."

"Say, "eat my pussy, James.'"

"Eat me, James," her voice came out as a hoarse whisper.

"No, say 'eat my pussy, James.' Say those words. I want to hear how much you want it."

"Eat my p-pussy, James." It was almost as if she was uneasy with such frank language but she'd soon learn.

"And tell me how badly you want this."

"I need it, James. I don't think I could stand it if you don't!"

He grinned at her in triumph. "Well, since you asked so nicely…" He lowered his head and ran his tongue along her pussy from her clit to her anus.

"Oh God!" Noelle screamed.

James lifted his head again. "It's James. Remember it." He stroked her with the flat of his tongue, swiping her cunt with broad licks. Noelle grasped his hair and bucked her pelvis against his face. In response, he caught her clit between his teeth and alternated between nibbling and sucking on it.

"James! Please I can't take anymore!"

She was not only going to take it, she was going to love it. James released the hot little nubbin and pushed his tongue inside of her and wiggled it around. He pulled it out and then shoved back in. While he did this, he took her clit between his finger and thumb and twisted it.

Noelle bucked her hips wildly and he knew she was close to her peak by the way her grip tightened in his hair and her juices began to flow more rapidly.

A scream ripped through the room signaling Noelle's release. James continued to lap at her pussy, unrelenting in his pursuit to drive her insane with lust.

He took her close to another sweet climax but pulled back. When she came again, he wanted it to be on his cock. James slid off the bed and quickly undressed, never taking his eyes off her. She looked so beautiful laying there in all her glory, ready to be taken by him. He'd been anticipating this moment for weeks and finally his fantasy was near its fruition.

James slid on top of her and gave her a long deep kiss. He was pleasantly surprised when Noelle's tongue shot forward to greet his. It was brief, but it satisfied him to see she was a quick learner. His cock was so hard it almost hurt and he could no longer put off being inside of her. Positioning himself on his knees, he pushed her thighs apart. Her dark eyes connected with his as he guided his dick to her slick opening. "Are you ready for this, baby?"

"Yes," she answered in a small whisper.

He thrust inside of her with one powerful surge. Goddamn she was tight! It would take a lot of willpower not to come right away. Noelle's pussy was like warm velvet holding his cock in a vise.

"James!" Noelle screamed her eyes wide in apparent surprise.

He wasn't a small man, he was in fact larger than average but his size rarely presented a problem. "Are you okay?"

She nodded with her lip between her teeth again. Sure she was tight but she didn't feel like a virgin.

"You have done this before, haven't you?"

"Once."

"Jesus Christ," he muttered. She might as well have been a virgin.

"No. Noelle. Remember that," she teased him with a shy smile.

Her comment caught him off guard, making him chuckle. It was a rarity to find humor in a situation like this even when it was killing him to be inside of her and remain still.

"Noelle, I'm going to have to move now. Will you be okay?"

"Yes. I was a little surprised. You're kind of big."

He braced his arms on either side of her head and eased several inches of his dick out of her cunt until only the head remained. James forced himself to go slow, pushing himself deep once more. He repeated this motion several times but when Noelle wiggled her hips beneath him, all bets were off.

He slammed into her harder and faster but Noelle didn't seem to mind this time because she met him thrust for thrust. She was a natural, made for this. Made for him.

"So good," he murmured. "*My* pussy."

Their sweat-dampened bodies slid together as James continued to conquer her pussy. He wanted this to go on for as long as possible but a climax so powerful tore through his body making it impossible to hold back. He shot his seed deep inside of her tight cunt before collapsing on top of her. James wrapped his arms around her body and continued to pump.

Noelle cried out and ran her nails down his back. Her pussy gripped his cock even tighter as she screamed her orgasm. "James!" She buried her face against his neck and clung to him.

James wasn't sure how long they held on to each other but the moment he realized their arms were wrapped around each other, he disentangled himself from her hold and rolled away. Noelle placed her hand on his chest but he flinched away.

"James?" He could hear the hurt in her tone but it couldn't be helped. He needed to establish how things would be between them from the beginning before she got any ideas. An emotion he couldn't quite explain tweaked his heart but James refused to acknowledge it. Noelle was no different from the others, and as soon she realized that the smoother things would be. No matter how much he wanted to stay and hold her he couldn't allow himself the luxury. Noelle was already under his skin but he refused to let her into his heart. He paused for a moment, realizing where his thoughts had traveled. James reminded himself of his plans and his future, a future Noelle did not belong in. With that in mind, he rolled off the bed and stood up.

"I'm going to get a drink. Would you like something?"

The bewilderment on her face was clear but he squashed the guilt rearing its head. "I'll take that as a no." And with that he turned his back to her and walked out the room not bothering to get dressed.

Watching James stroll away so nonchalantly was gut wrenching, Noelle wasn't sure whether to cry or be angry. She wondered how he could be so unaffected after what she thought was pretty special. One second she was on the highest of highs and now she felt lower than she had in a long time. Noelle was positive she hadn't imagined the connection between them. It went beyond physical. But she couldn't figure out why he'd leave her so abruptly. Doubt assailed her and she wondered if she'd pleased him.

Noelle lay on her side and stared off into space, not really seeing anything. When James returned to the bedroom she sat up. "Hi," she greeted shyly.

He gathered his clothing off the ground. "I'm going to shower in the spare room and then head out."

"You're not staying?"

"No." It was just a simple word but it came out so abruptly it sent a chill through her.

"Maybe we can go out for dinner the next time you come by," she suggested.

"Maybe." His noncommittal response gave her the impression he had no intention of taking her out anywhere.

Once he'd scooped up his belongings, James headed for the door. "I'll be in touch, Noelle."

Instinctively, she knew better than to ask him when that would be but she had to know the answer to the one burning question on her mind. "James."

He halted in mid-stride and turned back to her. She tried to keep her gaze on his face but it was hard not to take in his magnificent body. Her breath caught in his throat. The man was a walking, talking Adonis.

"What is it Noelle?"

"I was wondering, uh did you like it? I mean, did I please you?"

He remained silent long enough to make her squirm. At first Noelle didn't think he would answer. "You still have a lot to learn but you have a lot of potential."

"Oh." It wasn't the answer she'd expected.

He walked over to the bed, bent over and caught her chin between his fingers. James brushed his lips against hers. "You were fine, Noelle. I'll be in touch okay?"

She nodded feeling only slightly mollified.

As he headed for the door a second time, James paused. "Those store accounts you have access to—use them." And then he left.

In the blink of an eye he'd transformed from an attentive, passionate lover to a cold stranger. Noelle couldn't wrap her mind around the switch. She wished her body didn't still crave his. But most of all, she wished she had the strength to walk away before she was in too deep. Unfortunately, Noelle didn't feel as if she could get any deeper.

Chapter Nine

"I'm sorry I'm late," Simone greeted. Noelle stood up to give her cousin a hug. "I was meeting with investors for my boutique."

"No problem. I'm just glad you could make it. I've only been here for a little while anyway. I went ahead and ordered you lemonade if that's okay."

"That's fine. But why would you think I wouldn't come? I was glad to hear from you."

Noelle had wanted to call Simone every day since she'd moved into James' penthouse but didn't have the nerve. She was still uneasy about the way things had been left between them but Simone was family and they'd always been close. Remembering this, she finally broke down and called to invite her to lunch. "We haven't spoken in weeks. I told you I'd give you my number when I was settled in and I didn't."

Simone took a sip of her drink before responding. "I figured you were busy but I was wondering when I'd hear from you. I would have called you myself if I had your number. And since you're the last person on Earth to not own a cell phone, I had to wait."

Noelle pulled her cell phone out of her purse and placed it on the table. "I have one now." James insisted she have one if he needed to get in contact with her at a moment's notice but she wouldn't tell Simone that for fear of being lectured.

"I'm impressed. My little cuz has stepped into the twenty-first century. Did my eyes deceive me or did I see you rocking Kate Spade's latest handbag?"

"The sales lady said these were very popular."

"I got to admit, you look like a million bucks. Your hair looks nice."

Noelle touched her hair self-consciously. She'd never worn a weave in her life and was still adjusting to having foreign hair. James seemed to like it though he never came right out and said it. She could just tell by the way he liked to pull her long tresses during sex. Noelle had been uneasy about spending his money so freely but once she realized it was what he expected of her, she'd gotten a makeover from head to toe, including a brand new wardrobe full of labels she'd never heard of but cost more than anything she'd ever owned in her life.

"Thanks. I only wish I had your fashion sense. Speaking of which, how did your meeting with the investors go?"

Simone's grin widened. "That's why I'm late actually. They seemed really impressed with the location I've chosen and my business proposal. They said they'd get back to me by middle of next week but I believe my boutique will be a go."

"That's amazing, Simone. If anyone deserves to have her dreams come true, it's you."

Simone reached across the table and gave Noelle's hand a squeeze. "Aww, thank you girl. When I decided to take on this endeavor, I didn't think the ball would get rolling so quickly. You're the one who encouraged me to go for it and now, it's actually happening. I know they say seventy percent of businesses fail in the first year but I realized if I don't take this opportunity now, I'll wonder 'what if' for the rest of my life."

"You won't fail. Anything you set your mind to you end up accomplishing."

Their conversation was halted when the waiter returned to the table to take their order. Once he was gone, they resumed dancing around the subject that had caused their rift.

Finally, unable to take the underlying tension between the two of them, Noelle broke down. "Look Simone, I'm really sorry for the way things were left between us when I moved out. You've done so much for me I could never repay you for. I love you and I don't want us to be mad at each other. That's why I haven't called you. It was because I'm ashamed of how I acted. I know you meant well when you told me what you thought."

Simone shook her head. "No. I'm the one who should apologize. I was way out of line. You're an adult and free to do what you like. Even if I don't always agree with the decisions you make, I'll always be here for you, hon. All I'm concerned about is whether you're happy. Are you?"

Noelle nibbled her bottom lip. She wasn't sure how to answer that. She was happy when James took her until she was breathless. Her pussy got wet whenever she thought about their sexual escapades. But afterwards he'd pull away and become distant. There were moments when he'd share a little about himself but those occasions were rare. It was those times that kept her anchored to him, what made her yearn to be closer to James in not just the physical sense.

It frightened her but Noelle fell for him a little bit more each time they were together. However, deep down Noelle knew James would be finished with her if she admitted it.

She pasted a smile on her face. "Yes, I'm happy."

Simone didn't hide her emotions well either, and by the expression on her face, Noelle could tell her cousin still had reservations. "Well, that's all that matters."

Once that awkwardness was out of the way, the conversation flowed. It was nice having her cousin to talk to. She didn't have many friends beyond a few acquaintances at art school because she always felt self-conscious and insecure. Simone was one of the few people who put her at ease.

"So how have you been keeping yourself busy?" Simone casually asked over their shared dessert of a pear tart.

Noelle swallowed the piece of tart in mouth. "I watch a lot of movies and I shop. Nothing too productive, I'm afraid."

"Well you look like a million bucks. That outfit looks great on you."

Noelle snorted. "I wish I could take credit but all those highfalutin stores I have accounts with all have personal shoppers. They pick out outfits, I wear them."

"You wear them well, though. It's funny because you never liked going shopping with me."

Noelle still wasn't a huge fan of shopping but it embarrassed her to admit she only shopped because James expected her to uphold a certain image. Noelle realized her cousin wasn't fond of Noelle's situation; she didn't want to give Simone another reason. "Something to fill the time I guess." She quickly redirected the topic. "I've been baking a lot lately. I found my mom's old recipe books and I've been trying them out. She wanted to own a bakery one day."

"You never mentioned that about Aunt Dot."

Noelle shrugged. "The subject never came up. She used to be something else in the kitchen. I don't think I've been able to replicate Mom's baked goods but I'm getting pretty darn close."

"I'd love to try your baked goods sometime."

"I have a fridge full of chocolate cupcakes if you'd like to come back to the penthouse with me. We can walk from here. It's a nice day."

"You had me at chocolate cupcakes."

They chatted and giggled the entire walk to the penthouse. It felt like they were teenagers again.

"Oh, my God! Girl, are you serious?" Simone exclaimed when she stepped inside the penthouse. "This place is unbelievable!"

Noelle laughed uneasily. "Yeah, it's a bit overwhelming isn't it?"

"I wouldn't say that but it looks like you've moved on up like the *Jeffersons*."

Noelle giggled. "You're so silly."

Noelle gave Simone the full tour of the penthouse and then the two women browsed through the extensive Blu-ray collection in the entertainment console finally settling on an old movie they both enjoyed watching. Noelle popped some popcorn. It was like old times. The movie was only half way over when Noelle felt another presence in the room. The hairs on the back of her neck stood up. It was unnerving how easily she could sense James without having to lay eyes on him.

He'd never told her she couldn't have visitors but she felt guilty nonetheless. She slowly turned to see him enter the room. His jacket was slung casually over his shoulder.

Noelle stood up to greet him. "Hi, James. You remember my cousin, Simone, don't you?"

Simone, who had been engrossed in the movie, noticed James for the first time and stood as well. "Hi." The greeting lacked the warmth it had from their first meeting at the gym.

James, seeming unaffected, smiled at Simone, going into full charmer mode. "Nice to see you again, Simone. Noelle mentioned you were going into business for yourself?"

Noelle was surprised he'd remembered.

Regardless of how her cousin felt about James, he found her Achilles' heel. She beamed with pride. "I am. It's still in the beginning stages but thus far it's been an exciting process."

"It certainly can be. I remember when my first hotel opened. I wish you luck in your endeavor. Simone, would you please excuse us?"

"Uh, sure."

"Noelle, a word please?" James turned on his heel not bothering to wait for a response.

Noelle shot Simone an apologetic look before she followed James to the kitchen. James leaned against the island, his arms crossed over his broad chest.

"Is everything okay?" she asked nervously.

"I believe I made my conditions clear in the beginning. I want you available to me at all times, not entertaining guests at random."

"Simone is not a random guest, she's my cousin. If you had a problem with me having company, you should have made it clearer. I'm alone in this penthouse ninety percent of the time so I thought—"

"You're not here to think. You're here to do as I say. Get rid of her."

"But I haven't seen her since I moved here. And I..." The stony expression on his face shut her down.

"Then by all means, when she leaves you can go with her and the two of you can spend as much time together as you need."

Noelle didn't need clarification to understand what he meant. She bit the inside of her lip to hold back an angry retort. He'd just given her the opportunity to tell him to shove it but she couldn't bring herself to take it.

Not trusting herself to speak, Noelle attempted to leave the kitchen but James grabbed her wrist and turned her around to face him. "Are we understood?"

The moment she met his intense gaze she lost the will to fight. "Yes." Noelle snatched her wrist out of his grip and stalked out the kitchen.

"Is everything okay?" Simone asked as Noelle approached.

"Um, no actually. I was wondering if I can have a rain check to watch the rest of this movie. James…" She saw no need to finish when it was clear her cousin got the message.

Simone pursed her lips and shot a disgusted glare toward the kitchen. But to Noelle's relief, her cousin held in whatever it was she wanted to say.

"I'm really sorry. Maybe we can go out another time. Or I can come by the apartment with the movie so we can finish watching it together."

Noelle waited for Simone to collect her purse and walked her to the door. She stepped into the hallway with Simone and closed the door behind her so James wouldn't hear their conversation. "Please don't be mad at me," she pleaded to her stiff-backed cousin.

Simone released an exaggerated sigh and turned to face Noelle. She placed her hands on Noelle's shoulders, leaned forward and gave her a kiss on the cheek. "Sweetheart, I'm not mad at you."

"But you're annoyed. I can tell."

"I'd be lying if I said I wasn't. But it's not directed toward you. I can't tell you how to live your life, just know, no matter what happens, I'll be here for you. You'll always have a place to stay with me. And before you think I'm jinxing your relationship, I'm simply saying I have your back. Okay?"

Noelle's eyes welled with tears as she walked into her cousin's open arms. Noelle hung on to Simone for as long as she could. "Thank you. That means a lot."

"And you mean a lot to me." Simone gave her one last squeeze before letting go. "I'm going to take off now but don't take too long getting in contact with me again okay?"

"I'll call often. I promise."

"You'd better."

They hugged again before Simone left. Once her cousin was gone, Noelle quickly wiped away a stray tear that slid down her cheek. Leaning her forehead against the door, she worked up the nerve to go back inside. Part of her feared he'd be done with her because of this faux pas and the other half didn't think that was a bad idea. Once she was sure she wouldn't break down, Noelle went back inside.

James leaned against the bar, drink in hand.

"She's gone," Noelle announced. James took another sip from the tumbler he held in his hand. Unable to stand the tension, Noelle headed to her bedroom. She lay on the bed and closed her eyes, trying to make sense of his coldness. She might be his mistress but it didn't mean she wasn't entitled to a little courtesy.

Dealing with James' standoffishness after sex was bad enough but this outright disregard for her as a person was a blow to her spirit. He never told her his comings and goings. There'd be periods when he wouldn't show up for days, yet he expected her to be here to wait for him in case he did show. She only left the penthouse for a couple hours at a time to either shop or take a walk. At times she felt like a princess trapped in an ivory tower.

When she was in his arms Noelle felt special but when she wasn't she felt cheap. Soft foot falls alerted her to his presence. She lay still, making no attempt to get up.

"Noelle." The low timber of his voice was like a sultry music to her ears. The bed dipped beneath his weight. A strong finger moved down the center of her back sending a shiver through her body. He leaned over and kissed the side of her neck.

She didn't want to respond but her body's betrayal was absolute. Her pussy tingled and her heat index rose. Noelle squeezed her eyes shut as hard as she could to ward away the temptation he offered.

James tugged at her shoulder until she was flat on her back. "Open your eyes, Noelle."

Reluctantly she did. "James I—"

"Noelle, I realize I was unfair to you earlier. And you're right I never said you weren't allowed company. But there will be times when I visit that I need you right away and you weren't ready for me."

This was the closest James had ever come to apologizing and this was probably as good as it was going to get. "I understand but I haven't seen my cousin in weeks. There's only so much shopping I can do to pass the time."

"I'll tell you what; I'll have Paul call you when I'm traveling. At least then you'll know when not to expect me." She was surprised he conceded that much to her; it was then she realized how tired he looked. It was hard to stay mad when she caught something that almost seemed like sadness in his gray gaze.

"James, is everything okay with you?"

"I'm fine. I just need you, Noelle. Need you so bad." His gruff admission caught her off guard, leaving her mute. He took advantage of her slightly parted lips to push his tongue past them. The skillful mastery of James' kiss had her stomach fluttering and body quaking.

Noelle wanted him to open up and trust her with whatever secrets he currently guarded, but thoughts of his well-being were pushed from her mind as he continued to conquer her with his kiss. She kept her fists balled at her side, unsure of what he wanted her to do.

James stood up and placed his hands on either side of her head. "Touch me, Noelle." He bent over to brush his lips against hers, still holding her face.

His request almost sounded desperate and she wanted to demand he tell her what was bothering him. But the spark of sadness she'd glimpsed earlier touched her soul, making Noelle want to soothe whatever ache he felt. It suddenly dawned on her when he said he needed her it wasn't in the physical sense. He needed *her*.

She reached up and cupped the side of his face in her palm. "What happened? What's the matter, James?" she asked again, hoping he'd open up some more.

He didn't reply right away but he didn't break eye contact with her either. Finally he answered, "Nothing some time in your arms won't solve."

Chapter Ten

It wasn't the answer Noelle was looking for but she realized it was the most she would get out of him. He continued to hover over her, signaling for her to make the next move.

Noelle released the breath she didn't realize she'd been holding in anticipation of his response. She stood with him and pressed her mouth against his. He remained still, allowing her to take the lead. James usually took charge so this put her in new territory. The ire she'd felt shortly after he'd arrived at the penthouse was gone, to be replaced with the need to please him.

Noelle pushed James on the bed and straddled him. She locked gazes with him as she lowered her head to place light kisses along his jaw line. She cupped his face between her palms and captured his lips in a light kiss. She moved her mouth in different positions until their mouths fit together perfectly. The press of James's cock against the juncture of her thighs emboldened her to run her tongue across the seam of his lips before pushing it inside his mouth to fully taste him. She'd never been the aggressor in bed but her movements were led by instinct.

Noelle was cautious at first, flicking her tongue along the cavern of his mouth, savoring the taste of coffee, bourbon, mint and a flavor that was uniquely James. His tongue shot forward to greet hers, tangling and wrestling with it in a passionate duel of wills but still allowing her to be in charge. Noelle caught his tongue between her teeth, giving it a playful nip and then sucked on it. He moaned, sending a delightful vibration against her lips and a tingly sensation throughout her entire body.

Her core was hot and wet and she began to grind against his erection, wanting the pleasure only he could give. Breathlessly, she broke the kiss to stare into his deep gray gaze. His eyes were filled with hunger and a lust that took her breath away. The raw passion she saw in those depths made her shiver. Still maintaining eye contact, Noelle found the buttons on his shirt and slowly undid them, grazing her finger along each inch of skin she exposed. His flesh was heated and breathing shallow, which gave her a heady sense of power. She enjoyed the ability to turn this gorgeous man on.

Once her task was complete, she pushed the shirt off his shoulders. With James's assistance, she pulled his shirt off completely and tossed it to the floor. She next turned her attention to his shoes and socks, making quick order of pulling them off and discarding them. She then moved to his belt, clumsily unbuckling it.

James caught her wrists. "Take it easy, baby. We have the rest of the day and night."

Their eyes locked again and though no more words were exchanged, there was a wealth of meaning in that look. Slow and steady. With a nod, she followed his silent instructions and finished undoing his pants in unhurried movements and slid them down his muscular thighs. Noelle tried to be casual when disrobing him of his boxers but it was difficult to remain nonchalant when beholding such a magnificently cut figure. She bit her bottom lip to hold back a gasp. His body never ceased to amaze her. From his taut pecks to washboard abs, he was sheer perfection—Adonis in repose.

She'd deliberately skimmed over his burgeoning member. No matter how many times they had sex, it was quite an intimidating organ. Its girth alone had her shivering as she remembered how deliciously it stretched her walls until she begged for mercy. Noelle didn't realize she was staring until James' light chuckle reached her ears. "Go ahead and touch it. I know you want to."

She shot him an uncertain glance before returning her gaze to his cock. Noelle moistened her lips with the tip of her tongue and wrapped her fingers around his shaft. She'd only done this once since they'd been together and even then she'd barely gotten her mouth on it before he'd pulled her off and buried himself deep inside of her. This time around, she had a feeling that wouldn't be the case. She slid her index finger along the length of his shaft. James' sharp intake of breath indicated he liked it, encouraging her to continue. Noelle wrapped her fingers around the base and slowly stroked his cock from root to tip, gently at first but when he raised his hips she tightened her grip and sped up.

"Yes, just like that," he encouraged. His eyes were now closed, and face taut with tension. Deciding to turn the heat up another notch, Noelle lowered her head and flicked her tongue against the head. James jerked. "Yes, more like that. Do it again."

Noelle licked his tip like the top of an ice cream cone, reveling in the velvety texture of his skin. She circled the head with her tongue then slowly sucked his length into her mouth an inch at a time. When she took in as much as she could, Noelle pulled back until her lips rested at the mushroom capped tip again. She repeated the process several times. To her surprise, James dug his fingers through her hair and guided her along his shaft. She clenched her lips around his dick to create more friction. His moans were now loud and throaty and the sound of his arousal turned her on beyond her wildest imaginings. If someone would have told her how much she would enjoy pleasing a man in this way she would have scoffed, particularly after her first disastrous relationship. But here she was, loving the feel and taste of James's hard cock in her mouth.

She loved that she could bring this big powerful man to his knees with something so base and bawdy. It gave her a sense of power she didn't realize she had. Feeling more confident, Noelle used her free hand to capture and caress his balls. She fondled and gently squeezed them until he yelled her name.

"Noelle! Shit. So. Fucking. Good."

Though she didn't think it was possible, it seemed as if his dick got harder by the second. She could tell he was close to orgasm by how tight his muscles had become. But to her surprise James sat up and scooted back. He gently pushed her away. Reluctantly, Noelle let go of his cock with a wet pop. She looked up at him in bewilderment. "Didn't you like it?"

"You only have to see the evidence to know the answer to that, my dear. But I fear if we keep that up, I'd be finished before we get started."

"Wasn't that what you wanted? I don't mind if you want to…you know, in my mouth."

James grinned. "You've been here for over a month and there's still such a delightful innocence about you. You still can't say certain things. I believe the term is come in your mouth."

Her cheeks heated at his reminder. He'd mentioned it before and she'd tried to work on it, wanting to be as worldly as the sophisticated women he was used to. "If you want to come in my mouth, I don't mind." She said, this time proud of herself for getting the words out without stumbling over them.

James brushed her cheek with the back of his hand. "Cute, but not necessary. I have a more immediate need. Come here." Taking Noelle by her forearms, he pulled her on top of him until their lips met again. The kiss was hurried but no less passionate. He was the one to break away with a moan. "Now. I want you to ride me."

With a deep breath, she splayed her hands over his broad torso to brace herself as she straddled him. Noelle positioned her body until her pussy hovered over his erection. James grabbed his turgid rod and guided the tip until it rested against her damp slit. "Take me inside of you. I want to feel that tight cunt surrounding me."

She hesitated for just a moment, unsure of herself, but the desire she read in his eyes was all the encouragement she needed. Noelle was wet enough to lower herself onto his cock without trouble. She eased her way down until James was so deep inside of her she felt him all over her body. She let out a sigh of pleasure, thrilled to be so decadently filled with thick, hard cock.

"So tight. Feels so good. So damn good." He groaned, clasping her hips in a vise. He bucked his pelvis, sending him deeper than she thought was possible.

"Oh!" Noelle leaned forward to dig her nails into his chest. She moved unhurriedly at first, searching for her rhythm, and once she found it, she sped up just a little at a time. James assisted, pushing up as she pressed down, meeting her thrust for thrust.

"Play with your tits," he growled, becoming more aggressive with each shove.

Noelle cupped her breasts, pinching her nipples between her index fingers and thumbs. James dug his fingers into her hips and moved her up and down his cock, effortlessly demonstrating his sheer strength. Arching her back, Noelle thrust her chest forward and bounced up and down his length. She tightened her walls around his cock as an incendiary flame licked along every single nerve endings of her body, shooting straight to her core. Each time his cock hit her g-spot, she made it closer to her peak.

James sat up to capture a nipple in his mouth and he sucked and nipped on the tip like a starving man. When he bit down just hard enough to send her hovering over the line of pleasure and pain, an orgasm went spiraling through her. Noelle threw her head back and let out a hoarse scream. James continued to suckle her breasts, switching between them as she clung to his shoulders for leverage. All the while James pumped unrelentingly in and out of her.

She dragged her nails down his chest, breaking skin as he continued to hit her erogenous zone. Another swift climax hit Noelle, leaving her weak. James however kept going. To her surprise he rolled her over until he was on top. He was insatiable, plowing into her with long hard thrusts. When she reached her third peak, Noelle was on the brink of passing out from pleasure overload. Finally James tensed and thrust hard one last time, shooting his seed deep into her pussy.

James collapsed on top of her, but instead of rolling away like he always did, he stayed on top of her, resting his head against her shoulder. Noelle wasn't sure whether to offer him the comfort her instincts told her to give him because she didn't know if he'd pull away or not. After silently debating her next move, she decided to go for it.

Tentatively, she stroked the back of his head, preparing herself for his rejection. But to her surprise, he didn't pull away from her touch. "Won't you tell me what the matter is?" she whispered.

He knew he'd been unfair, a dick even, but he couldn't help it. There was something about Noelle that made him unreasonable, something he couldn't quite place. It was an irrational need to keep her all for himself. Something selfish and primal. With his other lovers, it didn't matter where they went when he wasn't here or if they entertained guests, as long as they didn't have sexual relations with other men while he was footing the bill for their living arrangements. With Noelle it did matter.

James found himself dealing with an emotion he wasn't used to and didn't like it one bit. He didn't enjoy obsessing over where she was when he wasn't here or who she was with. It made him lash out and even though it wasn't right, he couldn't help himself. And despite it all, she still showed a deep level of concern for him he hadn't experienced since his grandfather passed away. It made him uneasy and vulnerable, two emotions he wasn't equipped to handle.

Realizing he would either have to answer her question or withdraw emotionally as he always did, James chose the latter. He rolled off of her and sat up, already missing the feel of her skin against his.

"James?" Noelle reached over and touched his shoulder but he flinched away, knowing if he capitulated to her warmth he'd enter a space he wasn't prepared to go.

An audible gasp met his ears and he steeled himself not to respond. "I'm going to go grab a shower," he said more for the sake of breaking the awkward silence.

Without waiting for a response, he slid off the bed and grabbed his clothes. He didn't have to turn around to know her expression would be one of hurt. Noelle was the type who wore her emotions on her sleeve. He couldn't deal with it. Not on top of the emotional rollercoaster he'd already been on earlier in the day.

He rested his head against the shower stall as the water beat mercilessly down over his head. Squeezing his eyes shut, he attempted to force away the memories from earlier in the day but they assaulted him from every corner of his mind.

When Gillian's attempts to wheedle money out of him had failed, he didn't think her husband would have the nerve to contact him. But to his surprise, that's exactly what David had done. James wasn't exactly sure what to expect when David had walked into his office that day but the moment he crossed the threshold with that familiar knowing smirk on his face, James was instantly on guard.

James knew this meeting wouldn't end well before it even began. Not bothering to stand when David entered, he gestured for the other man to take a seat, bowing his head slightly forward in acknowledgement.

The smirk transformed into a knowing smile. "You're looking well. The good life suits you. Heard you were dating Eleanor Harrington. Also heard her father's company will be bankrupt within a year if they don't get an infusion of cash pretty soon. But I bet Harrington won't mind sacrificing his precious daughter so he can get his hands on some of that Rothschild capital." Instead of taking a seat, David walked around the office and casually inspected the décor, running his finger along the knick knacks as though accessing their worth.

Even after all these years, David knew exactly which arrows would hit their mark, but fortunately for James he mastered the art of never letting his opponent see him sweat.

James leaned forward on his desk with folded hands and met David's gaze. "I seriously doubt you've come to make small talk, David. So drop the bullshit and tell me what you really want."

David had always been quite the cool one himself, able to hide a wicked mean streak behind the façade of his all-American boyish looks. However, James wasn't fooled for a second. The other man raised his chin slightly with thinned-out lips. "Finesse was never one of your strong suits was it?"

"Neither is my patience. So do us both a favor and cut to the chase or else we'll end this meeting right here and now."

The flare of David's nostrils was the only sign that gave away his displeasure. Finally, he took the seat directly in front of James's desk. "I bet you're enjoying this."

"I enjoy classic rock when I'm driving, a good ball game on the television and the occasional glass of scotch... but this…this is a mild annoyance at best."

David shifted in his seat, looking slightly uncomfortable before once again gaining his composure. "Why pretend, James? You know why I'm here since Gillian has already paid you a visit."

"Did you really think she'd be able to bat those baby blues and I'd hand over money no questions asked? I find that insulting you think I'm so easily persuaded. I also find you to be a coward, seeing as you weren't man enough to come here yourself in the first place."

David bared his teeth in a silent snarl. "I'm here now, and as you know AlCore is in need of a significant infusion of cash or else we'll go under within a year. I've done the best that I can to stave off our creditors thus far but there's only so long they're willing to wait."

James steepled his fingers together and leaned forward. He could tell it had taken a lot for the other man to get that out, but he felt no sympathy for the twerp. Knowing David as he did, James was almost certain AlCore was in the position it was in because of his mismanagement.

Silence fell over the room as the two men stared each other down.

"Well?" David finally prompted.

"Well what? You're the one in the need of cash. I assume you have a business proposal for my perusal to make investing in AlCore worth my while."

"Business proposal?"

Shortly after Gillian's visit, James had his contacts quietly look into how much debt AlCore was in. So he knew they were in the red for millions. No one loaned that kind of cash without collateral or at the very least some kind of plan to future profitability. "Being the head of your organization, you should know more than anyone that if you want someone to invest in your company you need some type of proposal. I'm sure you didn't think you could come to me and ask for money on the strength of our tenuous connection. Any man worth his MBA would want a return on his investment."

"So you're not going to make this easy for me?"

James was now more than mildly irritated at David's arrogance in thinking he was the same boy who'd desperately wanted to please the people who'd constantly rejected him. It was clear to James, David still thought very little of him.

James took several shallow calming breaths before replying. "I'm not sure on what planet you can come unprepared to a business meeting to ask for a large sum of money for nothing. And on the strength of what? Why should I give AlCore a dime? The only way I'd even consider it is if I was offered a sizable stake in the company and at which point, I'd have my accountants running through the books with a fine tooth comb. Plus a management team of my choosing would be put in place, but that's only if there was a proposal for me to review."

"So that's it?" David sneered. "You want AlCore. I should have known better than lowering myself by coming here. I thought I could appeal to your sense of decency because we're…" he trailed off as if finishing the sentence would scorch his tongue.

James raised a brow. "What David? Say it. Because we're brothers? Isn't that what you used to tell me when we were younger so I'd take the rap for you? So you could use me when it was convenient for you and forget about me when it wasn't? If that's what you had in mind, that's quite unfortunate for you because those days are long gone. So, unless you have a serious business proposition, I'll have to decline any assistance you're looking for."

David bounded out of his seat. He no longer hid the disgust he probably felt from the second he stepped into the office. "Screw you, James. You think you're so mighty, lording your success over our heads. Behind the money and nice clothes, you're still just a junkie's son. Oh, you can buy your way into our circles but you'll never truly belong."

James's ears burned in his anger but he used every bit of will power he possessed to not to leap over his desk and beat the shit out of that self-important bastard. "Seeing as how you made the ultimate sacrifice by being in my lowly presence, I bid you a good day." And with that he picked up a pen and examined documents on his desk, not really seeing any of the words swimming on the pages. He wouldn't give that asshole the satisfaction of knowing he'd gotten to him.

"Son of a bitch," David cursed. He slammed the door behind him.

The confrontation with his half-brother had left James in a foul mood for the rest of the day as memories from the past resurfaced – memories he'd fought hard to put firmly behind him. Yet here they were again with a vengeance.

As if sensing his mood, Paul had tip-toed around him for the remainder of the day, although it did nothing to assuage James's ire. He'd barely managed to get through the remainder of the morning without completely losing his cool. Deciding he needed to get out of the office, he sought out one of the two things that always eased his tension, and as he didn't particularly feel like going to the gym, he headed to the penthouse.

James allowed the sting of the hot shower spray to flay his back, letting it administer scalding lashes. Despite turning the nozzle to its hottest temperature, the physical ache was easy to ignore with the various emotions warring through him.

He could do the decent thing and cut Noelle loose but something held him back. It annoyed him how she'd managed to get under his skin in such a short time. After all, Noelle was no different from any of the other women he'd kept. She was just a better actress. With that in mind, James managed to firmly stow away any residual guilt he'd experienced from their encounter. He wouldn't think about her beyond their arrangement and he most certainly wouldn't think about what transpired with David earlier.

He may have come from humble beginnings but now that he was on top, he intended to stay there. He'd have the life he'd always deserved: the money, the trophy wife and the social status. And no one would deter him from his goal.

Chapter Eleven

Noelle didn't hear from James for two and a half weeks, although Paul called to let her know James would be out of the country for a week. That didn't account for the other week and a half. And knowing he was in town and not visiting hurt like hell.

After he rolled out of bed the last time they were together, he headed for the shower and stayed there for a considerable amount of time. At the very least, she expected him to come by her room to say goodbye but he didn't, leaving her feeling used and discarded.

Most women would have packed their bags and got the hell out of there but she couldn't bring herself to walk away. The man seemed to have weighed her down with invisible chains she couldn't break from. There was another side to James he hid from her, a side he didn't think she saw. It was in his eyes the last time they were together. Noelle wanted to take whatever pain he carried away. But once again, he'd shut her out. What kind of masochist was she to take this kind of emotional abuse?

During his absence she stayed in the penthouse most of the time, trying out her mother's recipes and adding her own twists to them. She'd only leave the penthouse to take a walk around the block for the sake of getting fresh air. After a week with no word from James, she went out more, mostly to go shopping for things she believed James would like to see her in. She kept in contact with Simone via the phone and pretended everything was fine and dandy, despite the fact she was a big ball of anxiety as she waited to hear from James.

Noelle missed him so much she had trouble sleeping and could barely eat. The culinary confections she made were given to the guards at the front desk and the doorman. She went down one dress size.

After two weeks, she was tempted to call Paul and ask if James was traveling again but she had a feeling he wasn't. As it turned out, there was no need to contact Paul because he showed up two weeks into James' mysterious absence. Hearing the knock on her door one day startled Noelle because she wasn't expecting anyone. The only two people allowed past the guards without receiving a call from them were James and Paul. James never knocked so she knew it had to be Paul, though she'd only met him when she first moved in to the penthouse.

Her only interactions with him had been on the telephone when he called to check in on her to see if there was anything she needed. He was always polite, but very crisp and businesslike, making sure no familiarity developed between them.

"Hi, Paul," Noelle greeted once she opened the door.

He nodded. "Miss Greene? May I come in?"

She stood back, opening the door wider to allow him entrance. "Sure. And please, call me Noelle. I thought we settled this already."

The polite smile he shot her way told Noelle he had no intention of complying. "James wanted me to stop by and check the faucets. He said something about the water pressure being off the last time he was here. Have you had any problems with it lately?"

"No. I gotta admit I'm surprised to see you here. Normally, you just call to see if everything is okay."

"Usually when there's a problem with maintenance, I stop by to see for myself what's going on, so I'm able to accurately describe to the repairman what the problem is. "

The explanation seemed plausible enough but there was something about his statement that didn't really hold true. Noelle could sense there was something Paul was holding back but she decided not to call him on it. Besides, being the type of man James was, she doubted his EA would be here without his knowledge. "Okay," she finally responded. "You know where everything is. I'm going to finish frosting my cake."

Paul raised a dark blond brow. "You baked a cake?" The surprise was evident in his voice.

Noelle shrugged. "I didn't have much else to do. There's only so much shopping I can do before it gets boring."

"I can imagine. Well, if you'll excuse me."

"Sure."

By the time Paul returned from his inspection, Noelle was viewing her handy work. Not only had she tried a variation of her mother's recipe, she'd tried her hand at piping to recreate a cake she'd seen on television.

She didn't realize he'd entered the kitchen until he spoke. "Everything seems fine but I'm going to call the plumber anyway just to make sure. I'll call and let you know when you should expect someone."

Noelle barely spared him a glance as she continued to study what she'd created. "Okay. See you later."

"You made that?"

"Yes. What do you think?"

Paul approached the island. "I think that's pretty amazing. I didn't realize you were so talented. It's almost as fancy as those cakes you see in bakery window displays."

Noelle beamed under his approval. It wasn't often someone complimented her on something she did. "Well, how about seeing if it's as good as it looks. Let me cut you a piece."

He held up his hands in protest. "No. That's okay. I had a big lunch."

"So, I'll cut you a little slither. Please, won't you try some?" She wouldn't have pushed in other circumstances, but being alone in the penthouse for the past couple of weeks was driving her nuts, and having company broke the monotony. "Please," Noelle softly begged when she noticed his reluctance.

"Okay. I guess I can give it a try."

She had a feeling his capitulation had more to do with politeness than him actually wanting to try her concoction. Whatever his reason, she ignored it and sliced him a piece of cake, serving it to him on pristine china.

Paul forked a sizable bite into his mouth and froze. His eyes widened slightly before he began to chew slowly. "This…" He took another bite. "You baked this?"

"Yes. It's my mom's old recipe with a twist."

"And you decorated it and everything?"

"Yep. Don't sound so surprised," she responded dryly.

"I didn't mean to offend. Besides the cake looking great, it tastes fantastic, even better than the junk I've been forced to try with my sister."

"Your sister bakes?"

"Not on her spoiled little life. No, she's getting married at the end of the year and we've visited caterers and bakeries for the reception. I must admit, this beats all the ones we've tried so far, at least in my opinion. You have a gift."

Noelle grinned, content to have someone enjoy her culinary treats besides the security guards who claimed she was making them fat. Not that they minded because they always eagerly accepted whatever she had to offer. "Then I'll cut a piece for you to take to her."

He forked another mouthful past his lips and moaned. "To be quite honest," he spoke with his mouth full, "it may not make it to her."

"Then take the entire thing with you."

"I couldn't."

"Sure you can. I wasn't going to eat it anyway. It would only end up with the guards downstairs. But be prepared for dirty looks from them when they see you walk out the door with a cake."

"Seriously Miss—Noelle," he amended when she raised an admonishing eyebrow. "I don't want to impose."

"Please, Paul. You'd be doing me a favor. Besides, it's not like I need the extra calories. I just bake because it's one of the few things that relax me. My mother and I used to bake together when I was little. She worked hard to make ends meet, and there were times I rarely saw her because she was pulling extra shifts to pay a bill that got behind. But every week, she set aside some time for me and one of our favorite pastimes was baking. Doing this keeps her with me."

"How old were you when you lost your mother?"

"I was eight. It was especially tough since my father died before I was born—an accident at work."

"So where did you stay after that?"

"I went to live with my aunt and her husband." A shudder wracked her body as she thought of the years she'd spent in that house. Even though she hadn't lived there in over three years, she was shaken to the center of her being as the memories came flooding back.

"Noelle, are you okay?" Paul placed his hand on her shoulder.

"Huh?" She snapped back to attention.

"You were somewhere else for a second. Is everything all right?"

"Oh, yeah. Sure."

"I take it you weren't happy living with your aunt and uncle?" He turned a bright shade of red after asking the question as though remembering he wasn't supposed to be curious about her. He quickly removed his hand and straightened up. "My apologies. It's none of my business."

Noelle shook her head, not wanting him to feel uncomfortable around her and draw back inside his shell of professional politeness. "No need to apologize. I'm the one who bought it up. And no, things weren't great with them, but I guess I should be grateful for the roof over my head, the clothing and food they provided me. At least that's what they kept telling me. If it wasn't for my cousin, Simone, I don't know how I would have made it without going bonkers." It was weird finally saying out loud what she'd always felt about living with her aunt and it was even stranger the person she'd confess this to was James' Executive Assistant. All she knew was it felt good to unload. To her relief, Paul didn't seem put off by her admission.

With a sigh, he placed his plate on the island. "Noelle, may I be frank with you?"

She gulped. That sounded ominous. "Uh, sure."

"Look, I could possibly get fired for what I'm about to say but...I think I'm a pretty good judge of character, and you just don't seem like the type to walk away from this arrangement unscathed. Why are you really here?"

She opened her mouth to reply but as the meaning of his words suddenly hit her, she immediately shut it again.

"I think you know where I'm going with this right?"

She turned her back to him to hide her expression. "In other words, you don't think I'm good enough or glamorous enough to be here. But it really doesn't matter what you think does it? James chose me." Noelle wrapped her arms around her body, afraid to turn around and face Paul.

"Yes, he did and I can't imagine what he was thinking. But you and I may have our wires crossed here. I'm not saying you shouldn't be here because you're not good enough. I meant you're too damn good for something like this. Noelle, I'm not telling you this to hurt your feelings but you're not the first woman James put up in this penthouse. For as long as I've worked for him, there have been dozens. Some don't last more than a few weeks, some months, but none of them last past a year. But those are the kind of women who live the life. Most of them already have other rich benefactors not long after they leave. You just don't strike me as the type to give herself to someone for financial gain."

Her cheeks burned at his assessment. Even if the words were true, she didn't like being so exposed. She finally turned and faced him. "What do you know about it?"

He shook his head, his expression full of pity. "I'm the one who makes sure everything runs smoothly and makes sure the women are happy. You're not like the others, and that leads me to believe you're here because of your feelings. James can be very charming when he wants to be. Trust me, I've seen him in action. But as there have been others before you, there will be some after you."

Deep down, she knew he spoke the truth but to admit she was wasting her time with a man who only saw her as a convenient fuck was not something she was yet willing to accept. "And what makes you so sure?"

He rolled his eyes. "I'm not telling you this to be cruel. I just want you to be aware so when the time comes for this thing to end you won't be hurt."

"How do you know James hasn't developed feelings for me?"

Paul shook his head with that compassionate gleam entering his blue gaze. She was starting to hate that damn look. He reached into his pocket and pulled out his smart phone. After tapping a few buttons, he held it out to her. "Here, take it and read."

Noelle didn't want to but couldn't stop herself from reaching for the phone. On the device was an article from a local newspaper, the society section. Her heart seized in her chest when she spied a picture of James with a beautiful redhead clinging to his arm like a limpet. She was everything Noelle was not: tall, gorgeous, and poised, with an air of sophistication about her which screamed confidence. This was the type of woman she imagined a man like James would be with. Seeing this picture was like her worst nightmare come true. Under the picture was a caption of that read: *Hotel magnate James Rothschild and Socialite Eleanor Harrington at the Cancer Awareness Benefit. Sources have revealed an engagement is on the horizon for this couple.*

Noelle handed the phone back to Paul. She went numb. There was the evidence staring her in the face. Here she was holed up in this damned penthouse while James squired around his potential perfect trophy wife. But did she have the right to be upset when he'd made no promises to begin with? He'd been honest, and it was only her foolishness which made her ignore what was staring her in the face. He didn't care for her and possibly never would. But that glimmer of hope nestled deep in the recesses of her heart refused to die. And as long as the little kernel remained intact, she'd forge ahead. She bit the inside of her cheek so hard the coppery taste of blood filled her mouth. She focused on the physical pain so she wouldn't have to think about the emotional ache.

"Noelle, will you be okay?" he asked gently.

She stood still in an attempt to get herself together. It was several silent moments before she trusted herself to even move without bursting into tears. Noelle nodded. "I'm sure you're a busy man so I won't keep you. Let me wrap this cake up for you. And I really hope your sister enjoys it."

"Shit," Paul cursed under his breath as he raked his fingers through his neat blond hair. "I was out of place. I shouldn't have said anything."

Noelle shrugged as she moved mechanically, going through the motions of boxing up the remainder of the cake. "If you're worried whether I'll tell James about this conversation forget about it. I won't mention it."

"If I cared about that, I wouldn't have said anything in the first place. You're a genuinely nice person. And I just want you to be careful okay. May I have your cell phone please?"

"Why?"

"Please?"

"Fine," she let out with an exaggerated sigh. The phone was on the counter. It was the one James had provided for her in case he needed to get in contact with her. The one he never called. She picked it up and tossed it to Paul.

He began pressing buttons and before she could ask him what he was doing another cell rang. Paul reached into the inside pocket of his suit jacket and pulled out another phone and showed her. "This is my personal phone. The number is in your phone now. If you need anything at all, even if it's just to talk, give me a call."

She snorted. "Isn't that your job?" Noelle knew she was being surly, but facing the realization she was nothing more than a glorified whore kind of put a damper on her mood.

"Noelle, I'm serious. If you need anything, just call me okay? Either on my business or personal phone. Okay?"

"Sure you won't get in trouble with the boss for mingling with his side piece?"

"Don't denigrate yourself like that." He looked as though he wanted to take a step forward and offer comfort of some sort but thought better of it. "I'm really sorry, Noelle."

"Not as sorry as I am." She handed Paul the cake and turned her back to him again. She refused to let him see her cry.

And despite what Noelle was now aware of, she knew she'd stay.

Chapter Twelve

James sensed something was different with Noelle. Ever since he avoided the penthouse for several weeks something in their relationship had shifted. Noelle still gave herself to him freely, but still, something was off.

She dressed differently. Her clothes were flashier, more revealing and form fitting. Her hair had changed as well. He wasn't up on the latest coifs but he assumed she'd added hair extensions that fell down the middle of her back. Noelle even wore colored contacts, of various shades. When he'd visit, sometimes her eyes would be blue. Once they were green. Another time they were hazel. Rarely did he see her natural dark brown shade which secretly he preferred. She even wore more makeup than when he'd first met her. While she still presented an attractive package, he missed the fresh-faced women he'd met originally, though he'd never admit it.

Her dramatic makeover however, wasn't the most noticeable change in her. There was a distance between them on her end that hadn't been there before. He'd never required her to be his friend or even chatty. She no longer asked him about his day and Noelle no longer volunteered tidbits of information about herself. Now when he arrived, she dropped whatever she was doing and would head to the bedroom with barely an acknowledgment. Though he loathed admitting it, he hated the change. But to say something would somehow alter things in a direction he wasn't willing to take them in.

The smell of fresh baked goods infiltrated his nostrils the second he stepped over the threshold. Baking seemed to be the one thing that remained constant with her. It made the penthouse feel like a home. James headed to the bar to pour himself a drink, expecting Noelle to pop out of the kitchen to give him the vague greeting he had become familiar with recently.

He was halfway finished with his drink before deciding to go to her. Why hadn't Noelle come out to greet him? She must have heard him come in. It wasn't as if he'd been particularly quiet. When he walked into the kitchen, however, it was to find her hunched over the island, with white ear buds in her ear and a pencil in hand. Noelle appeared to be sketching something that held her attention to the point that she hadn't noticed him enter the room.

For the first time in weeks, her face wasn't caked with makeup. Her hair was piled on her head in a messy bun and she wore a simple black t-shirt and a pair of jeans. She reminded him of when he'd first met her. James couldn't tear his gaze from the sight of the innocent sensuality she presented, from the way she nibbled on her bottom lip to the way she'd periodically poke her tongue out to rest at the corner of her mouth. More than anything he wanted her attention to be on him so he could capture that tongue and suck it into his mouth as he fucked her senseless.

It was almost a shame to break her from the deep concentration she was obviously in, but seeing her this way did things to his libido that was probably outlawed in several states. His gaze drifted to the image on the sketchpad which looked to be a landscape. What really surprised him most was how good it was. He knew she was an art school dropout but he had no idea she was this talented. Taking a step forward to get a closer look, he brushed up against the island. The movement must have caught her attention because Noelle raised her head with a startled gasp.

She flipped the pad over in an obvious attempt to hide her work from him and popped out her ear buds. "Sorry I didn't hear you come in. Let me turn off the oven and I'll head upstairs."

Just like that he could actually feel that invisible wall she erected between them. Though James would never mention it, he didn't like it one bit. Noelle removed a muffin pan from the oven and placed them on top of the stove without a glance in his direction.

"It smells great, Noelle."

She stiffened momentarily. "Thanks," she replied matter-of-factly.

After plucking off her oven mitts and tossing them on the counter, she brushed past him. James reached out and caught her by the arm. "You don't have to hurry off."

Noelle looked pointedly at the hand restraining her, then raised her head to lock gazes with him. Her expression was closed and it drove him crazy; he couldn't read her mood like he usually could. "I'm kind of sticky from being in the hot kitchen for most of the afternoon. I need to go freshen up."

"You seem fine just the way you are. Have a drink with me."

She crinkled her nose, her bemusement obvious. "Why?"

"Do I need a reason?"

She opened her mouth and then closed it as if she thought better of it. "I guess not. Should I fix it for you?"

James wished he knew what she was about to say. "If there's something on your mind, you can tell me, Noelle."

She gave him a slight smile that didn't quite reach her eyes. "Um, thanks. So, what would you like to drink?"

He stifled a frustrated grunt. "I'll get it myself," he muttered leaving the kitchen.

She didn't follow him out to the living room immediately. As he waited for her he poured himself a glass of scotch and leaned against the bar, trying to figure out why the hell this change in Noelle bothered him so damn much. She was still accommodating which was all he really required. But her sudden personality change didn't sit well with him.

She finally came out of the kitchen with what looked like a glass of fruit juice. "I hope you don't mind but I don't think I can stomach any heavy alcohol right now, but I didn't want you to drink alone."

For the first time since he arrived, he noticed the strain on her face. Something was obviously bothering her and he needed to know what was going on with her. "Noelle. Something is bothering you. Tell me what it is."

"Nothing's wrong."

She answered too quickly. "Noelle…"

"I'm just not feeling one hundred percent is all. No biggie."

"Funny. You seemed fine when I came here," he noted before taking another sip from his tumbler.

She took a considerable pause before replying. "I'm sure you're not interested in discussing the state of my health, James. And for the life of me, I don't understand why we're even talking instead of heading to the bedroom." There was a slight edge to her tone one he'd never heard her use.

"You're here to fulfill any need I require. And right now, it would satisfy me to have a conversation with you."

Noelle squeezed her eyes shut and pinched the bridge of her nose between her thumb and forefinger. She let out an exaggerated sigh. "What do you want to talk about James?" Noelle sounded as if she couldn't be bothered.

He placed his drink on the bar and stalked in her direction, closing the short distance between them. James placed his hands on her shoulders. "Look at me, Noelle."

Slowly, she dropped her hand and raised her head. Her dark brown eyes glimmered with the sheen of unshed tears, her expression pained. "Noelle, what's going on? I realize I can be demanding but I'm not a complete bastard."

"In the grand scheme of things, I don't think it matters. When you've gotten what you want from me and walk out that door, I seriously doubt my concerns will be on your mind. Now if you'll please excuse me. I need to take something for my headache before it turns into a full blown migraine and heaven forbid if I'm unable to perform for you." She practically slammed her juice on the bar and tried to move past him, but he grabbed her wrist.

"Whoa. What the hell is that supposed to mean?"

"You've never been interested in having a stimulating conversation with me when you come by. Why now? You just want sex and I accept that. So you don't get to treat me like some mindless bimbo and then pretend you give a shit about whether something is bothering me. That's not part of the deal." She yanked her wrist from his grasp and maneuvered around him. This time he didn't stop her.

What the hell was that about? It had been six months since he'd set Noelle up as his lover and he'd come to depend on these visits as a sanctuary from his hectic work and social schedule. With Noelle, James wasn't quite as guarded. She never made demands on him as some of his previous lovers, and her presence always put him at ease. Sometimes he felt so comfortable around Noelle, he wanted to share things with her that he wouldn't with anyone else. He never did, but the fact that he even wanted to frightened him a bit.

He was playing a dangerous game keeping her as his mistress, because she posed a threat to all he'd worked for since he was a teenager. He wouldn't cast those ambitions aside for anyone, not even her.

Part of him wanted to go upstairs and smooth things over with Noelle but the other half said, "screw that." The second he caved to her whims meant he no longer held the upper hand. She accused him of treating her like "a mindless bimbo", which wasn't his intention, but he couldn't help the way she felt. As Noelle had pointed out, she was there because she wanted to be. James told himself he had no reason to be guilty.

The more James thought about it, his anger grew. She was no better than his other mistresses. Noelle was good at pretending she was the embodiment of sweet innocence but today proved otherwise. Her tirade had made him feel two inches tall. Long ago, he'd made a promise to himself no one would ever make him feel that way again. He'd be damned if he allowed Noelle to call the shots because of his lapse of judgment where she was concerned. Who the fuck did she think she was to rail at him as if she had a say-so? There were hundreds of women who would love to be in her position. Perhaps she'd gotten it in her head that she was irreplaceable. She probably expected him to follow her.

He finished the rest of his scotch and pounded the tumbler against the bar. James had actually looked forward to spending time with Noelle but the day was ruined. Glancing at his watch, he figured he could head to the gym and he'd call Eleanor to see if she wanted to have dinner. With that decided he headed out the door, trying to push down that nagging kernel of guilt that kept trying to resurface.

Noelle slowly opened her eyes, feeling a bit groggy and realized she must have fallen asleep. Glancing over on the nightstand, she noticed it was six o' clock. Instinctively, she knew James had left. A sickening sensation formed in the pit of her stomach. Was this the beginning of the end? Had she ruined any chances of penetrating that barrier James constantly wore like a shield? It was a rare occurrence when James showed any interest in her beyond the bedroom and today had seemed to be one of them. But she couldn't smile in his face and be sweet. She wasn't good at faking her emotions nor could she pretend she wasn't slowly dying inside to know she wasn't enough. After seeing that picture of James in the newspaper with that beautiful socialite, something within

Noelle had withered. That was why she'd lashed out at James. How could he do such wonderful things to her body and it not mean anything to him? It hurt so much, but he was an addiction she couldn't quit.

She'd tried harder to be more compliant, changed her look to the point she barely recognized herself. From the hair extensions to the ridiculous range of colored contacts, Noelle tried to give James what she believed he wanted but it never seemed to be enough. She cursed herself for trying to recapture those fleeting moments of happiness they'd shared on their dates.

Noelle wasn't sure how long she lay on the bed in a fetal position feeling sorry for herself, but she eventually got up to stretch her tense muscles. As she headed downstairs, the insistent ringing of her cell phone brought Noelle out of her miserable musings. She secretly hoped it was James and was slightly disappointed when she spied the caller ID and saw it wasn't.

"Hi, Simone!" Noelle attempted to inject as much cheer in her voice as possible but only managed to emit the pain she was in.

Her cousin picked up on it right away. "Cuz, what's the matter?"

"I'm fine. Why do you ask?"

"Noelle, don't lie. You sound like shit."

"Gee, thanks, Simone," Noelle replied dryly.

"I didn't say it to be mean but I can tell by from the sound of your voice you're not fine. Did James do something to you?" When Noelle didn't answer right away, Simone persisted. "He did, didn't he?"

Noelle knew better than to say anything negative about James around her cousin. She wasn't in the mood for a lecture. "Do you mind if we don't talk about James please?"

"But--"

"Please," Noelle begged.

"Fine. But if I find out he did something to you, I'm cutting off his balls."

Noelle rolled her eyes heavenward, thankful her cousin couldn't see her expression. "Duly noted. So, are you calling to find out the status of my relationship or just to chit-chat?"

"Actually, I wanted to invite you come out with me and some friends tonight. That's if you're allowed out of the ivory tower."

Noelle groaned. "Simone, please don't start."

"Sorry, but it's kind of annoying how you keep turning down my invitations to hang out because you have to wait around for James. It's almost like he's holding you prisoner."

"I can come and go as I please."

"So there's no reason why you can't hang out tonight."

"Other than the fact, I don't fucking feel like it. Now would you please get off my back about it?"

Silence greeted Noelle's outburst and instantly she regretted it. Simone didn't deserve that tongue lashing. This situation was really starting to get to Noelle but she had no right to take it out on her cousin. "I'm sorry. That was totally uncalled for. I know you mean well but I don't think I'll be the good company tonight."

The uncomfortable silence continued.

"Simone, are you still there?"

"Yes," her cousin finally answered.

"I'm really sorry, Simone. Please don't be angry with me. I don't think I could bear that on top of everything else."

"I'm more concerned than I am angry. I've bit my tongue for the most part but I have to say my peace and I promise, after this I'll try my best to not bring it up again. You're so much better than the situation you're in now. I don't understand what you see in this guy."

"Well, he's good- looking and I'm sure many would find a billion reasons why he's such a great catch," Noelle laughed trying to inject humor into this situation, though failing miserably.

"Hon, do you hear yourself talking? A billion reasons? Seriously? You sound like a gold digger with no self-respect. That's not you. And when I say you're better than this, I mean you deserve someone who will put you on a pedestal, and not be ashamed to be seen with you in public. You've completely changed for him and I think you were just fine before you met him. And if he can't see that, it's his loss."

On an intellectual level Noelle understood what Simone was saying but she didn't want to hear it. To accept her cousin's words would only reinforce what she was beginning to realize for herself: James didn't and would never love her. Most times she wondered why he'd chosen her in the first place. Had she been fooling herself all this time that he actually had a softer side to him? Noelle shook those painful thoughts away, not wanting to be pulled further into the abyss of depression.

"Are you still there, cuz?" Simone prompted.

"Yes," she whispered softly.

"Look, I'll tell you what. I'll call the girls and cancel our plans for tonight. I'll come over and we can pop popcorn and watch bad black exploitation movies. I can bring over my *Dolomite* collection."

"No. Don't cancel your plans on my account. You work hard so you deserve to have some fun."

"You need to get out as well. I can't have fun knowing you're cooped up inside that penthouse feeling down on yourself. Besides, there will be plenty more opportunities for me and the girls to get together."

Against her better judgment, Noelle caved. She wouldn't be responsible for ruining her cousin's plans because she knew Simone would be over like she said she would. "You don't have to come over. I'll meet you. Just tell me where."

"Really? You won't regret it. We'll have a blast. We're going to have drinks at that really snooty restaurant Isabella's and then we're going clubbing to get our grooves on."

"Don't you need reservations for Isabella's?"

"Only for the dinner section. They have a lounge with a bar in it. It's become quite a popular hangout. We're planning to meet up around eight-thirty so you may want to eat before we hang out."

After confirming the logistics, Noelle hung up with resignation. That nagging sensation in the back of her mind refused to go away. She had a feeling this would be a long night.

Chapter Thirteen

James glanced at his watch for the third time within the last ten minutes. While he found his dinner companion charming, beautiful, accomplished, and everything he looked for in a potential wife, he simply didn't want to be there. All he could think about was how he'd parted with Noelle earlier in the day. What should have been a relaxing afternoon of fucking turned into a test of his patience. He couldn't figure out for the life of him why he hadn't contacted Paul to arrange for her departure, as he'd done with his former mistresses who he'd grown tired of or who forgot their place. But he didn't. He'd almost made that call but something held him back. He couldn't stop thinking about her.

"James, did you hear what I just said?" Eleanor interrupted his thoughts bringing him back to the present.

"My apologies, I was thinking about a business call I have in the morning. What were you saying?"

Eleanor raised an auburn brow. "Ah, those Saturday business calls are the worst aren't they? No rest for the weary, I suppose."

"So they say."

"Anyway, I was mentioning how I was in need of an escort to my mother's charity event. I'd love if you could take me."

"When is it?"

"Three weeks from next Friday. Knowing how busy you are, I'm putting my request in early. My mother was just named committee chair so I'm obligated to attend even though you know these little events can be a bit dull."

"I don't see why I can't but I'll check with my secretary to make sure I have no schedule conflicts."

She flashed him a bright smile in response. "Daddy will be pleased. He really likes you, James."

James, who had been in the middle of sipping his wine, nearly choked on it. The cynic in him was well aware George Harrington was more interested in the capital he could bring to Harrington's ailing company, regardless of James's humble beginnings. A man like Harrington usually didn't acknowledge anyone in a social setting whose blood wasn't as blue as his or had the right social connections. But times were different from when Harrington had come up with the likes of the Rockefellers and Mellons. Most of the old-money families were either up to their ears in debt while still clinging to the names that had at one time gained them admittance anywhere, while others were savvy enough to align themselves with the *nouveau riche* to keep the champagne flowing freely. Harrington was a man who obviously saw his only chance at salvaging his lifestyle was marrying his daughter off to a man of James's financial situation.

James realized he was being used but what they didn't know was he was using them as well. They were his means to an end, and Eleanor was his ticket to a world where no one would ever look down their nose at him again. Along with the money and power he'd acquired, he'd have the name and connections that went along with it. His children would attend the finest schools and they would not bear the stigma of illegitimacy or poverty.

That he wasn't in love with Eleanor was of no consequence. He held no illusions she was in love with him either. Both of them knew the roles they were cast to play. This charade of a courtship would end in a proposal which she'd accept. There'd be several pictures of them as an engaged couple as they went about town together, which would finally culminate into a huge society wedding, which he'd probably end up shelling out a couple of million for. They would have two children and possibly even enjoy the sex required to obtain that "heir" and the spare. And then, he'd politely look the other way if she took a lover, and he'd keep a mistress on the side through the duration of the marriage. She'd be the perfect hostess and be a credit to his name. That's how it worked in the circles he'd worked hard to belong to.

"You two should get together for golf at the club," she continued.

James tilted his lips into a smirk. Not very long ago, her father barely acknowledged his existence. Pompous ass. "I'll have my secretary contact his and we'll set something up."

"You have to go easy on Daddy, though, he hates losing."

"I'm sure," he murmured and took a measured sip of from his wine glass.

"I'm losing your attention again, James. Maybe we should call it a night, since you can't seem to keep your mind off business." There was no petulance in her tone from what he could discern but she couldn't be pleased that his thoughts kept wondering off.

James paused to give her a suitable reply without causing offence but Eleanor spoke before he had the opportunity.

"James, may I be frank with you?"

He inclined his head forward in reply. "By all means."

"I'm well aware of the type of man my father is. Not too long ago, he would have made a stink if someone with your background even stepped foot in his club outside of a service capacity. He basically disowned my sister, Christina, because she married someone whose background he considered questionable. Steven is a good guy and makes a decent living, but it's not good enough for Daddy. He can be an insufferable snob at times, but he was just raised in a different era."

"I'm not trying to make excuses for him but that's the way he is. I don't need to tell you Harrington's is in trouble. The stock has plummeted and investors are getting antsy. The company is on the verge of ruin unless it gets a very generous investor. Someone like you. James, you can correct me anytime if I'm wrong but I think you're only with me to be connected to the Harrington name. Am I far off base?" She asked with raised brow.

Eleanor's bluntness caught him off guard. "You already seem to have the answers. You tell me."

Her scarlet painted lips curled to a half smile. "People talk, James. Though it's distasteful to speak of money in our circles, word gets around. Anyone who reads the financial news or follows the stock market knows the shape my father's company is in. And those people know he's looking to marry me off to someone who would be beneficial to Harrington's. So why would someone in your position be willing to infuse a huge chuck of money into an ailing company all for my hand in marriage. It isn't because you're madly in love with me. You've barely paid attention to a word I've said all night. So I can only conclude you want the family connection. As archaic as that sounds, it's still done in our world."

She'd hit the nail on the head. It should have made him uncomfortable how direct she was about the situation, but women like Eleanor were taught from birth how to be the perfect society wife. It was none of her business why he so badly wanted to be connected with an old-money family and he had no plans to share why, but he did owe her some type of explanation. "I suppose I should return your honesty with a bit of my own. No, I'm not madly in love with you and I don't think you love me either. But I believe we'd do quite nicely together. You'd compliment me perfectly with your beauty, education, poise and grace. I can't promise you a grand romance, but I will honor and respect you. You'll never want for anything."

She smiled. "That's good to hear. Just so you know, James, I'm usually not this forward, but if you could imagine some of the men my parents have been pushing my way lately you'd feel sorry for me. You're the first one I actually like. I don't love you but like you said, I think we'll rub quite nicely together. So we're really doing this?"

James didn't need her to elaborate to know what she was talking about. "When should we announce our engagement?"

Eleanor's smile widened. "After mother's gala. No need to take the spotlight from her."

"Is there any particular type of ring you'd care for?"

"I trust your judgment. I don't want anything too ostentatious but I'd appreciate something befitting the wife of James Rothschild."

James raised his glass in salute to his fiancé. "I'd say this calls for a toast to a successful union."

Eleanor lifted her wine glass and gently tapped it to his. "To us."

He had to hand it to her, when it came down to the nitty-gritty Eleanor was all business. While he appreciated that she didn't pretend this was some great love match, her businesslike manner took him by surprise. Everything he wanted was coming to fruition. So why couldn't he stop thinking about Noelle?

Noelle did her best to keep up with the fast chatter and merriment of the women surrounding her, but she simply couldn't get into the spirit despite the smile she'd glued on her face.

Simone placed a hand on her shoulder and gave it a rub. "Are you okay, sweetie?"

Noelle widened her smile to play off the fact she simply didn't want to be here. "I'm fine."

"Are you sure? Because you're really quiet."

"I'm okay."

"You've barely touched your drink, girl. You're making the rest of us look like lushes. Come on, bottoms up." Tanisha, one of the women at their table egged her on.

"I'm not really much of a drinker to tell you the truth," Noelle answered as politely as she could.

"You've been acting like a Debby Downer all night. Do you think you're too good to cut loose with us? Simone why is your cousin such a wet blanket?" Tanisha went on.

Out of all her cousin's friends, Tanisha made her the most uncomfortable. She was loud and one of those brutally honest people who didn't have a problem hurting someone's feelings in the name of telling it like it is. She reminded Noelle of the girls who used to make fun of her in grade school.

"Lay off, Tanisha. One of these days your mouth is going to get you in trouble." Simone glared at her friend.

"Whatever," Tanisha mumbled before taking a generous swig of her Long Island Ice Tea.

Needing to get away from the table for a moment, Noelle pushed her chair back and stood. "I need to run to the restroom. Excuse me."

In order to get to the restroom, she had to go through the restaurant portion of the building. As she walked by the patrons, she could have sworn she saw James out the corner of her eye. Of course it wasn't him. She had to be imagining things. The man occupied every corner of her mind all the time. She often imagined seeing him in places she went but it always turned out to be someone else.

In the bathroom, she washed her hands and checked her makeup in the mirror. She barely recognized herself. Tonight, she wore the gold contacts and her makeup was artfully done, although it was more than what she usually wore. It was all for him and he wasn't here to see it. James would probably never bring her to a place like this anyway.

She wiped away an unexpected tear that fell from the corner of her eye before it could leave a track down her rouged cheek.

"Are you okay?"

Noelle turned to see one of the most stunning women she'd ever seen. She was tall and willowy with dark red hair and large blue eyes. Dressed in designer wear from head to toe, everything about this woman screamed money. Noelle had seen her somewhere before but couldn't place where.

Noelle smiled at the woman and nodded. "I'm fine, thanks for asking."

"Well, if you're sure..." The other woman looked her over. "That's a lovely necklace by the way. Cartier?"

Noelle touched the necklace protectively. It was one of the few gifts James had given her. It was a diamond surrounded by smaller diamonds on a platinum chain. She rarely left the penthouse without it. "Yes, it is. Thank you."

"You have great taste in jewelry."

"Well, it was a gift actually."

"Ah, I see. Well it's lovely nonetheless." The redhead touched up her makeup and then smiled at her. "I hope your night improves."

"Thanks," Noelle mumbled.

"Keep in mind, no man is worth the stress, dear."

Noelle raised both brows in surprise. "I never said my problems were because of a man."

The redhead chuckled. "Isn't it always because of a man?" she answered airily before sailing out of the restroom. Women like her didn't have men problems. She probably had a slew of suitors standing in line for a chance to be near her. She was the type of woman Noelle envisioned James with. That last thought made Noelle wince.

Noelle chided herself gently. "Get yourself together, girl" she spoke to the mirror.

"Do you need some assistance, Miss?" the valet in the corner spoke for the first time.

"Oh, no, I'm fine." Embarrassed at being caught talking to herself, Noelle hurried out of the restroom and headed back toward her group. From the corner of her eye, she caught sight of the redhead from the restroom. Curiosity made Noelle slow her steps and glance over to see the lady's companion.

The room began to spin and air swooshed from her lungs. She couldn't move, breath or even comprehend the unlucky coincidence of the scene before her. Only a few moments earlier she'd supposed this was the type of woman James would be with and there he was, smiling at the redhead in a way he never smiled at her. He was attentive and seemed interested in what his companion had to say. More importantly, this was the woman he took out in public. It suddenly dawned on her that the redhead was the same woman she'd seen in the newspaper. She was even more beautiful in person, which was why Noelle hadn't immediately recognized her. Here was the irrefutable proof of James' disregard for Noelle staring her in the face. It literally felt as if her heart was crumbling into tiny pieces.

She wasn't sure how long she stood in the same position but she realized the longer she did, the greater the chance James would see her. She didn't want to look as if she'd stalked him. Forcing her feet to move, she headed back to her table feeling completely numb.

Simone seemed to notice something was wrong right away. "Noelle, you don't look so hot."

Noelle opened her mouth but no words came out at first. It took a considerable amount of concentration just to keep from crying. Finally finding her voice after a few moments, she said, "I'm really not feeling well. I think I'll pass on going to the club tonight."

Tanisha snorted. "I told you she'd come up with an excuse when she got out of the bathroom."

"Shut up!" Simone snapped at her friend before returning her attention to Noelle. "What's the matter hon?"

"I feel a migraine coming on." And that wasn't far from the truth. That familiar throb of her frontal lobes was merely a dull ache right now, but she knew if she stuck around much longer it would be a full-on thunderclap in her skull.

"I'm sorry, honey. I can go with you if you'd like."

"No! I don't want to ruin your night. I'll just get a cab, head home and lay down."

"Are you sure?" her cousin asked.

"Yes. Please enjoy your evening."

"Okay, but call me when you get back to your place. And if you need me to come over just say the word."

"Will do." Noelle made her hasty goodbyes to the rest of the ladies at the table and headed out, still trying to wrap her head around seeing her worst nightmares come true. Noelle was well aware of James's other life, but it was one thing to know and not think about it versus coming face to face with it.

By the time she made it back to the penthouse, her migraine was in full effect. She was in so much pain her eyesight was bleary. She probably handed the cabbie far more than the fare based on his effusive thanks but she didn't care, she simply needed to get inside and lay down. This was one of the worst she'd ever had.

"Miss Greene, are you okay?" the security guard asked as she stumbled past his desk. He probably thought she was drunk by the way she swayed from side to side as she walked.

"Fine. Just not feeling well," she managed to mumble, stumbling past him.

Nearly collapsing in the elevator, she barely stayed on her feet and practically crawled to her door. How she managed to unlock the door was pure testament to her determination because once she was inside the penthouse, she collapsed and fell into a blissful faint.

Chapter Fourteen

James wasn't sure why he went back to the penthouse, particularly after the way Noelle had acted earlier. He told himself he didn't need a reason but deep down he knew it was because he couldn't stay away. He had to see her. The woman was like a sickness in his blood he couldn't get rid of. She consumed his every waking thought. The sooner he was able to exorcise her from his system the sooner he'd be able to move on with his life.

A twinge of unease seared through him when he thought of her walking away. But he squashed those misgivings. What the hell was the matter with him? He didn't care if she left, beyond the fact it would create an inconvenience for him until a suitable replacement was found. Even as he tried to convince himself of this, James knew it wasn't true.

Perhaps he felt this way where she was concerned because things were going extremely well for him. James was used to dealing with one major stress or another but lately things were going swimmingly. Business couldn't be better, AlCore was crumbling and he was engaged to a woman of impeccable breeding. If only things would fall in line with Noelle, everything would be perfect.

By the time he was in the elevator on the way up to the penthouse, James had made up his mind to set Noelle straight. He would let her know in no uncertain terms who called the shots, and if she didn't like it she was free to leave. With that in mind, he managed to push away the excitement he felt at seeing her again.

James used his key to let himself into the penthouse; however, he was met with darkness. He didn't expect her to be in bed so early. When he flipped on the nearest light switch, he froze in terror at the sight which greeted him. Lying in a heap not too far from the door was Noelle. Her coat and shoes were still on as if she were about to go out or was coming home.

"Shit," he muttered, dropping down next to here to see if she was still breathing. Her face was more than a little warm. He gathered her upper body in his arms and gently patted her cheek.

"Noelle. Wake up! What happened?"

Her head lolled from side to side as she released a moan. "The light," she whispered.

"What?"

"It hurts. The light. Turn it off."

Whispering another curse, James hooked one arm beneath her knees and the other around her back and lifted her as he stood. He carried her the short distance to the couch and gently laid her down. "I'll call an ambulance. Don't move."

"No," she weakly croaked.

"You're not well. You need to see a doctor."

"No doctor," she whispered, her eyes still closed. "Just a migraine. I get these sometimes. I'll be okay. Just have to lie very still. In the dark."

"Does a migraine make you pass out like this? No, I'm calling the doctor."

"Stop. Yelling. No ambulance. I just need to sleep this off."

"I wasn't yell—," he sighed. James could imagine every sound was probably like an earsplitting jackhammer to her.

He modified his tone to a whisper. "At the very least allow me to call a doctor to come check you out.

"You're wasting your time. I have tablets. If I get a couple, I'll be fine."

James needed to strain in order to hear her. She sounded so weak and he felt helpless seeing her in so much pain. Noelle seemed to know best in this situation so he decided to go along with her request. He turned the light off and went back to the couch to collect her.

Noelle gasped when he lifted her into his arms again. He was careful as he carried her up the stairs and to her bedroom, holding her close like a fragile parcel. Once James laid her down in the center of the bed, he took extra care as he removed her coat, shoes. He stripped her down until she was in her bra and panties. Though her body encased in a black lace bra and panty set would have sent his hormones raging in other circumstances, he pushed away any urges he felt of a sexual nature. He pulled back the covers and tucked her in.

"Noelle, what pills do you need?"

He thought she passed out again but she finally answered after a long pause. "In the medicine cabinet in my bathroom. It's the only prescription bottle in there, you can't miss it. I only need two."

"I'll be right back." James had no problem finding the pills per her instruction. He left the two tablets on her nightstand and ran back downstairs to get her a bottled water to wash them down with. When he returned, he sat on the bed next to her and lifted her up. "Here take these," he prompted, feeding Noelle the pills.

She winced in obvious pain but opened her mouth to receive them. James took the water and pressed it against her lips. She took a few sips and swallowed. When James was satisfied Noelle had washed the medicine down, he lowered her on the pillow. He then went to the bathroom, found a washcloth and ran in it under icy water. James returned to her with the damp cloth and placed it over her forehead. "This should make you feel better."

"Why?" She groaned.

"Why what?"

"Why are you being so nice to me?"

Did she really think he was such a monster to do nothing while she was in such a weakened state? It hurt him a little to know she had such a low opinion of him. "What exactly did you expect me to do, Noelle? Leave you on the floor. Maybe kick you a couple times?"

"You're yelling again."

He silently counted to ten to get his ire under control. She was sick and probably not thinking clearly. He made sure to lower his voice when he spoke next. "Noelle, this is basic common courtesy. If I were ill enough to pass out, I'd hope someone would help me."

"It's no big deal. Like I said, I'm used to them."

"Have you seen a doctor about them? I've had headaches before but none have made me pass out."

"You've obviously never had a migraine headache. They're a million times worse. James, thank you for being here but you can go now. The pills should start working soon."

"I'm not going anywhere. Not while you're like this." He wouldn't be able to forgive himself if anything happened to her and he could have done something about it. James kept that last bit to himself, afraid to make this situation into something more than it actually was.

James slid off the bed and removed his suit jacket and shoes. He walked to the other side of the bed and slid next to Noelle.

"James?"

"Shh. Just rest. I'll be here if you need anything."

"You don't have to."

"I know I don't. I want to."

Noelle didn't say anything afterwards. The two of them lay in silence. After a while, James figured Noelle had gone to sleep. This gave James the opportunity to think. He was playing with fire laying her with her this way. He didn't want her to get ideas but he couldn't walk away from her either.

It had scared the hell out of him seeing her passed out on the floor. His heart nearly plummeted to his feet. He decided to not question why because it might lead him to an answer he wasn't ready to deal with.

Lying here with her like this reminded him of the period of time when he took care of his grandfather. His grandpa had meant the world to James. When he'd gotten sick James had taken a break from school to take care of him. It was an emotionally and physically taxing time. James never thought he'd find himself taking care of anyone like this again, although the situations were vastly different.

James must have dozed off because the next thing he knew, he was being nudged awake. "James?"

It took several seconds for James to remember where he was. He sat up and looked over at the clock on the nightstand. It was two in the morning. Sometime when he'd fallen asleep, Noelle had gravitated toward him and his arms were wrapped around her.

"Yes? How do you feel?" He held on to her, relishing the feel of her in his arms.

"Better, thank you for staying here with me but I would have been fine by myself."

"You were doing so well by yourself you were passed out downstairs by the door. These migraines, how often do you get them?"

"Not very often but mostly when I'm stressed or upset about something."

"And what upset you so much that you got sick?"

"Do you really want to know or are you asking out of politeness?"

"I wouldn't have asked if I didn't want to know."

"James, I think some things are probably better left unsaid."

Now James was even more determined to find out what the problem was. He didn't like her keeping secrets from him, especially when he suspected they were about him. "Is it about earlier?"

"James, have you ever done something you knew wasn't good for you but you kept doing it anyway?"

He wasn't sure what she meant by that but he figured it was her roundabout way of answering the question. "Yes. Actually I have."

She chuckled lightly. "I find that hard to believe. You seem to be the most together man I've ever met. You're very sure of yourself and you know what you want. I can't imagine you wasting your time on something you know is futile."

He shrugged. "Believe it or not, it's true."

"Tell me about it." She gently prompted.

This was the part where he'd usually shut down but for reasons he couldn't explain he shared with her something he'd never told another living soul, not even his grandfather. "When I was younger, I was the new kid in school. Mind, you this was a special school that went from kindergarten to twelfth grades. I didn't start until I was around nine, so for the most part most of kids who attended that school had known each other for a while, and groups had been formed. Like most kids my age, I wanted to fit in. There was a boy there, his name was David, who seemed like a nice kid, at least I thought so. But then things started happening, he'd say nasty things around the other kids, steal things and blame it on me, basically he was a bully in every sense of the word."

"That sounds awful, James. This kid must have been a real jerk."

"That he was. But you see at that age, all a kid really wants is to belong and I desperately wanted that, so I put up with his antics for a couple years, even when I knew deep down this kid and his friends would never accept me." A lump formed in his throat as he recalled those days when he was constantly reminded about his addict mother and how his grandfather had been nothing more than a lowly gardener. At the time he would laugh it off when the other kids teased him about it, not letting them see how deeply their barbs had cut.

Noelle empathized with him. She knew what it was like to be ostracized. "I'm guessing you got past that. How did you do it?"

"I reached my breaking point. Sometimes you have to be figuratively smacked on the head to eventually wake up. And I did. I saw David for what he really was. I eventually did my own thing and the teasing eased up some. By then I learned to be a little more cautious around people."

"Whatever happened to David?"

James smirked. "Oh, he's having his just desserts as we speak. Now it's your turn. I shared with you and now you have to answer my earlier question. Were you upset with what happened earlier?"

Noelle hesitated. "I don't want this to turn into an argument."

"Who's arguing?"

"James, to be quite honest, I don't know how to act around you sometimes. I want to please you but I never know what you're thinking. I'm on pins and needles when you visit."

This admission took him by surprise. He knew this was no mere act no matter how he tried to convince himself otherwise. James didn't want to be the reason Noelle was in pain, but he didn't twist her arm to become his mistress. "If you didn't please me, you'd know. But you never really answered my question did you? You're just dancing around the issue."

"James, I think if I told you things would never be the same between us again. Can't we just put it down to me having a bad day? Please?"

There was a desperate timbre to her voice. Whatever it was Noelle didn't want him to know. He decided not to press. Besides, he felt if he did force the issue it would break the warmth of this unguarded moment between them. James knew once he let her go things would return to the way they had been. He needed this moment and he suspected Noelle did, too. "Okay. Tell me something else, then. When I came by earlier I saw you sketching something. I actually caught a glimpse of it and was very surprised. I never knew how talented you we were."

"Hmm, I'm okay. I'm no Picasso but I do okay."

"When you told me you were taking a break from art school, I assumed it was because you were no good at it."

"I never said I sucked, but I'm just not at a level I think I should be at. At least not at the level my professor thought I should be. That guy was always on my case. He always used me as an example and class to point out what not to do. I'd leave his class in tears most of the time."

"From what I saw, you're very talented. Maybe that professor of yours was jealous. They say those who can't do, teach."

"I don't know about that. He's pretty respected in the art community."

James had a feeling no matter how much he complimented Noelle on her work she wouldn't believe him, so he stopped trying. "So what were you drawing?"

A small smile touched her lips. "I was sketching a cake I wanted to try."

"A cake? It looked more like a landscape of some sorts."

"It was, kind of, but I've been watching these televisions shows about bakers who make the most fantastic cakes into wonderful works of art. I wanted to give it a shot. After all, I have a lot of time on my hands."

"Is this something you've done before?"

"No. I've got the baking part down so now I'm going to try my hand at the crafting part. I've done a lot of research on the internet. Seems like a fun hobby to take up."

"I'd love to see what you come up with."

"I doubt my first attempt will come out that good but it should be fun trying." He could hear the enthusiasm in her voice. Even though the lights were off, James could see the sparkle in her eyes. Unable to help himself, he bent down and dropped a light kiss on her lips. He pulled back after that taste.

Noelle stroked the side of his face. "Don't you want to finish what you started?" she asked expectantly.

For reasons he couldn't explain James felt sex would ruin this moment. "If it's all the same to you, I'd rather just lay here."

Noelle snuggled closer to him and continued to stroke his cheek. This was nice. James could get use to this. He wished Noelle and he had met under different circumstances and…he shook his head to dispel those thoughts. It was too dangerous to let his thoughts dwell into that territory.

"James?" Noelle asked after several minutes of silence.

"Mmm?"

"I wish it could be like this all the time. But I know after tonight it will go back to the way it was, won't it?"

He wished he could give her the answer she sought but refused to lie to her. He kissed her forehead. "Go to sleep, Noelle. You've had a rough night."

Thankfully, she didn't say anything else. James held her until her slow even breathing indicated she was asleep. And even after she was out he held on for as long as he dared. He didn't want to fall in love with her, especially when he wasn't sure if that particular emotion actually existed. He'd worked too hard to achieve his goals to throw it away now for something he wasn't certain of. If he didn't end this arrangement soon, one of them would end up hurt and he was almost certain it would be him. But letting her go right now simply wasn't an option, as irrational as it was.

It was close to dawn when he finally let go of Noelle and slid off the bed, leaving Noelle alone. He didn't look back as he walked out of the room because the temptation of rejoining her was too great.

Chapter Fifteen

Once again, the dynamic changed between Noelle and James. She saw James even less after the night he took care of her when she was ill. Noelle thought things would be different after what he'd done and the things he'd shared with her. But was he even more distant than before. Even the sex was not the same. While still earth-shattering, but there seemed to be a piece of him missing.

Noelle believed his interest was waning. They were coming up on a year of their arrangement and she continued to hold on because her heart wouldn't allow her to leave.

Paul told Noelle she'd lasted longer than any of the other women who'd resided in the penthouse. At first that made her feel a little better because she thought it had to mean something. But after a while, Noelle knew she was only fooling herself. James still appeared in the papers with the redhead from the restaurant. It was obvious he wanted to keep Noelle as his dirty little secret.

Noelle didn't visit her cousin as much as time went on because her appearance had changed. She'd lost more weight and wasn't sleeping. She'd often go through the day with huge bags under her eyes, which she'd cover with a ton of makeup. Her migraines occurred more often and, according to her hairdresser, her hair was thinning.

One of the bright spots in the months that passed was Paul. The two of them had managed to form a friendship that Noelle could never have expected. He listened to her vent and he'd often stop by to keep her company. The other thing that gave her pleasure was her baking. She'd gotten good at decorating and sculpting cakes. Noelle discovered she had quite a talent for it.

Whenever she felt particularly low, she'd try a new recipe and call Paul to come try it as she had no appetite, which is where she found herself now. She fiddled around with one of her mother's old recipes and made a few modifications to it. She texted Paul to come over when he got a free moment. He immediately answered back to say he'd be over right away which meant James was away and not on business. James was probably with his redhead.

She hadn't seen James in over a week and the last time he showed up, he had been more than a little annoyed with her. Noelle typically only left the penthouse when she knew he would probably be in the office. On that day in particular, she decided to get out of the penthouse for some fresh air. She ended up walking several blocks. By the time she made it back, she'd been gone a couple hours.

She'd been surprised to find James waiting for her, his eyes slightly narrowed. *The reason I gave you a cell phone was so you'd answer when I called," he said without a hello or how are you.*

Noelle wished she was surprised by his tone but all he seemed to do lately was snap at her. "I'm sorry. I forgot to take it with me. How long have you been waiting?"

"It doesn't matter if I've been here five minutes or five hours, I expect you to be here when I arrive. Is that understood?"

She nodded. "Yes, of course but – " she was just about to point out she hadn't been gone for five hours when he grabbed her and practically ripped her coat off. He pulled her against him, crushing her breasts against his chest.

His mouth was over hers in a kiss so hungry and angry she could barely breathe. James wove his hand through her hair and yanked back so hard she thought her neck would snap. This wasn't the first time he'd been this rough with her, but she was ill- prepared for it.

She managed to tear her mouth away from him to catch her breath. "James, just give me a minute. I just need – "

"You don't call the shots here. Don't you ever forget it." He bit down on the tender flesh of her neck until she cried out. She didn't understand was happening but James didn't give her a chance to figure it out either.

He covered her mouth again as he cupped her ass and lifted her against the thickness of his erection. She gripped his shoulders and wrapped her legs around his waist as he carried her across the room. James didn't take her upstairs as she thought he would, instead he pressed her against the living room wall.

His kiss dominated her, seeming to rob Noelle of her very essence. He roughly moved his hands between their bodies and fumbled with the buttons and zippers of their pants until she felt his cock against her wet opening.

Noelle adjusted her position just enough to allow him the entrance he sought. Once his member was aligned with her wet opening, he thrust forward so forcefully she felt it all over. James was on a mission to conquer with no plans to take prisoners. And despite the roughness of his movements, her pussy gushed for him. She loved the way he plowed into her, claiming her body for his very own in a primitive dance as old as time.

No words were exchanged. The only sounds made were ones of grunts and moans. Noelle clung to him trying to give him everything he needed, though deep down knowing it would never be enough. Whatever had gotten a hold of him, she couldn't soothe. Realizing she was simply a temporary vessel to ease whatever demon drove him, she still held on as if her life depended on it.

Her climax came hard and fast yet he continued on, not slowing down, grinding into her as intensely as he began. She wasn't sure when he stopped but when he did, his arms tightened around her to the point where she had to gasp for air. Finally when he let her go, Noelle felt like a bowl of jelly. Her rubbery legs wouldn't support her without his support, so she slid down the length of his body in a heap at his feet.

He stood over her for several minutes, his breathing ragged. When he finally spoke, her blood ran cold. "Next time, answer your phone."

He walked away and headed upstairs to shower. By the time she found the strength to get to her feet and fix her clothing, he was back and heading out the door.

"Aren't you staying?" she called to him.

"No," was his curt reply.

She collapsed to her knees.

Noelle shuddered at the thought of how he'd used her and then left without a backward glance. The only thing missing from that scene was the pile of money the john usually threw at the whore when he was finished with her. At least that's how she'd felt afterwards.

"Earth to Noelle. Come in Noelle."

She snapped out of her daydream when she realized Paul stood in front of her, waving his hand in her face. She shook her head of the haze she had fallen under. "Paul, when did you get here?"

"A few minutes ago. You were in your own little world. I rang the doorbell and when you didn't answer I let myself in and found you in here spacing out. What the hell have you been doing to yourself lately? You're a mess!" He looked her up and down with a discerning stare.

"Gee, thanks friend. I call you over to try my latest treat and you insult me."

"I only tell you this because I am your friend. Sweetheart, have you been eating?"

"Of course," she said defensively. "I've just been counting calories lately."

"You're an awful liar Noelle, and there's only so much make up you can use to cover up those bags. Why do you torture yourself like this? He's not worth it."

She raised her chin defiantly. "That's for me to decide. If I wanted a lecture, I'd call my cousin."

"Noelle, I hate seeing what being James's mistress is doing to you. You're not handling it well."

"Can we not talk about it?"

"Fine, we won't talk about it now, but when will we? When you're in the hospital? I know about the migraines. I'm the one who gets your prescription refilled."

She shrugged. "So what? I get migraines. It's not so uncommon. Look, are you going to try this cake or not?" Noelle grabbed a plate and knife. Ignoring that pitying look on his face, she cut him a generous slice. "Here you go." She tried to inject as much cheer in her voice as possible.

Paul looked as if he wanted to say something but decided against it. "Sure. I love to try whatever you make. I come for the company but stay for the cake."

She relaxed now that the subject had changed. Noelle watched with anticipation as he forked a generous amount of the sweet treat into his mouth. No matter how many times he gushed over her creations, she was always anxious to get the verdict when she made something new. His eyes widened for a moment before closing in what appeared to be pure ecstasy.

"What the hell did you put in this cake? Crystal Meth? Crack? This is…" He took another bite and then another until the slice was nearly gone.

She grinned at his pleasure. "Glad you liked it."

"Liked it? That's putting it mildly. I've tried just about everything you've made and its all be fantastic but this is a whole other level. You have a gift, woman."

"You're exaggerating. But I'm glad you like it."

"I never lie about my food. Your cake is out of this world. Mind if I take some home to my sister? She's liked everything you've made so far as well. She wants to know why you haven't gone into business for yourself. And I completely agree. This is better than anything I've ever tasted in any bakery."

Noelle shrugged, a little embarrassed about the praise he heaped upon her. "It's something I enjoy doing. It makes me feel closer to my mother."

"And I think she'd be very proud of you if she tasted this."

She could feel a blush warm her cheeks. "Thanks Paul. It's really sweet of you to say."

"If you ever get serious about your passion then I could help you. Since I've been your guinea pig, I've taken all your leftovers home and shared it with my sister and her roommate. They love your baking as much as I do. And as you know my sister is getting married in about five months. She's contracted all of her vendors except a baker. My sister is very particular about what she wants and she wanted me to ask you if you'd considered doing the cake for her wedding."

Noelle gasped. She was honored to be entrusted with such a task but she didn't believe she was ready to share her creations for commercial consumption. "I just bake for fun. I find it hard to believe there isn't at least one bakery your sister likes."

"We've tried over thirty bakeries and establishments in other states. We even drove two hours out-of-state to try a cake from a bakery she'd seen in a bridal magazine. Nothing is as good as what you've made. You'd be compensated. Name your price."

"I've never made a wedding cake before."

"But I've seen what you can do. With your artistic background, you could make something delicious and pleasing to the eye. Would you at least think about it before you say no?"

"Well…"

"Please?"

Paul had really been a good friend to her. It was hard to say no especially since she enjoyed baking so much.

"Okay, I'll think about it."

He moved around the counter and gave her a big hug. "Thanks friend! You're the best."

Noelle laughed. "I didn't say yes yet."

"Maybe not but I can be very persuasive."

Noelle had no doubt about it. She only hoped if she did agree to do this for him she wouldn't be in over her head.

"We can duck out of this thing as soon as we finish making the rounds." Eleanor's left hand rested casually on his arm, the five carat diamond engagement ring he'd gifted her with the night before glistened on her finger. They'd ultimately decided to wait a few months to announce their engagement in an attempt to not make the courtship look like an arrangement of desperation on either side.

James stared at that elegant hand, so smooth and perfectly manicured. He wondered what his ring would look like on a different hand, one with shorter fingers, skin that was extra smooth and dark brown. He quickly shook that thought from his mind. What the hell was wrong with him? Was he deliberately trying to sabotage himself with these ridiculous fantasies? Maybe this was a sign that it was time to make a change.

Get rid of Noelle.

As a matter of fact, no more mistresses until after he was safely wed and Eleanor was pregnant with their first child. Noelle had become more of an irritant lately, inconveniently creeping into his thoughts at the damnedest moments. Whenever the temptation became too great for him to stay away from her, Noelle would stare at him with her big doe-like eyes. He felt guilty for even touching her. He didn't need that shit.

He'd end it tonight.

"James?" Eleanor tapped him on the shoulder.

"I'm sorry, Eleanor. What were you saying?"

She gave him an accessing look. "You have a habit of drifting off into space when we're together. It can't always be about business. Is it another woman?"

Eleanor was too perceptive for her own good. Even if she was correct, there was no way he'd ever admit it. "Why would you think that, when I'm standing with the most beautiful woman in the room?" He took her hand and raised it to his lips, for a light kiss.

"Charming." She smiled. "But we both know this isn't some grand love affair between the two of us. I don't mind your extracurricular activities as long as you're discreet. Requiring your full attention when we're together shouldn't be too much to ask, however."

"You're right of course, my dear. Shall we mingle?"

She smiled at him. "Yes. I see Daddy over there. Let's go over and say hello. He was quite pleased when I told him about the engagement. I'm sure my mother has already called the local papers. There'll probably be an article about us in the society pages tomorrow."

They were stopped several times before making it across the room to Eleanor's parents. Most of the interceptors were interested in doing business with James while the others had already heard of their engagement and wished to congratulate them.

By the time they got over to the Harrington table, James was ready to leave. There was nothing that bored him more than making small talk with people he wouldn't associate with outside of these tedious functions.

"James! Good to see you here old boy," Gregory Harrington greeted him a little more robustly than necessary, grabbing James by the hand and slapping him on the back.

James couldn't help but be more than a little amused at the man's warm attitude toward him. What a difference a few years and bad business deals made. "Good to see you as well, George."

"We should have a round of champagne to celebrate the wonderful news. Champagne for the entire table," he gestured grandly. Never mind the champagne was free, it was all about the show.

Maryanne Harrington sauntered over to them with her arms outstretched. "I was so pleased to hear the news." She grabbed James's hands and squeezed them. "Welcome to the family, James." She leaned forward and brushed air kisses on each cheek. She then turned to her daughter. "You know this means we have tons to do before the wedding. We have to book caterers and find the perfect venue and go shopping for your trousseau. You two simply must consider honeymooning in Fiji. Your father and I went there when we were married. Oh, listen to me go on." She giggled in a way that reminded him of a school girl rather than a mature matron.

"Now, dear, we'll have plenty of time to talk arrangements." George then led James away from the table just out of earshot of Eleanor and his wife. "So you finally did it, my boy. I couldn't be more pleased."

James smirked. "Thank you. I appreciate it."

"I'm sure you're aware Eleanor could have married anyone she wanted. Thad Richardson had been sniffing at her heels for ages. I was quite fond of him, you know. He and Eleanor practically grew up together. His parents were great friends of ours and he's a fine upstanding young man, but my daughter had her heart set on you and I'm loath to stand in her way."

In other words, Richardson had a more suitable background was what George actually meant. The Richardson family however, had fallen on even harder times than the Harringtons, and George was willing to settle for money over pedigree. The message was quite clear. Even though the man needed James way more than James needed him, the older man couldn't let things be without getting that dig in to put James in his place. "And I aim to make Eleanor happy. She won't regret her decision."

Harrington nodded. "Let's see that she doesn't. Now that we're practically family, perhaps we can meet up for golf this Sunday morning for a seven o'clock tee time. Afterwards we'll brunch. I have a tip on an investment you may be interested in."

And so it began. James was expecting this but he didn't think it would be this soon. He glanced over his shoulder to see Eleanor speaking with her mother, probably discussing wedding arrangements. He happened to catch her eye and she smiled and winked at him.

Yes, he'd definitely picked the right partner and soon the life he worked so hard for would be his. And things would go even more smoothly once he ended things with Noelle.

Chapter Sixteen

James and Eleanor stayed at the gala longer than either had intended. Once word of their engagement had gotten out, they were bombarded with several well-wishers and people haggling for wedding invites. Eleanor seemed to take all the attention as graciously as he expected her to, while James was slightly annoyed. He couldn't figure out why he wasn't happier.

By the time they left the function, Eleanor suggested they go back to her apartment for a nightcap. After a few drinks their light chatter turned into kissing and heavy petting. While Eleanor's kisses were pleasant and aroused him as they would with any man, something wasn't right. The chemistry was missing; it was as if both of them were simply going through the motions. James figured it was something they could work on. He refused to acknowledge his disinterest had anything to do with Noelle.

After a few more awkward attempts at foreplay, Eleanor finally put an end to their make-out session when it was clear neither one of them was really into it.

"We have to save something for later," she'd laughed. James, secretly relieved, didn't argue and they made arrangements to see each other again over the weekend. It was just past midnight and while he could have gone to the penthouse to see Noelle, something held him back.

The following day at his office James stopped himself from instructing Paul to make arrangements for Noelle's departure from the penthouse. He couldn't bring himself to do it. Paul was another issue in itself. There was something different about his Executive Assistant. He was as efficient as ever but the other man seemed aloof and more than a little peeved whenever they spoke. The more James thought about it, Paul's affable demeanor had turned to something that was almost hostile. Instead of the pleasant good mornings and polite inquiries, Paul was abrupt and to the point.

Several times James had asked his EA if there was a problem, but Paul always answered with a clipped "no." James hoped the younger man would get over it soon because it was getting old. While he didn't expect them to be buddies, James did care about his employees well-being.

He called Paul's office. The younger man answered on the first ring.

"Yes, Mr. Rothschild." And that was another thing. While most of his employees addressed him formally, Paul was one of the few who called him by his first name. Or at least he used to.

"If you have a minute, do you mind coming to my office?"

"Sure. I'll be right over." Paul hung up.

A few minutes later, a tap on his office door indicated Paul was outside his door.

"Come in."

Paul came in and closed the door behind him before walking over and halting in front of James' desk. "What can I do for you?"

"Actually, it's more about what I can do for you. Please have a seat."

The other man seemed surprised but sat down.

James gave him the once over. There it was: that hostility. Paul seemed to be looking through him instead of at him. "You're probably wondering why I've called you in here. Don't worry, it's not about your job performance. I have no complaints in that department. However, I have noticed a change in you."

"I'm not sure I understand, Mr. Rothschild."

"Right there. Since when did you become so formal with me?"

Paul shrugged. "You're my boss."

"Let's not split hairs here. I've always been your boss but only in the last several weeks you started calling me Mr. Rothschild. You seem upset about something. I know I may just be your boss, but if there's anything going on in your life or perhaps in this office that's giving you a problem perhaps I could help you."

If he wasn't paying close attention, James would have missed how Paul narrowed his eyes ever so slightly. "I really don't know what you're talking about *Mr. Rothschild.*"

"Paul. Cut the bullshit. What's really going on?"

"With all due respect sir, I feel if I were frank about my feelings they may cost me my job so I think I'll keep my opinions to myself. And I'd appreciate it if you didn't ask me again."

What the hell? "I am asking. You can speak openly without fear of losing your job because I asked you to."

Paul flexed his jaw as if he were trying to hold back whatever it was on his mind. Finally, "Okay, but remember you asked. It's about Noelle."

James stiffened. Paul had been with him for the last five years. In that time, there had been countless women in and out of James's life. Paul made sure they were taken care of and he often checked on them at James's behest. Not once, however, had he mentioned any of them, or seemed to be remotely interested beyond what his job required. James was instantly suspicious. "What about her?" he asked tightly.

"I think the way you're treating her is atrocious. Not to mention—"

Paul was cut off by the sound of a loud commotion outside of James's office door.

"Miss you can't go in there!"

The door flew open and a red-faced Gillian stormed into his office. Her eyes shot fire and she was practically foaming at the mouth. Her hair was slightly mussed and her clothes were wrinkled. James had never seen her look anything less than elegant. Right now however, she appeared to him like a raving mad dog.

"I'm so sorry!" Stella apologized, running into the room behind Gillian.

Two security guards burst inside and grabbed Gillian each taking an arm. "We're sorry sir, she got past us. It won't happen again. We'll call the police."

"Get your damn hands off me!" Gillian screamed struggling like a wild woman.

James held up his hand to halt the security guards from dragging her away. "Let her go. I'll talk to her."

"You're damn right you're going to talk to me. Who the fuck do you think you are ignoring my calls. I know your lap boy here must have told you I wanted to see you." Gillian slammed her palms on his desk.

He received the messages, but he had no intention of returning any of them. James chuckled at her outburst. "So this is what happens when you're ignored? What happened to all those elocution lessons from finishing school? Show a little decorum, sweetheart."

Gillian circled around his desk, her fist balled with the clear intention of hitting him. One of the guards restrained Gillian before she could assault James. "Son of a bitch!"

"Seriously Gillian, pull yourself together. No one in this room appreciates your tantrum. There's no need to be so dramatic about AlCore's turn of fortune. You knew it would eventually go bankrupt."

"You asshole! This is your fault. All David needed was a little boost. You could have helped. I swear to God if he dies, the blood is on your hands!"

What the hell was she talking about? James was well aware of the precarious state of AlCore but he had no idea what his former lover was talking about.

James nodded to the security guard. "Let her go. Wait outside and close the door behind you," he dismissed him. "That goes for the rest of you too."

Paul and Stella seemed only too happy to leave while the two guards hesitated until James made a sweeping motion with his hand, signaling them to leave.

When they were alone, James focused his attention on Gillian and saw tears streaming down her checks. Real tears. Not the fake crocodile ones she produced when she'd told him they could never be together. No, this time her eyes were red, her massacre was slightly smudged.

"Explain to me why there'll be blood on my hands? Who's dying? The old man? Hasn't he been at death's door for years now?"

Gillian's lips trembled and her fists clenched and unclenched. "David, you ass! He's crashed his car earlier today."

James froze. Even though David had been his nemesis since they were children, he didn't wish the man physical harm. "I'm sorry to hear that Gillian."

She pointed her finger at him, her body shaking. "You drove him to it!"

"I can hardly be blamed for a car accident."

"He crashed his car into a tree. There was no alcohol in his system or skid marks on the street. Can't you see, he wanted to die?" James barely processed her words before she was next to him, delivering a sound smack across his cheek. When she would have hit him again, James caught her wrist and stood up.

"That's enough. I'm sorry David was in an accident but if he did it deliberately as you think he did, the person you need to blame is him."

"If you would have only—"

"What? Blindly given him the money to save an ailing company he had no solid business plan to save. All that would have done was delay the inevitable. I didn't appreciate how he had the gall to send you to see me in the first place when you had no clue about the business. And then for him to show up and expect me to bail you guys out on the strength of our flimsy familial connection—a connection he made damn sure to deny until it was convenient for him to acknowledge it. Well, too little too late, Gillian. Now he has to deal with the mess he's made and you'll have to live with your choices as well." He let go of her wrist, bent down and pressed the speaker button to call the security phone.

"Yes, Mr. Rothschild?"

"Please see that Mrs. Alexander is escorted out. And going forward, she's not allowed back in the building."

Gillian backed away from him, almost stricken. "You don't even care do you?"

"About what? About David? It's sad, tragic even, but people get into accidents every day."

"He's your brother," she whispered, hand to mouth.

"And he's your husband. Shouldn't you be at the hospital with him? Did you come here in hopes I'd save you from the mess you're in? I'm not as gullible as I used to be."

He could tell by the way she flinched, he'd hit his mark. Gillian might have been genuinely upset but she was more worried about her own future than she was David's. "You didn't use to be this cold."

"I am what you, David and the old man made me. The three of you labeled me as a nothing, a non-entity. So you don't get to come in here and lay this shit at my feet."

Just then security showed up, discreetly tapping on the door before entering. One of the men grabbed Gillian by the elbow but she yanked it out of his grasp. "Don't touch me." She ran her hands down the front of her outfit before shooting James a glare that could have killed him on the spot if she had that ability. "I hate you."

"The feeling is quite mutual."

"Go to hell."

"I've been there Gillian and when I visited, I noticed there was a spot reserved for you."

She glared at him before turning on her heel.

When he was by himself again, James sank in his chair. A cold chill swept through his body. As he'd told Gillian, he was not responsible for David's action. So why wouldn't his hands stop shaking?

For years he'd forced himself not to feel, channeling all his past frustration and pain into a singular goal. From James's earliest memory, the Alexanders had given him nothing but grief. He should be celebrating their downfall, but the deep wounds they'd inflicted over the years wouldn't allow him his victory. It made him angry… angry because the old man was too incapacitated to realize just how much trouble the company he'd built was in. It also pissed him off that David tried to take the easy way out. Gillian's barbs had hit their target. James did feel guilty and he had no reason to. The Alexanders were still fucking with him without effort and it drove him crazy.

James couldn't concentrate at the blurring words on his computer monitor. His eyes were sore from strain and his temples throbbed. Damn Gillian and her dramatics. She had no right to come here and accuse him of anything after what she'd done—they'd done—to him.

Realizing he wasn't going to get another thing done, he powered down his computer and packed up his laptop. He called Paul to let him know he could go for the day, mentally reminding himself to continue that conversation they'd started earlier. Right now, however, he was too distracted to concentrate.

He barely responded to the security guards' good nights as he strode out the building into the parking garage. Instead of heading to his house however, he ended up driving. He got on the highway without a destination.

His mind drifted to the first time he met the imposing figure of Sheldon Alexander, which ironically was at the funeral of James's father, Stephen. He had been nine and had already learned some of the harsh realities of life. His grandfather having suffered a stroke and had become wheelchair bound. His mother was hardly home and when she was, she was drunk or high. He'd spied his mother shooting up in the bathroom once. When she saw him, instead of telling James to leave she asked him to pull the strap around her arm tighter while she gave herself some special 'medicine'. It wasn't unusual for things to go missing around the house. His grandfather tried to cover for her, but James knew his mother stole the items to sell for more drugs.

James pretty much took care of himself because of his grandfather's limited mobility and his mother's drug addiction. School wasn't much better. The children made fun of his worn clothes that were two sizes too small or large. He was often dirty because something was always getting cut off. He was lucky to get one square meal a day let alone three.

So he was surprised one day when his mother, who had been surprisingly lucid, brought home a brand new suit and shoes that fit perfectly. It was the best thing he'd ever own.

"Make sure you get behind the ears. Don't get out of the tub until you're squeaky clean." His mother claimed she was taking him someplace special. It must be because he couldn't remember when she ever paid this much attention or showed any interest in his hygiene or appearance.

His mother also took great care with her appearance, something she hadn't done in a long time. She actually looked pretty again. She'd artfully covered the bags under her eyes and the sores and scars on her face. Her clothes concealed the track marks on her arms, and how painfully thin her frame had become in her drug use. Her long blonde hair was arranged in a classy-looking bun. And she seemed sober.

He didn't ask questions as they rode the bus and walked three blocks to their destination, which turned out to be a church. He hadn't stepped foot inside of one since his grandfather's stroke. As they walked in, solemn organ music played and James realized this was no ordinary church service. It was a funeral. He'd only ever saw one on television. His mother chose a seat in the back as they listened to the dour minister give the eulogy. At the front of the church was a closed coffin with several flower arrangements on top. Beside it was a framed thirty by forty picture of a man who looked oddly familiar though Jaime was sure he'd never met him before.

His mother clutched him tightly, which was almost the most affection she'd ever shown him. She held on as tears ran down her face and he couldn't figure out why she mourned this man. Then he heard the name Stephan and he knew. That man was his father. His mother had mentioned that name many times yet this was the first time he'd seen his face. James's attention remained on that picture as he tried to commit every feature to memory from the gray eyes, like his own, to the ink black hair, also like his.

Sometime during the service he got the sensation someone was watching him. When he turned slightly to the left, his eyes collided with a man with iron gray hair and a stern demeanor. James wasn't sure how long they looked at each other before the old man turned back around.

Once the benediction was read, the pallbearers surrounded the coffin and proceeded to roll it down the aisle. It was followed by a tall, thin blonde woman, and with a small blond boy clutching her hand. The boy looked to be around James's age.

As the coffin passed them, his mother reached out to touch it. The blonde woman glared at his mother. "What are you doing here? You weren't invited," she hissed.

Kelly raised her chin defiantly. "My son has the right to pay his final respects to his father." She said it loud enough for the people around her to hear.

Then the man with the gray hair approached them and looked at James. He scrunched his face as if he'd smelled something unpleasant. "So this is the little bastard." It was all he said before ushering the woman and the boy out the church.

James didn't know how he ended up in the parking lot of Noelle's penthouse. Tonight he needed to just lose himself in her. When he walked through the door however, she looked to be on the verge of walking out the door. He didn't know where she intended to go but she'd have to change her plans.

Noelle was barely recognizable from the girl he'd first met. She wore way more makeup than she needed and her outfit, while well put together and obviously expensive, seemed wrong on her. Had he imagined her to be something she wasn't? Like Gillian who'd made a fool of him. The longer he stared at her, the angrier he grew. Everything from earlier hit him all at once and he wanted to lash out.

She fidgeted beneath his gaze. "I uh…I was just going to meet my cousin and some of her friends for drinks."

He didn't speak, as he continued to stare her down, taking in every single detail of her appearance from the high heeled boots to the jeans that provocatively hugged her hips. She'd lost weight since they'd been together but her curves were just as tempting. His cock stirred and all he could think about was how he planned on sinking himself into her tight wet pussy.

She ran her tongue across her gloss covered lips. "Well, I wasn't expecting you, so I didn't think it would be such a big deal to go out. I'm stuck in the penthouse most of the time and I—"

"Call your cousin and cancel your plans." He strode past her and made his way to the bar. After the shit day he'd had, James was in no mood for arguments.

"No."

He went about his task without missing a beat. "Take off your clothes, Noelle."

"Did you hear what I just said? I'm going out with my cousin. It would have been nice if you'd called ahead."

James slowly pulled out a glass and a bottle of whiskey. He poured himself a drink and took a sip before he acknowledged her. "I heard what you said; now take off your clothes."

"You can't order me around like this!"

He'd had enough from her. If she wanted to act like a child, he could certainly accommodate her. He refused to put up with her tantrum. "Five seconds, Noelle or I come over there and do it for you. And if I have to come over there, I'm going to paddle that delectable ass until you can't sit for a week."

She literally stomped her foot on the ground with her hands clenched into fists at her side. "James!"

"One." He took another sip of his drink.

"You're being unreasonable."

"Two." He licked his lips making eye contact with Noelle, leaving no doubt of his intentions.

"I'm a grown woman, and you have no right to treat me this way."

"Three." He put the glass down.

"Stop this."

"Four."

Despite her protests, he could tell Noelle wanted him just as much as he wanted her. She trembled and her lips quivered. The outline of her nipples peaked through her shirt just begging to be sucked and licked.

"Five." He walked from behind the bar and stalked toward her. He bent down just enough for his shoulder to catch her midsection as he lifted Noelle off her feet.

She let out a sound between a squeak and a scream.

As he carried her to the bedroom he swatted her ass. "I think it's time for a little reminder of who you belong to."

Though Noelle whimpered and kicked earning her another swat, James refused to change course. Once he tossed her on the center of the bed, he paused for the briefest of seconds and their eyes collided. That look in the depth of her big brown eyes made him flinch. In the back of his mind, he knew she didn't deserve this but he could think of no other way to exhume his pain. After this night, she might hate him, but it wouldn't be as much as he hated himself.

Chapter Seventeen

"Are you going to be okay?" Simone walked into Noelle's bedroom and sat on the bed next to her.

A week had passed since Noelle left the penthouse with only the things she'd come with. All the designer clothing, jewelry and items she'd brought with the money James had given her were left behind. The Mercedes he'd gifted her was left in the building garage and she'd closed the bank account he had opened for her and donated the money for charity. She wanted no reminders of her stupidity. It was embarrassing how she'd put up with James for nearly a year.

She fell in love with an imaginary figure she'd built up in her head. But in reality, James was a controlling egomaniac only concerned about himself. She'd been a convenient bed warmer for him and nothing more. The hardest part was finally admitting it.

"Yes, I'll be okay."

"Noelle, sweetie, you're allowed to mope for a few days but you have to come out of your room sometime. You're letting that bastard win. Do you think he's sitting around thinking about you?"

"I don't know."

"Yes, you do. He's taking his fiancée around town and has probably set up another woman in the penthouse."

Simone's words were exactly what Noelle needed to hear but it fucking hurt. "You're right," she whispered. "What's wrong with me? How could I have put up with that for so long?"

"Because you have such a good heart and you want to believe in people. I don't know how many times I have to tell you how strong and wonderful I think you are. But I'll keep doing it until you finally believe me."

Noelle sniffed. "I'm not strong. A strong woman wouldn't have let this man tread all over her for so many months. She wouldn't have to go crawling back to her cousin with her tail between her legs."

"That's not true. You didn't come crawling back. I invited you back because this is your home and I love you."

"I love you, too, Simone. Thank you for putting up with me. I swear I'll find a job and start contributing to the household bills more. In the meantime, I can use the money I'd set aside for school to help out."

"No. I want you to use that money for when you need it. If Aunt Dot were alive, she'd want you to put it to good use."

If her mother was still alive, Noelle doubted she'd be in this situation. "I wouldn't have this money had you not helped me. If you hadn't hired that lawyer on my behalf, Aunt Frieda would have spent it all. I'd probably be married to Walter."

Simone grunted in disgust. "I wish I were surprised at what they tried to do to you but my mother has done far worse." Her cousin's lips twisted in derision. Noelle knew that the disdain Simone held towards her mother, stepfather and brothers hid a secret pain she rarely spoke of. It made Noelle even more grateful to have someone who cared enough to take her out of a situation that could have ruined her life for years to come.

Noelle smiled at her cousin. "Thank you."

"No need to thank me. Like I said, this is your home too."

"No." Noelle shook her head. "I wasn't thanking you for letting me stay here but for being there for me. I know it was hard for you to maintain contact with me over the years because of your falling out with Aunt Frieda."

Simone looked slightly uncomfortable for a moment but she quickly shook it off. "I wish I could have taken you with me when I first left, but I knew they wouldn't let you go as long as they were receiving money for your upkeep."

"Have you heard from any of them lately?"

Simone broke eye contact and looked at her nails. "Not for a while." She was lying. But Noelle wouldn't press her. The mental abuse and isolation she'd suffered was nowhere near what Simone had dealt with. Though her cousin had only told her some things that had happened before she left home, Noelle could only imagine what she didn't reveal. Simone always seemed so strong and sure of herself, but now Noelle wondered if it was all just a front.

Her cousin was stunningly beautiful but she rarely dated. Noelle thought it was because Simone was so focused on her career and now getting her boutique up and running, but now Noelle had to wonder if her cousin still fought her own demons.

"I promise I'll get out of bed today. I think I'll take a walk to clear my head and figure out what I want to do with myself. You said I could stay here forever if I wanted but I'm going to need to learn to stand on my own two feet. I don't have much work experience beyond retail but maybe I can find something at an entry level."

"What about your art?"

Noelle shrugged. "I dropped out of art school, remember?

"There are lots of people who make a living doing caricatures or working with the city to beautify walls that have been covered in graffiti. You might also try private art lessons. I don't think you need a fancy art degree for that."

"To be honest, I've lost my passion for it. Don't get me wrong, I still love it but it's not the path I want to take. I believe the only reason why I went to art school in the first place was because art was one thing I was actually decent at. When I was a kid, it made me feel good when the teacher would tell me how realistic my drawings looked when most kids were still making stick figure people. I liked doodling in my notebook. I enjoyed art class and learning different techniques. I even enjoyed some of my art school classes, but when I think about trying to make a living out of it, I just can't fathom it."

"Wow. I thought that's what you wanted. I never would have pushed you to apply if I'd known that's how you felt."

"No. It's good that I went because I learned it wasn't what I wanted. I wish I were more like you. You love fashion and you've always wanted to open your own boutique with your designs. And look at you. Your shop is opening soon and it's going to be a huge success. I can't think of anything that gives me that same drive."

"There's got to be something that makes you happy."

"Well, I have my mom's old recipes that I've been playing around with. Paul says they're the best he's ever tasted. He asked me to do a cake for his sister's wedding. He even suggested I make a business out of it. That sounds crazy, doesn't it?" Noelle laughed before Simone could tell her how dumb an idea it was.

But her cousin didn't. "Does baking make you happy?"

"It makes me feel closer to Mom. I think about how happy we were in the kitchen when we baked together."

"Then maybe Paul is on to something. Why not give the wedding cake a shot as a test run and go from there."

"That's crazy."

"Crazy is having a dream and then sitting on it. Do you want to wonder 'what if' for the rest of your life?"

"But I'm not like you."

"And thank God for that. If you were like me, then you'd have more hang-ups than you can deal with. I can barely deal with them myself at times." Simone laughed. "I'm not the smooth operator you think I am. Do you think leaving a very comfortable, well-paying job was easy for me? I was terrified, but what scared me even more was not trying. You can't live your life comparing yourself to others. I have faith in you. Think about it." Simone leaned over and gave Noelle a kiss on the cheek. "I need to get ready. I'm meeting with some interior designers today to put the finishing touches on my boutique. I'm so excited to see my vision come to life."

"I'm really proud of you, Simone."

"Thanks hon." She got off the bed. "There is some leftover turkey sausage on the stove if you want any."

"Thanks."

Simone smiled and waved goodbye as she sashayed out the room. There was an extra spring in her step. With her cousin gone, Noelle fell back against her pillow. The dull ache in her chest where her heart beat throbbed. One of these days she'd get over James, but it didn't look like today was that day.

James read the letter twice to confirm he wasn't imagining things. "Son of a bitch." He picked up the phone and punched in Paul's number.

"Yes, Mr. Rothschild?"

"In my office now!" James slammed the phone back on the receiver without waiting for a response.

When summoned, Paul usually made it to James' office in under a minute but today it seemed like his employee took his sweet time. Paul tapped on the door before poking his head in the door. "Yes, Mr. Rothschild?"

"Get in here and close the door. I'm sure you know why I've called you to my office."

Paul didn't reply. He took the seat in front of James's desk.

James held up the letter. Paul seemed unimpressed with him, making James even angrier. "What the hell is this?"

"My letter of resignation."

"Are you not being compensated enough?"

"My paycheck has always been more than adequate." Paul's face remained expressionless and James tried to figure out what game the man was playing.

"Were you offered another job?"

"Nope."

"Okay, I'll bite. Why are you leaving a well-paying job without one to replace it? I've always pegged you for an intelligent man."

"With all due respect, Mr. Rothschild, now that my resignation has been tendered to you and Human Resources, the only thing you're owed is the two months of my time it takes for me to find my replacement and train him or her."

James had had enough of Paul's passive-aggressive attitude of the last several weeks. "Bullshit. What the hell has been your problem? You've been walking around with a major chip on your shoulder."

Paul's eyes narrowed. "Why does it make a difference why I'm leaving the company?"

"Because I want to know."

"And what you want trumps all, right?"

"What the hell is that supposed to mean?"

"It means you're so used to getting your own way you don't care how you go about getting it, even if it means hurting someone."

James instantly realized they were talking about two different things. The hostility in Paul's voice was so palpable he could touch it. Noelle. The conversation that had been interrupted by Gillian's hysterics came to mind. What had Paul been on the verge of telling him then?

"And you believe I hurt someone?" James said with more calm than he felt.

Paul's face turned bright red as he gripped the arms of his chair. James could tell the other man was close to losing his cool. "I don't just believe, I know." Paul leapt from his seat.

"Sit down," James barked.

"No. You don't get to tell me to jump and I ask how high. Not anymore. You're going to listen to what I have to say for once." Paul leaned over and pounded his fist on the desk. "I've followed your career closely and have admired how you've managed to turn one low budget hotel into an international chain. I idolized you, and to land a job working directly for *the* James Rothschild was a dream come true. You've been a tough but fair boss and I've learned so much from you. I knew when I took on this job keeping order in your personal life was a part of the package. But then Noelle entered the picture. Any idiot could clearly see she wasn't cut out for that lifestyle. Those other women were seasoned pros, but Noelle was different and I think you knew it, too. But you chose her anyway and treated her like crap."

James could feel the heat in his face as his temper threatened to explode. He didn't appreciate the tongue lashing even if every bit of it was true. "How I treat my lovers is between me and them. You get paid to do as I say, not question how I do it."

"I won't be quiet about her."

James felt the vein throbbing in his forehead as he forced himself to remain seated. He feared if he moved an inch he'd fly across his desk and beat the shit out of Paul, not because of his insubordinate tone but because it was now clear to him the other man had feelings for Noelle. "Get out."

"Gladly." Paul pivoted and stormed out of the office, slamming the door behind him.

As tempting as it was to simply let Paul go and pay him in lieu of that two month notice, James needed him in order to ensure the transition went through smoothly.

What exactly had been going on between Noelle and Paul? Did they have their own little affair behind his back? James would have bet a million dollars Noelle wasn't the type to take on more than one lover at a time but then again, it wouldn't be the first time a woman had fooled him. The thought of another man touching her ate at him. But the worst part was if it was true, James feared he'd driven her to it.

The ache was still raw upon discovering Noelle was out of his life for good. He tried to tell himself it was for the best, but it was a lie he had yet to swallow. His heart squeezed in his chest as he remembered when he learned she'd left.

He'd fucked up.

James knew it the second he rolled off of Noelle. She turned over, exposing her back to him, drawing her knees up to her chest and hugging herself into a ball. For reasons he couldn't explain even to himself, he reached out and touched her shoulder but she flinched away from his touch.

He'd been a lot rougher than usual, a bit mean and had said things he shouldn't have. In all his years of considerable experience, he'd never treated any woman as harshly as he had Noelle and his only justification was she had defied him. She stood up for herself and he didn't like it. He didn't like that she'd changed and wouldn't tell him why.

Unable to handle the shame of what he'd done, James slid out of bed and hastily gathered his clothing. Without a backward glance, he left the room not having the nerve to look her in the face. She was probably well within her right to curse or scream at him but she didn't. After a quick shower in the bathroom down the hall, he dressed and went back to his house.

James, lacking the concentration to make it through the next business day, had taken off early and headed to the penthouse with flowers and a diamond bracelet in hand. The second he stepped through the door, he immediately knew something was different. The warm scent that used to cling to the penthouse of something freshly baked was gone. Noelle was nowhere in sight, and upon further inspection he realized she wasn't there at all. It gave him no relief to see her clothing and all the jewelry and gifts he'd given her were still in her room, because the place seemed hauntingly empty without her there.

Instinct drew him back downstairs to the kitchen. Sure enough when he stepped inside the room Noelle seemed to favor, there lay a note on the island. With shaking hands, he picked it up and read the hastily scribbled words.

By the time you read this message, I'll be gone. I'm sorry I can't be who you want me to be. I can no longer pretend I'm someone I'm not. Good luck in all your endeavors. I hope you get everything you want. Best wishes. Noelle.

The note said so little yet so much at the same time. He wasn't sure what her cryptic message meant but he was certain of one thing; Noelle was gone and wasn't coming back. And an ache he thought he'd never feel again barreled its way into his heart. But this time it was much worse.

"Shit!" he yelled out in frustration.

Chapter Eighteen

"You did it babe! Do you have any idea how much business we're going to get from this event?"

Noelle chuckled, feeling nothing but relief now that the event was almost over. Though she was a guest at the wedding reception, her gaze kept straying to the cakes she'd baked and designed. "Please tell me you weren't soliciting business for our bakery at your sister's wedding. Alyssa will ring your neck if she finds out."

Paul waved his hand dismissively. "She's too busy playing princess for a day. Besides, I didn't have to say a word about the bakery. Once people walked into the banquet room and saw your work they were amazed. And when they tasted them, they were sold. People were asking Alyssa and Craig who the baker was. I already have a few clients lined up who'd like to do a consultation with you."

"The bakery isn't even open yet. It was tricky enough making the cakes in your kitchen, but if I have to fill more orders, those renovations to our bakery will need to be finished soon. I need a larger kitchen to bake in."

Paul slung his arm around Noelle and handed her a glass of champagne. "Relax, I'm handling this. The contractors assured me the renovations should be done by the end of next week. After that, the decorators will come in and do their part. We're still on track to have the shop open for business at the end of the month."

"You're amazing, Paul."

He leaned over and kissed her on top of her forehead. "No, you are. Without your creations, none of this would be possible."

It was hard to fathom six months had gone by since she'd moved out of James's penthouse. The first week, she'd lain in bed, crying most of the time, refusing to eat and cursing herself for believing someone like James was capable of loving anyone but himself. She'd been fooled by his smooth charm and those few tender moments they'd shared.

A couple weeks after she left the penthouse, Paul paid her a visit. She was surprised to learn he'd handed in his resignation. Horrified at the thought of Paul giving up a lucrative position over her she insisted he rescind it but he wouldn't budge. Paul had another idea, however. He'd saved a good chunk of money over the years and was looking to invest in a business so he could be his own boss. Noelle thought that was a great idea. Someone as smart and ambitious as Paul would do well going into business for himself. It was only when he'd told her what type of business he had in mind did she balk.

Paul was looking to open a bakery. He planned on handling the operation, advertising and finance side of it, while a partner would be in charge of the actual baking and direct supervision of employees. Baking for friends was one thing, but making a living from it was crazy. She had no experience running a business, and she wasn't used to making her confections for a large group of people. Paul assured Noelle she was indeed good enough to sell her baked goods to the public. He also pointed out how her artistic experience would be useful for the specialty designs and sculptured cakes that had become a recent fad.

Simone also seemed to think it was a good idea. It was only when Simone gently reminded Noelle of her mother's dream that she began to give it serious thought. She was quite good at putting random ingredients together to make scrumptious desserts, and she did love doing it, but she felt she needed more training in making those fantastical cake sculptures people went crazy over.

When Noelle expressed her concern to Paul, he found classes she could take to make designer cakes. It seemed he had it all planned out, right to down to a location for the proposed bakery.

When Paul wore her down with the help of Simone, Noelle agreed to his scheme, though she insisted she contribute to the startup costs. Since she had no plans to return to school, she decided to use her excess money to invest in her share of the business. After signing a contract and a handshake, they became business partners.

The site for their bakery was only a block away from Simone's new boutique. They decided to specialize in cupcakes, designer cakes and muffins to start out, and expand as their business grew. Paul immediately started to drum up business before the store opened by sending out samples of Noelle's baked goods.

Noelle took several cake decorating classes, from how to make a proper icing flower to how to sculpt cakes to look like anything. Most nights she practiced and tested out recipes while mapping out what would get baked on a daily basis versus what would be special order only. Starting up a business was harder than she thought, but it kept her busy and thoughts of James at bay.

Now with the store set to open in another month, Alyssa's wedding was the test. This was her first wedding cake...well, cakes. Alyssa had wanted three cakes, the main one, a cake for the bride and another for the groom that reflected their personalities. What she had come up with was a large cake that resembled the ball room the wedding reception was being held at, complete with a spiraling staircase with a bride and groom perched on top. It included tiny details from the paintings that adored the walls to the crystal chandelier hanging over the ceiling. That of course had been no easy feat, but she'd pulled it off after literally working on it for two days straight. For Alyssa's cake, she created a cake that looked exactly like a pink and white Louis Vuitton purse. And for Craig, she'd designed a small football field with players included.

Much to her pleasure, the guests "Oohed and aahed" over all of the cakes as if they'd never seen anything like it before. It made her happy to see all the hard work she put in was appreciated.

"I'm just glad this event is over. I barely slept for the last three days trying to get the logistics of these cakes just right."

"And that's exactly why you'll need to hire a few assistants. There's no way you can do this part on your own. I saw how much work you put in to it. And lucky for you, the shop will be open next month because I just secured us a party that will put your cakes on the map."

"Wasn't that the purpose of this wedding? There are over two hundred people here."

"Yes, small potato stuff. But apparently Craig's distant cousin is some big time philanthropist who has an interest in the arts."

"And what exactly does that have to do with our business?"

"She also owns one of the largest art galleries in the city. Apparently it was recently expanded. There's going to be a huge grand re-opening with a lot of big names in the art world in attendance. Mrs. Fontaine, that's her name by the way, wants you to create a cake sculpture replicating a famous piece, maybe the statue of David or the Venus de Milo. She also talked about cakes with paintings on them."

"Are you kidding me? Working out the logistics of something like that could take longer than the actual making."

"You know I'll help you out any way I can."

"The last time you tried to help me, you nearly burned the kitchen down. No thanks. When is the big event?"

"End of next month?"

"Sheesh. That's when the bakery is opening. It's not going to give me much time to do what I need."

"The kitchen will be ready if you need to use it. And I can place some help wanted ads in the newspaper to get you the assistance you require. "

"I don't know much about running a business, Paul, but it seems like everything is happening so fast. You're getting me more orders than I think I can handle, not to mention the day-to-day baking I'll need to do for regular menu items."

Paul squeezed her shoulder. "Don't worry. You can do this."

"I wish I had as much faith in me as you do." Though she complained, secretly it pleased her to know how busy she'd be. This ensured she'd have no time to think about James and soon she'd be over him. If only soon would hurry up and get here.

"James, thank God you're here!" Eleanor didn't look her usual put-together self. Her hair was slightly messy and her clothes were a bit askew as if she'd gotten dressed in a hurry. Her face bore no artifice, making her look years younger than the thirty-two he knew her to be.

He cupped the side of her face to comfort her. "Any news?"

"No, the doctors are still working on him. They've been in there for almost an hour. I've been pacing the floor driving myself crazy. I've probably worn my heels down an inch. I'm glad you're here. I know how busy you are."

"Eleanor, you're my fiancée, where else would I be?" He kissed her forehead. "Have you eaten anything?"

"Who has the stomach to eat at a time like this?"

"You have to take care of yourself otherwise you'll be of no use to your father. When was the last time you ate?"

"Mother and I had lunch at Pierre's around two."

"So tell me what happened."

Eleanor sniffed. "Mother, Daddy and I were at the club for dinner. We were in the middle of giving our drink orders when Daddy complained of chest pains. One of the waiters who happened to be a second-year med student managed to give Dad CPR and got his heart pumping again. I was paralyzed with fear. Mother was crying hysterically and all I could do was stand there and watch. I felt so useless."

"Try not to beat yourself up over this. It's difficult to know how you'll handle a situation unless you're in it. Let me get you a cup of coffee and a little something to nibble on from the cafeteria."

"I'm not sure if I can eat but thank you. James, what's going to happen if Daddy dies? His company is already in trouble. Now with this—"

"Let's not get ahead of ourselves. We'll wait to see what the doctor says first." James looked over her shoulder and noticed Maryanne huddled in the corner looking completely lost. "Why don't you go over to your mother and sit with her. I'll be back shortly." He kissed her forehead again.

James let out a sigh of exhaustion as he headed to the cafeteria. It had been close to ten when he left his office that night and his plans were to have a lengthy work out to release his stress. On his way out of the office, however, he received a call from a crying Eleanor informing him that her father had collapsed at dinner. It capped off an already shitty day—and an even shittier few months.

His new Executive Assistant Celeste, was a nightmare and caused him more work than necessary. What made things worse was she seemed to be under the impression that flirting was part of the job. Celeste spent more time throwing herself at him than actually doing what he hired her for. Also, she and Stella clashed. It was a no brainer; he'd have to fire Celeste before the probationary period was up.

She was the third in a string of terrible EA's since Paul's departure, and James was beginning to think Paul had cursed him. Damn Paul. Why the hell couldn't he just do his damn job and leave Noelle alone? Out of all the women he'd dealt with, why her?

Some of James' former mistresses had been models and pageant beauties, yet it had been Noelle Paul had given up a six-figure position with stock options for. James would lie awake at night obsessing over whether the two of them were together. When he imagined Paul touching Noelle, kissing her, fucking her, James became physically ill. Even though it had been months, thoughts of her still consumed him.

Since Noelle left, he hadn't taken another lover, telling himself he wanted to focus his attention on Eleanor, but he deep down James knew that wasn't the case. He even found himself visiting the penthouse and sitting in the kitchen. Guilt flayed at James when he thought of how he'd treated Noelle. When he'd set his course to obtain his ultimate goal, he knew there would be casualties. What he didn't realize was how great a price he'd have to pay. Despite how chaotic his life had become with her, at least his fiancée didn't disappoint.

Eleanor was a good woman. Despite her background, she didn't look down on people as most women in her circle did. She was beautiful, smart and unaffected by the trappings of her wealth. She appreciated the good things in life and made no secret of her expensive tastes, but she was basically a kind person. She never made catty remarks and James genuinely liked her. He wished, however, he could drum up enthusiasm for their upcoming nuptials. It was decided they'd marry the following year to give her and Maryanne time to plan the lavish wedding befitting a Harrington.

"This is what you wanted," he chided himself softly. James forced himself to push away the dangerous thoughts that led him down the path of regret.

James bought three cups of coffee for Eleanor, her mother and himself, along with a couple of sandwiches. When he returned to the ER waiting room, Eleanor and Maryanne were talking to a doctor and holding each other. Joining them, he listened to the tail end of the conversation. "We'll be taking him in to surgery first thing in the morning, but tonight our objective was to stop the seizures and get him into a more stable condition. Trust me, Doctor Pradesh is one of the top cardiac surgeons in the field. Mr. Harrington will be in great hands."

"Will the stroke leave him paralyzed?" Maryanne asked, shuddering as if the very thought of it was enough to make her faint.

"We won't know until he's recovered from his surgery. In the meantime, we're moving him to the Critical Care Unit. Visiting hours are over, but we'll let you look in on him briefly."

"I'd like to request a private room. I'm sure the family wishes to preserve Mr. Harrington's privacy," James spoke up.

"I'm sure that can be arranged. Do you have any more questions?" the doctor directed toward the three of them.

James looked to the two women seeing they were clearly shattered. So he took it upon himself to speak for them. "What time is the surgery tomorrow?"

"Surgery is scheduled for seven A.M."

James nodded. "Someone will be here all night, so if you can please keep us posted with any changes in Mr. Harrington's condition we'd appreciate it."

"Of course. I need to go confer with my colleagues but I'll be in touch." The doctor shot them a sympathetic smile and patted Maryanne on the shoulder before leaving the waiting room.

Eleanor turned to James. Her expression was one of despair. "What are we going to do if Daddy doesn't make it through the surgery tomorrow? What's going to happen to me and Mother? How are we going to pay off—"

"Eleanor!" Maryanne shushed her daughter. "We'll only think positive thoughts. I'm sure your father will pull through and everything will be just fine. Besides, James is here." Maryanne shot her daughter a narrow-eyed stare that spoke in volumes. It was no secret the Harringtons were in financial straits despite the lavish lifestyle they still led. But it was clear to James Maryanne wouldn't admit it out loud even if no one was around to hear.

James handed Eleanor a cup of coffee. "Here, take this. It'll calm you down. I brought one for you as well, Maryanne."

The older woman smiled gratefully. "Thank you, James, but I'll pass. I can't stand the Brand X coffee they use in these places. It's probably been sitting in a pot for ages." She curled her lip in distaste. "Were you serious about us being here all night? After I see George, I think I'd rather sleep in my own bed tonight. He won't even know if I'm here or not anyway."

"Mother, Daddy is in there fighting for his life. Can't you think of someone other than yourself for once?" Eleanor raised her voice, emitting an anger that surprised him. Eleanor, who was usually so poised, was not the type to make scenes but obviously her mother's blasé attitude had pushed her to the edge.

"Sweetie, I know emotions are running high right now, but your father wouldn't want us to be here all night in discomfort. James, can you take care of this?"

She made it seem like her husband was going to have a wart removed and not major heart surgery. "Of course, I'll make sure someone is here. I'll call a driver to come for the two of you and see you home. I'll stick around for as long as I'm needed."

"Oh, you're such a dear." Maryanne patted him on the cheek. "But then again, you're probably used to dealing with unsavory situations."

"Mother!" Eleanor's face turned bright red.

"What, dear? I only meant how useful it is to have someone like James around. Stop being so dramatic, dear." She patted her perfectly coiffed hair. "I need to go to the little girl's room. I hope to God the janitorial staff has given it a thorough cleaning."

James barely registered much after that jarring statement. *People like him.* How many times had he heard that before? It became clear to him right then and there no matter how much money he had, or how many connections he made, he'd always be the bastard son born to a drug-addicted daughter of a gardener.

No matter how hard he tried to fit in, he never would.

Chapter Nineteen

"Girl, I'm so proud of you! This place looks fabulous!" Simone walked around the shop, checking out every nook and cranny, and all the knickknacks that were placed strategically around the shop. "This place is so cute! And whenever I'm in the mood for something sweet, I can walk from my boutique to your bakery. I don't expect the family discount but if you want to..." Simone batted her eyelashes and gave her a huge grin.

Noelle giggled. "Of course you'll get the discount. I'll take off five cents from every item you purchase."

Simone's face fell.

"You know I'm just teasing. As much as you've done for me, anything you want at all is yours. And I'm sure Paul wouldn't mind either," Noelle teased.

"So, are you excited about the grand opening next week?"

Noelle raised a brow at the abrupt change of subject. The few times she noticed Simone and Paul interact it was clear to Noelle her friend had it bad. Whenever Simone walked into the room, Paul would literally stop what he was doing and his eyes would follow Simone wherever she went. Simone on the other hand was friendly with Paul but distant, not her usual gregarious self.

A blind man could see there was an attraction between the two of them. Paul seemed more than willing to act on it but Simone maintained that unspoken distance. Paul would constantly pump Noelle for information about her cousin, and when Noelle would bring the subject of Paul up, her cousin would conveniently change the subject. Like now.

Noelle decided not to press the issue for now. "I'm so nervous about the opening. Paul has been working like crazy on the marketing end. I hope a lot of people come in."

"I thought it was a great idea for you guys to hand out samples to the local businesses. You'll at least get a lot of customers on that front. Imagine all the office parties you'll bake cakes for. And I've already put out the word to my friends to come by. Word of warning, Tanisha is going to expect a hookup when she comes by so be prepared."

Noelle snorted. "I don't even like her. The only free thing she can expect from me is advice."

Simone raised her brows. "Wow, look at you cuz. I like this new backbone you've suddenly developed. It's about time."

"I like it, too. It's always been hard asserting myself, but I'm tired of being a door mat. It's like Aunt—" she broke off. Even if Simone had her own issues with Aunt Frieda, she was still Simone's mother.

"It's okay. We both know my mom is a piece of work. Go ahead, finish what you were about to say."

"It's just that, for so long I've bought into the things she used to tell me, like how I was stupid and no good. And Derrick and Damon didn't help matters with their constant harassment. I guess that kind of wears on you after a while. Living in that place felt like a slow death every day. And life with Walter would have been equally miserable." Noelle shuddered when she thought of her narrow escape from that fate.

Simone scrunched her nose. "Eww. I still can't believe how my mother tried to push you off on that old-ass man.

That was low even for her. I'm glad you're starting to realize they were full of shit."

"Yeah, but this confidence thing is new to me. I'll still have slip-ups and insecurities but I don't want to go back to the way I was. Thanks for letting me talk about it with you."

"Anytime."

Noelle reached out and pulled her cousin into an embrace. "Likewise, Simone. I'll be there when you need me." Though Noelle wasn't ready to discuss her year with James, talking about her experiences with her ultra- religious and hypocritical aunt made her openly aware of where her insecurities had originated. Slowly she was disabusing those beliefs that had been drilled in her head since she was a child.

She'd loved herself so little and she'd looked for that love in a man who was way more damaged then she was. There were times when Noelle couldn't help but think about James, but then she'd immerse herself in her work. Thank goodness she had something to distract her with or else she'd go crazy.

"So what are you ladies gossiping about?" Paul walked into the shop with a large box in his arms followed by Donna, one of the assistants they'd recently hired.

Simone pulled away from Noelle. "I think I need to get back to the boutique. I told Melissa I'd only be gone for a half hour. I'll see you later Noelle. Bye Paul."

Noelle had never seen her cousin move so fast. She was running and from the determined gleam in Paul's eyes as he watched her leave, he'd be in pursuit soon enough.

Noelle focused on the box to ease the awkwardness. "Are those the fliers you're carrying?"

"Huh?" he broke out of his trance.

"The box? Are the fliers inside?"

"Oh yeah," Paul said, still a bit distracted.

"Donna, could you take the box in the back and I'll join you shortly to start working on the fondant."

"Sure boss," Donna complied cheerfully, taking the box of fliers from Paul.

When Noelle and Paul were alone, she grabbed his hand and directed him toward one of the tables by the window at the front of the bakery. "Okay, when are you going to ask Simone out on a date?"

"Are you kidding me? How am I supposed to ask her out when she runs away whenever I get close? You saw how fast she hightailed it out of here like I had cooties or something. I haven't felt this rejected since I pissed my pants in the first grade." He threaded his fingers through his blond hair.

"I'll just think of a way to get the two of you alone. Simone's a little gun shy when it comes to dating." That wasn't exactly true. Simone had a lot of guy friends, none of them who she viewed as serious but Noelle didn't have the heart to tell Paul.

"She doesn't seem so shy to me. Maybe I'm the problem. Is it because I'm white?"

"She doesn't care about that."

"Do you think she may be interested in someone else?"

"She hasn't mentioned it. To my recollection, Simone hasn't dated since she started the boutique."

"I can't see why. Simone is gorgeous."

"I think she just wants to focus on her boutique right now. And seeing as how we just opened our own bakery, you can hardly blame her for that. Give her some time okay? I'm sure she'll come around eventually."

"I wish I was as sure about this as you."

"Paul, I wouldn't encourage you to pursue her if I didn't believe she likes you, too. I'm not the most perceptive person in the world, but I saw that look she gave you when I first introduced the two of you. Be patient, Simone is worth waiting for."

"And how about you?"

"What about me?"

"When do you think you'll dip your toes in the dating pool again?"

"Right now, my number one priority is the bakery. I have so many orders lined up I'll be lucky to fit in a nap."

"Don't use the business as an excuse."

"I'm not, it just that Ja—"

"Go ahead and say his name. You can't heal until you're willing to talk about it."

Noelle sighed. "You're right, but I just don't trust myself to choose someone who won't totally walk all over me. I feel like such an idiot for putting up with him for so long."

"You thought you were in love with him. It's understandable."

"I was in love and probably still am. When I allow myself to think about him, it kills me a little to know he's probably moved someone else into the penthouse and hasn't given me another thought."

"I'm not so sure about that, Noelle. When I worked out my two months' notice, he didn't mention the penthouse once, so I'm pretty sure he didn't replace you right away if he did at all. And I'm not so certain he didn't feel something for you."

"You don't have to say that to make me feel better."

"I'm not. I believe you've known me long enough to realize I'm honest, brutally sometimes. James may not be my favorite person right now but I can say the man works like a demon. Those times when he couldn't come around to see you, he wanted me to check in on you. On several occasions, he asked me how you were doing. He never did that with any of the other women. If I didn't know better, I would say he actually cared."

She snorted bitterly. "He had a funny way of showing it. He's engaged to another woman. I was stupid for thinking I actually had a connection with him. It was just sex."

"Unfortunately, most people in his income bracket don't marry for love."

"That really doesn't make me feel any better. I'm just surprised he considered me worthy enough to share his bed in the first place."

"Stop selling yourself short. Remember, we agreed you wouldn't do that anymore. You're beautiful, smart and talented. You have a lot going for you. Without you there'd be no shop."

"You're giving me way too much credit. If you weren't for you, I wouldn't have known where to begin."

"You can't have a business if there's nothing to sell and you make a damn fine product."

Noelle was truly humbled by Paul's praise. He had come to mean so much to her over the past several months. She cherished the friendship they'd formed. "Thank you, Paul. I just want you to know, your friendship means the world to me. But I have to ask, why me? What made you give up your job for me?"

"You reminded me of Alyssa. I've been more of a father to her than a big brother since we were kids and I guess my protective streak came out. But don't look at my resignation from my former job as me making a sacrifice. I see it more as me moving on to the next chapter of my life. I wouldn't have stayed in that position indefinitely. My goal was always to start a business for myself and be my own boss. And now with your help I have that opportunity, so I'm just as grateful for you as you are for me. We're going to make both our dreams come true. Noelle, you're one of the sweetest, kindest women I've ever met and once you recognize how great you are, you'll be a force to be reckoned with."

Tears welled in her eyes. Her cousin had basically told her the same thing over and over again. Noelle didn't want to just believe it this time; she wanted to act on it. She vowed to herself then and there, even if she had to go through years of therapy, she'd always walk with her head held high.

James wished he was somewhere else, but he promised Eleanor he'd escort her to this event thrown by one of her friends. Besides, he would have been a total cad to deny her anything with all she'd dealt with in the past month. Her father, having suffered a massive heart attack followed by a stroke, had miraculously survived, but not without severe trauma to his body. The stroke had left George Harrington paralyzed.

According to the doctors, it could still take weeks before they knew for sure what the complete damage was and what needed to be done to get him to some semblance of a normal life. Best case scenario, George would regain some of his motor skills and get some of his independence back. At worst, he'd need around-the-clock care for the remainder of his life.

Eleanor had been devastated by that news. Maryanne, on the other hand, seemed more interested in moving the wedding plans forward. Eleanor and James decided to postpone the wedding until they knew for sure what was going on with George's condition much to Maryanne's annoyance. It seemed heartless how Maryanne couldn't bring herself to worry over her husband's condition beyond playing up the drama among her country club friends. Eleanor had confided in James her disgust of Maryanne's behavior.

James did his best to help Eleanor out in any way he could but things were changing between them. Eleanor spent most of her time at the hospital. She didn't call as often and barely spoke of the wedding. Her obvious withdrawal might have bothered him if he weren't changing, too.

Lately, he'd wondered if marriage to Eleanor was what he really wanted. He'd fought hard to make it to where he was today, but James wondered if he'd been chasing the wrong dream all along.

It was painful to realize he'd become the very person he used to despise. He had plenty of material wealth and possessions but each night when he finally turned off his laptop, he'd go to bed alone, whether it was in his mansion or one of the several hotels he owned. And most of those nights he'd think of Noelle. He missed her. But he was too ashamed to track her down and give her the apology she deserved. He'd been callous and mean to her for reasons he couldn't explain at the time. But the realization of what he'd done had come to late and because of it, he'd lost someone very special.

"James, we don't have to stay long if you don't want to. I still have to go by the hospital to see Daddy before I go home tonight anyway." Eleanor placed her hand on his arm as she brought him out of his deep thoughts.

It took James a moment to remember where he was before he could respond. "I'm sorry, Eleanor. No. We can stay as long as you'd like. No rush."

"Are you sure? You seem a bit…distracted tonight. But then again, you've been that way a lot lately. Is everything alright?"

"Yes. I was just thinking I'll have the most beautiful date on my arm tonight."

She smiled. "You're a charmer, James Rothschild, but I know a lie when I hear it. I'll forgive you though since you've stroked my ego."

He relaxed a little under her teasing. James appreciated her sense of humor among the other good qualities she possessed. For a second he was tempted to tell her what he'd been thinking, but Eleanor was already going through so much. He couldn't pile on to it by voicing his doubts about their impending nuptials.

Eleanor had told him this event was in honor of her friend Susan Fontaine's art gallery re-opening. James wasn't a huge art connoisseur but he appreciated good work when he spotted it. He owned several valuable pieces and figured he'd add to his collection if something caught his eye if nothing else came of the night.

When they walked inside the gallery, the party was in full swing. There were silver and black decorations everywhere. Waiters in tuxedoes walked around with hors d'oeuvres on silver platters, and patrons chattered with gaiety while discussing the artwork surrounding them as they moved from piece to piece.

James was already bored.

"I wonder why everyone is circling that statue. Isn't that Rodin's *The Thinker*?"

James followed the direction of where she pointed. "Yes, that's what it looks like but I'm surprised to see it here. Maybe the artist did one of those modern modifications, otherwise I don't see why it's drawing such a big crowd."

"You could be right, but I wouldn't mind checking it out to see what the fuss is about. Let's take a look."

"Sure." He escorted her over and as he got closer, James could see why people marveled at the statue that looked damn close to the original. It wasn't a statue at all, but a cake. He could smell the cloying sweetness of the artistic concoction. Surrounding the life-sized cake were five more cakes. They were round layered cakes with a smaller layer stacked on top on the next. Each one was painted with a famous work. James immediately recognized Munch's *The Scream,* Van Gogh's *Starry Night,* and Grant's *American Gothic*. Whoever created these marvels had managed to overshadow the rest of the art.

"This is amazing," Eleanor gasped. "I've seen fancy cakes before but this is top notch. Susan went all out with this opening."

"They're almost too fancy to cut into," one of the patrons murmured.

"But they smell so good," someone else mentioned.

James, too, was fascinated by the culinary art, but something drew his attention away from his observations. He had the feeling he was being watched. James looked around and then froze. Standing several feet away and looking in his direction with a wide-eyed stare was Noelle. She'd haunted his dreams for the last several months. Surely this was all in his imagination.

Just to make sure this wasn't an illusion, he shook his head to clear it of any daydreams, but there she stood. The long hair she used to sport was now replaced with short, soft-looking curls that hugged her scalp. Her face bore only a minimal amount of makeup and she wore a modest little black dress that still managed to lovingly hug her curves, showing them off to her advantage. She looked more beautiful than he remembered. Noelle reminded him of the day he'd first met her, innocence and sensuality mixed in one ball of temptation. His body immediately reacted to her. As if on their own volition, his feet moved toward her.

It was then Noelle backed away with a shake of her head. James halted in an instant when Paul appeared by her side, shooting him a glare that could melt ice. The blond man casually slung his arm around Noelle's shoulder and James wanted to rip that arm off for daring to touch Noelle. She was still his, dammit!

But then James remembered. He'd fucked things up with her so badly he didn't have the right to be angry. Besides, with Eleanor next to him, it would have made him an even bigger ass to act on his emotions.

Their gazes remained locked however. Noelle was frozen like a deer caught in headlights and he couldn't look away even if his life depended on it. Finally after what seemed like an eternity, Paul steered Noelle away until she was out of sight.

"She looks familiar," Eleanor casually noted.

"Excuse me?" he asked, still looking in the direction where Noelle had been. He wondered what Noelle was doing here with Paul. The sight of those two together tormented him far worse than anything he'd experienced before.

"The woman you were staring at. She looks familiar. I think I've seen her before but I can't figure out where."

James felt guilty he couldn't give Eleanor the attention she deserved. "I'm sorry, Eleanor."

"It's okay, James. We never pretended this was a love match did we? Anyway, I'm trying to place where I've seen her before. I'm almost sure I've had a conversation with her."

Where could those two have interacted? James had always been careful to keep his worlds separate. Before he could reply, they were joined by Eleanor's friend.

"Eleanor, sweetie! It's so good to see you." The tall brunette greeted.

Eleanor turned to her friend and the two women hugged and air kissed each other's cheeks. "James, I'd like you to meet my friend, Susan. This is her gallery."

James took Susan's hand in a friendly handshake. "Pleased to meet you."

"Likewise." Susan grinned at Eleanor. "He's even more handsome in person than in the paper." She winked at James before releasing the firm grip she had on his hand.

"Everything looks great, Susan," Eleanor complimented.

"Thank you! Tonight has been a hit. I was surprised when you RSVP'd. I would have completely understood if you couldn't make it so I'm thrilled you did. How's your father, by the way?"

"His condition is stable. Thanks for asking."

"Please let me know if there's anything I can do for you. And send my love to your mother. This can't be easy for her, I'm sure."

"It's not easy for any of us."

"How is your father's health affecting your wedding plans?"

It was obvious to James that Susan wasn't the most sensitive of people but he remained silent during the exchange.

"Actually, we've postponed the wedding until Daddy makes a full recovery."

"Oh, well, of course. That seems like the sensible thing to do but don't make this handsome devil wait too long." The brunette batted her eyes flirtatiously at James.

James smiled politely, trying to pay attention to the conversation but he couldn't stop thinking about Noelle.

Eleanor tactfully changed the conversation. "I see quite a few art critics here. That must be exciting."

"Yes, and sales have been fabulous. I fought tooth and nail to keep the gallery in the divorce and I'm sure Timothy is eating his heart out. He didn't want it anyway. He just didn't want me to have it, the bastard. I hope that little slut he's with now takes him for every cent he has. I hear he didn't make her sign a prenup. What an idiot. The girl is trash and will bleed him dry. You know what they say, you can take the girl out of the trailer park but you can't take the trailer park out of the girl."

The more she talked the less James liked Susan Fontaine. Eleanor thankfully switched topics again. "So where did you get these cakes? I've never seen anything like them before."

Susan gushed. "Aren't they the bee's knees, darling? I think the cakes are getting more attention than the art," she laughed. "I took a chance on someone new and it paid off. The baker was just here a few seconds before I walked over. I was actually going to thank her for the display. I guess I'll have to catch her partner, Paul, later."

This latter part of the conversation caught James attention. "Paul Winters?"

"Yes? Are you familiar with him?" Susan asked.

"Yes." James answered without offering any explanation. So Noelle had made the cakes. He knew she liked to bake and was aware of her artistic talents, but he never could have imagined she was capable of something so extraordinary. And it shamed him that he'd wasted the chance to learn more about her beyond his own selfish needs.

He was thankful when Susan finally excused herself.

"James, I can see you're not really into this and honestly I'm anxious to see how my father is doing. Can we leave?"

"Yes."

"I just need to run to the powder room, okay?"

"No problem."As he waited for Eleanor to return, Noelle came into his line of vision again. She was headed toward the exit and Paul was nowhere in sight. James couldn't let this opportunity get away from him. He didn't know what he would say to her but he had to be close to her again, even for a few seconds.

Chapter Twenty

Noelle could feel his eyes on her before she saw him. No one could make goose bumps form along her skin or the hairs stand on the back of her neck without even touching her except James. Seeing him at the gallery tonight had stunned her to the point where she couldn't function. If Paul had not come along and practically pulled her away from where she'd stood, Noelle would still be rooted to the spot.

He looked every bit as handsome as she remembered. But there were also subtle differences to his appearance. He wore his hair slightly longer than she remembered and his face looked slightly gaunt denoting a recent weight loss. One thing that hadn't changed was how intensely his stare seared right through her. As he held her under his gaze, just like that Noelle became the same weak-kneed girl she'd been upon their first meeting.

Only when Paul ushered her away was she able to breathe again. After hyperventilating in the bathroom for several minutes, she was determined to make a quick exit from the party. She made her apologies to Paul who offered to take her home, but she knew how much this gallery opening meant to their business so she made him promise to stay behind.

She was almost out the door when James's hand fell on her shoulder. His touch practically scorched her skin. Noelle couldn't turn around. She didn't have the courage to face him. She'd imagined this scenario in her head over and over again where she'd be confident enough to tell him to fuck off but instead she was trembling like a leaf.

Mustering up as much bravado as she could, Noelle took a deep breath and shook his hand off her shoulder, forcing her legs to move until she was outside. Noelle only stopped when she was several feet away from the building. The scent of James's cologne wafted to her nostrils. He smelled so damn good. She silently prayed for the strength to make it through this confrontation without making a total fool of herself.

"Hello, Noelle."

She'd forgotten how his dulcet tone made her shiver. Slowly, she turned to face him. "James, what a surprise." She forced herself to sound nonchalant even though she felt far from it.

"Yes, it is." He hesitated in his response almost as if he didn't know what to say to her. "You look, well, beautiful actually."

When they had been lovers, a compliment like that would have been enough to melt her, however she remembered the drop dead gorgeous redhead at his side. Squaring her shoulders, she raised her chin and met his gaze. "So does your fiancée. Shouldn't you be in there with her? Heaven forbid you're seen in public with me."

"Don't."

"Don't what? Say out loud what you never actually did but showed me in every way possible? I wasn't good enough then so don't come to me now like we're old buddies with things to catch up on. I'm not even sure why you followed me out here."

"I...I wanted to see you."

"Right, because it doesn't matter what I want even if that's to be left alone. James, I just can't with you. I'm going to walk away now and I don't want you to follow me." She attempted to leave while she still had the will, but James caught her arm in his grasp.

"Let go," she hissed getting angry. How dare he even approach her when his fiancée was still inside? "Aren't you forgetting someone?"

"Eleanor isn't the jealous type."

At the mention of his fiancée's name, she found the strength to yank her arm out of his grip. "Just leave me alone."

"Noelle, I just wanted to say—"

"I don't want to hear it. Whatever you have to say, save it." She tried to walk away when he called out to her.

"I'm sorry."

She was tempted to keep walking but pivoted to face him again. Those two simple words should have given her the closure most women could only hope for at the end of a failed relationship. Instead it pissed her off. She saw red. "And what exactly are you sorry for, James?"

"For the way things ended."

"Oh," she snorted. "Just sorry for that? Not for making me feel like I wasn't good enough to be seen in public with you? Not for treating me like dog shit every time you came by the penthouse? I know I walked into our arrangement with my eyes wide open and I was foolish to think…well that doesn't matter now. But I deserved to be treated with a little respect. I have feelings and I'm not going to let you stand there and give me some half-assed apology to assuage your guilt. Take your 'I'm sorry' and shove it up your ass." Still functioning on rage, she turned around and stalked away. Only when she was inside her car did the tears come.

Finally she was able to say the things she'd been holding in for so long, but the pain refused to go away. It wrapped itself around her and squeezed tight. Once she was inside of the bakery van, she lost it. Tears streamed down her face as body racking sobs burst from her mouth. She rested her head against the steering wheel and cried until her throat ached.

And even though she'd finally told him off, it killed Noelle to know she wasn't over him.

Noelle's outburst didn't hide the underlying hurt James had heard in her voice. It hurt him that he'd done that to her. The joy and light he'd seen in those pretty brown eyes when he'd first met her was gone. As she laid into him about his treatment of her, he wanted nothing more than to take her in his arms and hold her tight until all the pain was gone. He had wanted so badly to hold her but knew she wouldn't accept his embrace. James hated himself for denying the truth he'd known all along but wasn't brave enough to admit. He'd fallen for Noelle. Hard.

He had been too much of a coward to act on his feelings, and now he only had himself to blame for the predicament he found himself in. He wished he'd been brave enough then to tell her how he'd felt instead of punishing Noelle for his feelings. She was one of the few genuine people he'd met in a long time and he had destroyed her. For once in his life, James didn't know how to fix it.

He didn't know how long he stood outside before he felt a tap on his shoulder. Eleanor had come looking for him and from the disheartened look on her face, he was almost sure she had heard bits of the conversation he'd had with Noelle.

His suspicious were confirmed as he drove her to the hospital. Halfway there, Eleanor broke the awkward silence hanging between them. "James, that woman you were talking to outside, I remember where I saw her from."

At first he didn't answer. He didn't know what he could say. In the end all he could say was, "Oh?"

"Some months back when we were dining at Isabella's, I saw her in the bathroom. I couldn't place her at first because she wore her hair different and wore a lot more makeup. I remember admiring her necklace."

"I see."

"She was crying. Now, I may not be a genius on the level of Steven Hawking but I can put two and two together. You were involved with her. And I'm guessing she saw us in the restaurant together and it upset her. I also surmise that things must have ended for you shortly after we announced our engagement because you changed somehow. I could tell you were relieved when we decided to postpone the wedding. James, I knew this would be a marriage of convenience when I agreed to marry you but this just isn't going to work is it?"

This conversation did nothing to assuage his guilt. If anything, it made it worse. Not only had he hurt Noelle, but he'd hurt Eleanor. Could he be any more of a fuck-up? With a heavy sigh, he found a safe spot to pull over.

Once he cut the engine off, James unbuckled his seat belt and turned to face Eleanor who remained stoic in the face of the deterioration of their engagement. "Eleanor, I don't know where to begin but I owe you an explanation."

"I knew there would be other women, James. You don't have to explain anything to me."

"But I do, because when I asked you to marry me, I was making a promise to you. I thought we could work because you were the embodiment of the ideal wife. In my own warped mind, I never expected you to be more than a pretty arm piece. I know that's a bunch of misogynistic bullshit but that was my thought process when we first met. You were supposed to be the last piece of the puzzle to complete the image I wanted to project to the world, but I have a dark side, one I didn't think any high society wife would tolerate. I enjoy sex. Lots of it. And I've been told quite often how dominate and rough I am in bed. So I took mistresses. I set them up in one of my properties and saw to their financial needs, and in return they would provide me with all the hardcore sex I required." He paused for a moment to gauge Eleanor's reaction.

Eleanor trembled slightly, but James couldn't tell if it was from distaste or excitement. Her gaze was unwavering, and her expression gave nothing away so he wasn't sure what she was thinking.

When she remained silent, James continued. "In my mind, the kind of wife I wanted wouldn't enjoy my brand of sexual pleasure. I felt whoever she was would be disgusted and blame my humble beginnings for acting like such an animal."

"But that's outrageous. You'd be surprised what some of these so-called society women are into. Why would you think you'd be judged on your sexual performance?"

"It's happened before, but I won't bore you with details. Eleanor, you guessed right. That woman you saw, her name is Noelle. She and I were lovers."

"Your mistress?"

"Yes. No. She was more than that. She was very sweet and shy and has a smile that lights up the entire room up. I wanted that light for myself the minute I laid eyes on her, but I was too stubborn to admit I felt more for her than any of the other lovers I'd set up in similar arrangements. Hearing that you actually encountered her on one of our dates and how she was upset makes me feel like an even bigger bastard than you probably think I am. I kept pushing her away and finally I pushed so hard, she'd had enough. This is the first time I've seen her in about eight months. But from the looks of it, she's moved on. With my former employee no less," he finished with a painful lump in his throat. James pounded his hand against the wheel in his frustration as he remembered how comfortable Paul had been putting his arm around Noelle.

"James, there's no need to beat yourself up over this. You're in love. Nothing trumps that, right? And if it makes you feel any better, from the looks of things, I don't think she's moved on as far as you think. She couldn't take her eyes off of you either. I'd say there are some lingering feelings there." Eleanor reached over and patted him on the shoulder in a comfortable gesture, making him feel like an even bigger asshole. Here he was breaking up with her and she was the one offering him comfort and giving advice.

"Shit. I'm sorry, Eleanor. The last thing I want to do is cause you embarrassment so however you want to handle this I'll take your lead. If you want to say you broke up with me or if you need compensation for all the time you spent planning this wedding, it's yours."

She drew back slightly, licking her red tinted lips. "Um…actually. I was hoping you would say something along those lines," she said hesitantly.

"Eleanor you can ask me anything. I never intended for you to walk away from this with nothing."

"James, I…I have a confession of my own to make. You see…I've been having reservations about this wedding for a while myself, even before my father fell ill, but I've been thinking about my future a lot lately because of it. I know the precarious state of my father's company. It's on the verge of collapse, even more so now that his condition is uncertain. I was supposed to be their key to saving the company, but not in the way they expected." Eleanor paused with a sigh. A far off look entered her emerald gaze.

"I'm not sure I follow."

She glanced out the window for several silent seconds and when she finally turned to face him again, there was something different in her expression. Anger. "They expected me to marry well, we both know that, but James, I'm not some empty headed decoration. I attended Yale. I have an MBA. I'm a member of Mensa. Did you know that about me, James?"

He knew Eleanor was well-educated and had graduated from Yale Summa Cum Laude. He'd had her thoroughly investigated before he began courting her. But he'd made the assumption she'd simply gone to school like most women of her background did, to get their "Mrs. Degrees.". It had never occurred to him that her accomplishments had meant anything to her and she'd never given any indication otherwise. "I did."

"Well, I didn't go to college to be some man's empty-headed trophy wife, but that's exactly what my father expected me to be. You see I'm not the son my father hoped for but that didn't mean I couldn't be an asset to them. From the time I could walk and talk, it was drilled in my head what my duty was. My father had no problem allowing me to attend college but I fought tooth and nail to attend grad school. He only agreed because I threatened to apply for grants and scholarships and that would have been an embarrassment to the family. Once I received my degree, however, he made it clear no daughter of his would work a nine to five. I even begged him to let me work for Harrington's but he felt I should spend my days shopping and hosting charity events alongside my mother. And when my sister, Christiana, refused to toe the line, their focus on me doing the right thing almost became an obsession with them. James, I know how badly Harrington's is bleeding right now. I've read the papers and have gone through my father's business documents. I have fresh ideas that could help the company but my father never wanted to hear them. You have no idea how many men my parents have pushed my way in hopes I'd choose one who could basically save Harrington's and keep them in their lavish lifestyle. I never wanted to marry any of them."

"So why did you agree to marry me?" James asked softly.

Eleanor moistened her lips with the tip of her tongue. "Because I knew you weren't really interested in me. I mean, you went through the motions but I knew you were only marrying me for the name and I actually liked you, James. You weren't a snooty asshole like most of the men I dealt with and I thought the two of us could get along. I figured, if I played my cards right, you might even allow me some latitude in joining your company or perhaps taking a hand in helping

Harrington's. At the very least, I believed you'd allow me to start up my own business. Despite your reasons for wanting to marry me, you didn't strike me as someone who'd treat me like a mindless idiot. I've seen my father talk down to my mother all my life, and she seemed perfectly okay with that as long as she was kept in the latest designer fashions and her credit cards remained limitless. To be perfectly honest..." she took a deep breath but didn't finish.

When the silence stretched to an uncomfortable tension within the car, James gently prompted Eleanor, knowing she wanted to get something off her chest but couldn't find the words. "Please go on. This is a no judgment zone."

"I'm trusting you to keep this next part to yourself."

"Of course, what's said in this car stays here."

She gripped his hands, her eyes wide and an air of desperation clung to her.

"Yes. I swear on my grandfather's grave."

"I'm going to trust your grandfather actually meant something to you for you to make that statement, so here it goes. I never wanted to get married: at least not to a man."

James furrowed his brows instantly understanding her meaning. "You're gay?"

She nodded. Her eyes welled with tears. "That was like pushing a boulder off my chest. I've never told a soul but I've always known I was different even when I was little girl, all my friends were fantasizing over the latest teen idols while I had a crush on my ballet instructor. I knew it was something I could never confess to anyone so I tried to be what my parents wanted. I really tried. I enjoy fine living just as much as anyone else, but I envisioned myself either working alongside my father or in some other *Fortune 500* company, building my own portfolio and thereby negating the need to marry and depend on a man. Barring that, I thought I could be the wife you wanted, but since my father's heart attack, I've done a lot of thinking." She released his hands to fold them in her lap.

"I realize just how tenuous my position is. My father is in no condition to run the company. The board is already in talks of who the next successor should be and there are even talks of liquidation. I don't want to see that happen. I'm working to get power of attorney for Daddy's business affairs, which is currently in the hands of an executor who I don't believe has Daddy's best interests at heart. Once I get power of attorney, my shares, along with my parents', will be enough to take over the board, and I intend to appoint myself as the next CEO. I'd like your help."

James didn't know what to say at first. He wished he would have known about this sooner. It bothered him that she'd suffered in silence. Not seeing Eleanor's dilemma only compounded the mistakes he'd made lately. "Eleanor, you seem to have put a lot of thought into this."

"I have to think of my father. If the company goes bankrupt our stock is worth nothing. We've been living on credit for years and our bills are going to catch up with us soon. My father will need round-the-clock medical care for God knows how long, and my mother hasn't worked a day in her life. She'll be lost if someone can't provide for them. If you can help me, perhaps guide me through this whole process while I find my legs, I'd be so grateful."

Her request wasn't unreasonable. It was the least he could do. "Of course I'll help. Will you be able to handle the medical expenses for your father?"

"He still has first-rate medical insurance so that shouldn't be a problem while he's in the hospital. Thank you so much." To his surprise, she wrapped her arms around his neck and began to cry; he could only imagine how it must have been for her holding in her secret, and the relief it was for her to finally get it out.

Eventually she pulled back with a sniff and wiped her eyes. "I'm sorry about that. But you're the first person I could be honest with."

"Maybe one day I won't be the only person you can be honest with."

"I hope so. One day." She sniffed again. "I guess I should give this back to you," she attempted to remove her engagement ring but James covered her hand with his.

"Keep it. Do whatever you like with it."

"Thank you. You know, James, I think we may actually become friends."

James smiled. "I'd like that."

"Good. Since we're friends, can I offer you a little friendly advice?"

"Depends on what that advice is," he chuckled.

"I've lived this lie most of my life and I've been miserable. If you can find a way to be happy in this sorry existence we call life, go grab it, hold on tight and never let go. And remember, sometimes what we think we want isn't what we need. Go find that girl and do whatever you have to do to get back into her good graces."

"And if I fail?"

"Then at least you can say you tried. Failure is a better than wondering 'what if.'"

More than anything James wanted to do exactly that, but he wondered if he'd damaged things with Noelle beyond repair.

Chapter Twenty-One

"Paul, I'm only one person. You're bringing orders faster than I can fill them. The kids are only here part-time and since Donna had that family emergency we're swamped. Do you think we can hire another full-time baker?" Noelle sat down at the table across from her business partner, coffee in hand. The shop was blissfully quiet for the first time that day.

Before they'd opened their bakery, Paul had told her things may be slow in the beginning until they built up their clientele so she hadn't expected to be this busy. The designer cakes she'd made for Alyssa's wedding and the art gallery had garnered them a lot of business, but the cupcakes Noelle baked daily had taken off as well.

Running the bakery was hectic and rewarding at the same time. Most nights she'd go home so bone tired she'd be out before her head hit the pillow, Noelle wouldn't trade this feeling for the world. She was proud of herself to be doing something she enjoyed and making a living from it. She only wished her mom was alive to see her namesake, Dot's Bakery.

"Relax, Noelle. I'm on it. I'll send out an ad for another baker and hire another part-timer to help out in the front. Actually, I was thinking maybe we should have a full-time person to just handle the cash register."

"We're just starting out. Are you sure we should be taking on all these people so soon?"

"I think our budget can handle it. We're already getting a lot of business in the shop but orders for specialty cakes are coming in much faster than I expected. You're going to have to work around the clock in order to fill them unless we get you some help."

"The baking part is easy, but the orders we've received lately have been for really detailed cakes. Not all bakers have a knack for that, and it will take more time for me to train someone to help than actually doing it by myself if we don't find the right person. I think we should look for someone with an artistic background for the job. And as much as it pains me to say this, I think we'll need to turn away some of these projects."

"You're right, Noelle. I guess I got a little overzealous. I just have this fear of falling flat on my face."

Noelle was surprised to hear this. She'd never seen Paul uncertain in anything unless her cousin was involved. "Is it my turn to give you a pep talk?" she teased.

"I guess a little ego boost couldn't hurt right now. I want to feel validated for walking away from a well-paying job to start my own business. I'm aware of how many businesses fail within the first year and I don't want us to be one of them."

"We're doing well, Paul. Relax. So, what's the new order you mentioned earlier?"

'"I wrote down the details. The client wants you to call them back to discuss the order further. They said price was no object."

"Okay, I'll call at the end of the day. Since we have some down time, I think I'll try out a new recipe I've been fiddling with."

Paul held up his hand to stop her. "Hold on for a second, I wanted to talk to you about something. How are you doing?"

"I'm fine. But I'm sure there's a reason why you're asking."

"We haven't really had a chance to talk since the gallery function."

She stiffened. "Because I didn't want to talk about it. So what? I saw James. Big deal."

Paul gave her a long accessing stare. "If you don't want to talk about it, I won't push. But I'm here if you need to."

"Thanks, Paul. I think I'll head back now."

Just as Noelle walked to the kitchen the bell dinged, indicating a customer coming into the shop. She turned around with a smile and was surprised to see her old professor from art school.

"Miss Greene. You work here? This is a pleasant surprise."

"Professor McGregor, this is a surprise, but I'm not sure if it's a pleasant one," she answered honestly.

The man who had made it his life's mission to make Noelle miserable actually chuckled. Outside of the classroom setting, he actually seemed human. "I know I'm not one of your favorite people, Miss Greene, but you were definitely one of my favorite students. I was sorry when you dropped my class."

"Actually, I left school altogether."

"Yes, I found that out. It's a shame. You had a lot of potential."

This was news to her. "Pardon my bluntness, but you only had criticism for my work."

"Miss Greene, I've gained a reputation for being harsh but I think I'm fair. I was only coming down on you because you weren't living up to your true potential. You were one of the most talented pupils I've had in a while. Technically your work was flawless but something was missing. The passion wasn't there."

"I didn't know you felt that way. Why didn't you just tell me instead of being so harsh?"

"Because I suspected and you probably figured out for yourself that the type of art I asked you to produce wasn't your calling. So, there's been a lot of buzz surrounding this place. What do you recommend?"

"Everything is made fresh daily, but if you're looking for an individual treat, I'd suggest a cupcake. Try the salted caramel, they're our most popular."

"I think I will. Box four of them and I'll take one to go."

Once she rung him up and handed him his purchases, he took a bite into one of the cupcakes. "Mmm. I can see why these are so popular."

"It's a spin on my mother's recipe."

He smiled. "Seems like you've found your passion after all."

When he left, Noelle couldn't help but smile. All that time in art school she'd doubted herself when all along the problems wasn't the work but her lack of interest in it. She was still riding on the high of her former professor's compliment when she heard the bell ring again. As she looked toward the door, her smile fell.

Noelle looked around the shop to see Paul had disappeared. He was probably in his office and couldn't act as the buffer she so desperately needed. "What are you doing here?"

James strode over to the corner with a slow swagger. Noelle willed herself not to react to his handsome visage and his hypnotic gray gaze. "Is this the way you greet all your customers?"

"I'm surprised you've lowered yourself to visit this humble establishment. Felt like slumming today?"

"Don't degrade yourself like that, Noelle."

Was he for real? If she didn't know him any better she'd think he was actually sincere. "Oh, so you're the only one allowed to degrade me? I'm sure you have a reason for being here so why don't you tell me and then leave. I have a business to run."

He flinched. "I never meant to hurt you, Noelle."

"Wow. For someone who didn't mean it, you were pretty damn good at it. Look, I can't do this now. Please leave."

"All I need is just ten minutes of your time. Could you at least hear me out?"

She had a feeling he wouldn't go away until she listened to what he had to say. "You've really got a lot of nerve. Do you know that?"

He smiled humorously. "Well I didn't get to where I was by taking no for an answer."

"How nice for you," she muttered. "Let me get someone from the back to watch the register."

"Thank you."

"I'm not doing this for you. I just need you to say what you have to say to get you out of my life."

Noelle went in back and asked Gabby to come out front. She bypassed Paul's office not wanting him to know James was out here. Paul still held a lot of animosity toward James.

"Okay, let's go outside. I don't want this conversation to be overheard."

James nodded and followed her outdoors.

Noelle put as much distance between them as possible and crossed her arms over her chest. "So?"

James stared at her as if he were committing each of her features to memory. If he continued to look at her like that, Noelle would crack. "Take a picture, it'll last longer."

"I can't help it. You're so beautiful. I like your hair that way."

Noelle self-consciously touched her short curly afro. She'd taken out the weave, and shaved her head close to the scalp, feeling a lot like a butterfly coming out of its chrysalis for the first time. She found wearing her hair in its natural state suited her, but it still felt weird to hear James compliment her on it when she'd altered herself so drastically for him. "I doubt you're here to discuss my hairstyle."

"I didn't, but it's the truth." He cleared his throat looking uncomfortable and unsure of himself. She'd never seen him look anything other than the confident and mostly arrogant man he was. She hated seeing this humbled version of James; it robbed her of her anger. It saddened her that James couldn't be this way when they were together.

Noelle sighed, feeling weary. "James, if you're not going to say anything, I have to go back inside."

"Wait." He placed his hand on her shoulder.

She jerked away from his scalding touch. They hadn't been lovers for months but her body hadn't forgotten him.

James backed away, holding his hands up to show he meant no harm. "I'm sorry. I'm making a mess of this." He raked his hands through his hair. "I'm not sure where to begin and five minutes won't be enough time. Have dinner with me tonight."

She held herself rigid against his invitation. "I don't think that's a good idea."

"Because of Paul?"

"Paul? What does he have to do with this?"

"You two are seeing each other now, aren't you?"

She wasn't sure where he'd gotten the idea she and Paul were a couple, but she decided not to disabuse him of the idea. He'd put her through way too much for her honesty. "That's none of your business. We're nothing to each other anymore. We were never anything to each other, were we? Look, I appreciate your apology earlier. I'm sure it wasn't easy for you but I'm letting you off the hook. You don't have to give me some long drawn-out explanation for why you were such an asshole. I'm just as much to blame because I allowed you to treat me that way, but I'm not going to be your doormat anymore."

"Eleanor and I are no longer engaged," he blurted out.

Months ago this information would have caused her to leap for the moon but now it was too little too late. Even if he was no longer engaged, it changed nothing. "Good for her."

"You're not ready to listen, are you?" James asked with a hint of defeat in his voice.

"What tipped you off?"

"What's going on out here?" Paul stepped outside and glared at James.

James's lips tightened and his fists clenched at his sides. "Nice to see you again too, Paul."

"I didn't come out here to exchange pleasantries with you, Rothschild." He turned his attention to Noelle. "Is he bothering you, honey?"

Noelle raised a brow. Honey? Paul never used that endearment with her before. She wondered if Paul was only trying to rile James, not that she minded. "Er, uh, yes. I'm fine. James was just leaving."

James looked as if he wanted say something else but decided against it. He left without another word.

Once James was out of sight, she turned to Paul. "Honey? Did you by any chance tell him you and I are an item?"

"No. But when I let him have it for the way he treated you, he put two and two together and came up with five. It's not my fault if he thinks we're more than friends. What was he doing here anyway?"

"He said he wanted to talk and that I deserved an explanation."

"In that case, I shouldn't have interrupted you two. When I saw him, I went into big brother mode. I'm sorry for breaking in on the conversation."

"I'm glad you came out. As embarrassing as it is to admit, I'm still in love with him. After what he put me through, am I crazy for feeling this way?"

"No. Strong feelings like you had for James don't simply disappear at the drop of a hat. If that were the case, there wouldn't be so many sappy love songs on the radio."

"I probably should have heard him out, but on the other hand it felt so good to finally tell him what I didn't have the courage to a year ago."

"That's called growth, my dear. You're not that same meek little mouse I first met. You are a lioness."

Noelle giggled at his analogy. "I don't much feel like one now but thanks for being a good friend."

Paul put his arm around her shoulder and gave her a kiss on the temple.

As they went back into the shop, Noelle couldn't shake the feeling that this wasn't the last she'd see of James. Not by a long shot.

"What the hell are you doing here? I should fire the entire staff. Oh yeah, that's right, I forgot. I don't have any except that cantankerous, half-blind old man who refuses to leave out of some misguided sense of loyalty. More likely, he has no place else to go." David shook his head before taking a healthy swallow of the amber liquid in his glass.

James wasn't expecting a warm reception but he wasn't going to let his brother's hostility ward him off. This talk was a long time coming.

"Mind if I have a seat?" James asked.

"I doubt I could stop you." David took another gulp from his glass.

James took a seat on the couch adjacent to the chaise lounge David reclined on. His brother looked a complete mess. His hair was tussled, there was several days of unshaven beard on his face, and he looked as if he had slept in his clothes. His eyes were bloodshot and red-rimmed. Gone was the spoiled heir of AlCore James had cast as villain in his own personal life drama. In his place was a man defeated.

David narrowed his eyes. "So what are you here for anyway? Wanna rub salt in the wound? Mother is in Europe with her third husband, Carlo. He's some Italian count who's my age and has a raging coke habit from what I hear. She couldn't be bothered to listen to my pedestrian problems, as she put it. The old man is still alive unfortunately. And Gillian has decided she can't live like this. She gave me some speech about needing some space to find herself but the truth is, she's basically checked out of the marriage." David chuckled humorlessly and finished the remainder of his drink.

"Last I heard, she was in the Hamptons with her latest lover. And you already know that AlCore is kaput. The house is in foreclosure and it's only a matter of time before the repo man comes knocking. So there you have it, my life in a nutshell. And you're still doing swimmingly I hear so I guess you win. Congratulations." David stood up to walk across the room to the bar.

James had imagined this moment for as long as he could remember. The Alexanders were ruined while he came out on top. He'd always imagined he'd feel triumph, but the reality, however, was nowhere near the fantasy. He took no pleasure in this moment. He didn't like seeing David so defeated and pathetic. All these years he'd spent hating his half-brother and the Alexanders, the truth was, he didn't hate them.

He hated himself.

It was a bitter pill to swallow to finally acknowledge the only person who had been standing in his way of happiness was him. And because of his pigheadedness, he'd lost the one good thing in his life. Noelle.

James sighed, trying to find the words to say to his brother. David probably wouldn't be receptive toward them but he had to try. "David, you may not believe this, but I didn't come here to gloat, and this isn't about winners or losers."

"You could have fooled me. Gillian's favorite pastime is rubbing your success in my face. She never stopped loving you, you know. Throughout our entire marriage, she always founds ways to compare me to you. Too bad she's so impatient, she'd be living it up right now."

"I'd say I made a lucky escape."

David pursed his lips. "Must be nice to be over her so easily. Fool that I am, I actually still care for her. The bitch."

"The way she came storming into my office, blaming me for your accident, I'd say she cares for you, too."

"The only person Gillian cares for is Gillian. Don't read more into her actions other than those of a woman bent on creating her own little melodrama. She lives for that shit. So what the hell are you here for again?"

"To talk. It's time we cleared the air."

David huffed. "Now that's a laugh. Tell me another one."

"I'm serious, David. Don't you think it's time for us to hash things out? I'm not suggesting we become best buddies but we are brothers, whether either of us want to acknowledge it or not."

"You sound like a goddamn woman. What are we supposed to do? Sit here and talk about our feelings? I've thought of you as many things but a damn pussy wasn't one of them."

James bit the inside of his lip to stop himself from retaliating in kind. James recognized David's petulant façade for what it was: a cover for his pain. James had carried his own hurt around for so long he could see David was suffering, too. James took a measured breath to calm down before replying. "If wanting to clear the air makes me a pussy, then so be it. If you have nothing to say, I have plenty."

David shrugged. "It's not like I can stop you." He moved from behind the bar and headed to a large bay window in the corner presenting his back to James.

"David, for a very long time I blamed you and anyone who bore the name Alexander for anything that went wrong in my life. I blamed our father for casting my mother aside and essentially turning her into a drug addict. I hated you for all the torture I suffered through in school and I was jealous when Gillian dumped me for you. What really sent me over the edge was Grandpa Lou's death. I held the old man personally responsible for that one. That changed me."

"Well, I guess you'll have the last laugh then," David spoke in a tone devoid of emotion.

"No. I haven't laughed in a long time, actually. I always imagined seeing the downfall of this family would make me happy but it hasn't. Whether you believe it or not, I didn't have a hand in AlCore's failure."

"Gillian said you bragged about ending the contract between AlCore and Rothschild Holdings."

"I think we both know Gillian has trouble with the truth. I did say things I shouldn't have to her but I don't make my business decisions based on emotion. One of the hotels my group acquired already had a contract in place with AlCore, but the only reason we didn't renew it was because I already had a vendor in place that was more cost effective and produced a higher quality product. That's it."

"So you're basically saying you didn't dance for joy when you heard of AlCore's troubles. How noble of you."

"David, I'm human, so of course my initial reaction was to gloat but when it was all said and done I wasn't happy. My focus was to be accepted by the people who used to reject me. I turned into the people I used to despise and I ended up hurting someone important to me. I don't want to be that person anymore. I just want you to know, if you need my help for anything, you have it. No strings attached."

David without turning around, placed his now empty glass on a nearby end table and slow clapped. "Brava. All we need now is some sappy orchestra music as this scene fades to black."

"David—"

His brother turned then with red-rimmed eyes. "What exactly did you expect me to say after that? Let's be brothers? Let's start over again and be chums? If you've come here to appease your guilty conscience then fuck you. Go to a priest because you'll get no absolution from me."

James stood with a heavy sigh. "I'm sorry you feel that way. I'll leave my card on the table for you to call me."

As James headed to the door he was stopped when David called out. "Yeah, now you can go behind my back and laugh at what a pathetic state you found me in. I'm sure you'll sleep better tonight because of that sanctimonious little speech. You act like your world was so terrible but you got a free education at one of the best schools and have women throwing themselves at your feet. Now you're a billionaire. Boo freakin' hoo, life was so hard, wasn't it? Even now you sit on your high horse and tell me we treated you like shit, yet you forgive me? Who the fuck do you think you are?"

James silently counted to ten to keep himself from saying something equally crass but his temper got the best of him. He whirled around and answered, "I never asked for my education to be paid, but do you honestly think it was free? Do you have any idea what he wanted in exchange for that *free* education? No, you probably don't because you're the precious heir."

"Are you kidding me? I know exactly what that bastard wanted. It's the same thing he wanted from me and any other little boy who caught his eye."

James stilled. "He did it to you, too? I thought...."

"Of course he did. He's been doing it for years. What? Did you think you were special? Why do you think dear old Dad took the easy way out?" David laughed almost maniacally.

"What are you talking about?"

"You didn't think our father died of natural causes do you? The old man did the same thing to him as he did to me and you apparently. Why do you think this family is so fucked up?"

Shortly after the funeral, James had learned the old man who'd called him a bastard was his paternal grandfather, Sheldon Alexander, head of AlCore. The second time James had seen Sheldon was at the reading of the will. He remembered sitting outside of the lawyer's office waiting for his mother to come out. When she finally stormed out of the room, she had been furious.

"I can't fucking believe he left me out of the will. And all you got was tuition to that snooty-ass school. Too bad you're not going just so you can walk around the house thinking you're better than me. Come on." She grabbed his arm roughly.

Just then, the old man came out of the office. "I would think you'd want your child to have a proper education, although in my opinion, Stephen was foolish for leaving this little bastard anything. With you for a mother and that uneducated buffoon for a grandfather, I can already see he'll end up exactly like you. A big fat zero. Just don't come knocking on our door for any more handouts."

James could see the distress on his mother's face and though she was rarely nice to him, she was still his mother and he still loved her even if she didn't reciprocate. "You shut up!" James shouted. "Don't be mean to my mom. You're a big jerk."

"Jamie, be quiet," his mother hissed and pinched his arm.

James rubbed the inflamed skin his mother injured as he glared up at the old man.

The old man chuckled. "Well, at least you have some spunk. Young man, nothing in the world is free and one day you'll have to pay the piper."

"Sheldon, can't we get out of here? I'm getting dizzy from the smell of cheap perfume. Haven't I suffered enough by being in the same room with my husband's paramour?" said the blonde standing by the old man's side.

"In a second, Cassandra." He focused his attention back to James's mother. "And just so you know, if you come begging for money again, that free ride your son is getting will cease. I don't care what's in my son's will. I will contest it and have it tied up in court for years and for no other reason than because I can. Good day to you." The way he said it made it clear he didn't mean those last words of nicety.

His father had left James a modest trust specifically to pay for James' elementary through high school education at the prestigious private academy all the Alexanders had attended. That so-called gift left by his father turned out to be a living nightmare and James found out the meaning of "nothing in life being for free". It wasn't the last time he'd have a run-in with the old man. But he wished to God it had been.

"It was only one time," James whispered, almost shaking at a memory he'd desperately tried to suppress. "I thought he'd done it because…because he wanted to humiliate me. He denied my existence in public so what better way to show me I meant absolutely nothing to him. I just wanted…" Remembering how he'd felt as those cold hands fondled and violated him, and how Sheldon had pushed James against the wall. James had struggled all while that old bastard laughed and told him nothing in the world was free.

"Just once? You got off easy then. Try once a week. And get this; he said he was doing it to make me a man. To make me strong. I actually made the mistake of telling my mother once, but she smacked me across the face and told me not to say those things out loud. Not because she thought I was lying, you see. She just didn't want to hear it. I'm sure my father might have mentioned something to her in his drunken ramblings, but my mother has a way of blocking out all things that aren't about her."

He hadn't realized David had suffered too, and probably more than James had. "I had no idea. I wish I would have known or…well, we weren't exactly friends in school were we? We hated each other. You went out of your way to make me miserable, but I guess if I would have known—"

"You would have done nothing. There wasn't anything you could do and me for that matter. And I hated him and you. He may not have acknowledged you in public but he kept tabs on you. According to him you did everything right, from those stellar grades to how well you did at sports. He loved to point out how well my bastard brother was doing. Even when you became this great success, he told me I wasn't half the man you are. I could do no right in his eyes, and you know what he said to me?"

It made James' skin crawl to know the old man had had him monitored. "What?"

"On more than one occasion, he told me he wished I was the illegitimate one and you were the heir. At least then he'd have a grandson to be proud of. And when he wasn't abusing me with his dick, he was doing it with his fists because I wasn't you! So yes I hated you. I hated everything about you. You didn't have to deal with that asshole and you still managed to outshine me in his eyes." David picked up the glass off the table and hurled it across the room. It shattered against the wall into tiny pieces. James was speechless but David wasn't with finished his tirade.

"That's why I made things difficult for you. But somehow you kept coming out on top. Except with Gillian. She was the one thing I got over you but that was thanks to her greed. But the joke was still on me, wasn't it? I actually ended up falling for the greedy bitch. And let's get one thing straight here: it was Gillian's idea to see you. I didn't send her. She did that on her own accord thinking you'd bail us out. I only went to you in a last ditch effort to save my marriage. Gillian was on my case about seeing you so I caved in and made an appointment with you. I didn't have a business proposal as you pointed out because I never intended for you to save AlCore. I only wanted to give the appearance to Gillian that I was fighting for the company's life."

"I'm not sure I follow. If you didn't want to save the company you could have lied to her about meeting me."

"I didn't want to leave it to chance for Gillian to find out I didn't."

"Then why did you get so upset with me when I told you no. And why don't you want to save AlCore?"

"Because I still resent the hell out of you and I got angry. As for AlCore, I want to see everything that old bastard worked for crumble to the ground. After that boating accident that left him incapacitated, he had no choice but to give me the reins. I could have done a great job running the company, but even from a wheelchair he tormented to me to the point where I just said fuck it. I didn't want any of it anymore. I've systematically set out to destroy that company and since I have the controlling shares, no one has been able to stop me."

"Why didn't you just prove him wrong and make AlCore a success?"

"Like I said, nothing would have been good enough for him. The highlight of my life now is visiting the old man's room to share with him how far our stock has plummeted. I'm surprised he hasn't had a heart attack over that. If I had my way, I'd stick him in a substandard nursing home but Gillian said it wasn't good for appearances. So there you have it. And I'm not telling you any of this because I want your goddamn pity. I actually don't know why the hell I told you that."

"So you're letting the company go bankrupt. I understand you may resent your grandfather but what about all the workers who'll lose their jobs?"

David shrugged. "Isn't it a sign of the times? Big companies go under, people lose their jobs."

James wanted to point out how unfair it was to punish innocent people in order to fulfill a vendetta but he stopped himself. Hadn't he done exactly that? Besides, David wasn't in the right frame of mind to listen. Maybe he'd look into purchasing AlCore to salvage as many jobs as he could but for now, he'd allow David his vengeance.

"What will you do now?"

David shrugged. "Maybe I'll bum around Europe for a while and then buy a little hut in the Caribbean and set up a harem of island girls. I have a nice little egg nest stashed away in the Caymans Gillian doesn't know about. That should set me up comfortably for a while. Maybe I'll even start my own little business, if for nothing else than to prove to myself I'm not the piece of shit the old man thinks I am."

"If you need my help—"

"I need to do this on my own. Receiving help from you would defeat the purpose."

"Fair enough, but even I've needed help building my empire. At the very least, I can offer you advice."

David opened his mouth but closed it with a nod.

James wasn't sure what else he could say, so he made a move to leave. "Well, I'm glad we had this talk. I don't know if we can ever be friends but hopefully we won't stay enemies. Take care of yourself."

James was almost out the door when David said, "Our father…he wasn't a bad man. He was just incredibly weak. I think he would have acknowledged you had it not been for the old man. That's why he provided for your education. It was his way of saying sorry."

"Thank you for that," James said softly before walking out the door and finally letting go of a past he'd misinterpreted.

Once James got into his car, it was as if his own inner GPS led him to Noelle's bakery. He had no right to be there and knew she didn't want to see him but his soul called out to her. If only he could see her face he'd feel better.

He found himself parking in front of the bakery and heading inside. Like the last time he'd visited, the shop was quiet, but judging from the near empty case in the front, they'd been busy earlier.

A teenage girl was at the register while another girl stood behind the counter. "Welcome to Dot's Bakery. How can I help you?"

"Uh, I was wondering if Noelle was in."

The blonde behind the counter smiled. "Sure. I'll go get her." She went to the back and returned with Noelle who had flour stains on her apron and a bit of the white dust on her cheek.

Her lips thinned to a disapproving line the second she saw him. "I thought I told you—"

"Please, Noelle. I need to speak with you. Please."

She hesitated for a moment. Perhaps she heard the desperation in his voice but after giving him a long stare down, she finally nodded. "Fine. Come to my office."

She led him to the back through the bakery area, to a small office where a desk took up most of the space. The table was full of sketches of cakes and cupcakes and what looked like recipes.

Noelle closed the door and then folded her arms across her chest. "Well?"

James was so overcome with emotion he didn't know where to start. He walked until they were only inches apart and the floodgates suddenly opened. James fell to his knees, brought his hands to his face and cried.

Chapter Twenty-Two

Noelle was stunned. She'd never seen a grown man break down like this before. It was hard to believe this was the same James she'd parted with. His shoulders shook and his sobs were loud and pain-filled. It sounded as if he was crying from the pit of his soul and someone had ripped his heart in two and left him broken.

Even though he'd hurt her, Noelle took no joy in seeing him so shattered. Unable to take any more of James' suffering, Noelle went to her knees and wrapped her arms around him in comfort. He pulled her closer and buried his face against her neck.

Noelle doubted these tears were about her but he chose to share them with. She figured it must have taken a lot for him to become vulnerable in front of someone else. She rocked him gently from side to side and stroked the back of his head as the tears flowed down his face. Noelle wondered how long James had carried this burden as she wished she could take it all away.

She wasn't sure how long they remained on the floor locked in a tight embrace but finally James tears subsided to muffled sniffles. When she felt the brush of his lips against her neck, Noelle believed it to be a mistake but then he did it again. She stiffened, releasing her hold on him and planting her palms against the wall of his chest. "James, not now."

James held her tighter. "Noelle, please," he murmured and rained kisses over her face. His cheeks were stained with tears, his eyes were red and his pain was still evident. She told herself this was for comfort, but her body said otherwise. Her nipples pebbled to painful peaks and an almost unbearable warmth built up within her core. What had started out as a means to sooth a fellow human turned into so much more.

She turned her head to dodge his seeking lips, not wanting to surrender so easily, but James was not deterred. He untied her apron, pulled it over her head and immediately began to fumble with the buttons on her blouse.

She should have pushed him away but Noelle missed the feel of James against her. Noelle responded to him like a fine tuned instrument under the hands of a musical virtuoso. As he pulled her blouse apart and buried his face in her cleavage, Noelle fumbled with his belt buckle. Managing to get the belt undone and his pants unzipped, she reached inside his pants until her fingers circled his hardness.

Noelle shivered in anticipation, desperately needing him inside of her. She'd regret this act later but for now all Noelle could focus on was how good his cock felt in her hand and how it would be even better plowing into her pussy. Already her juices flowed and her body ached with need for him.

James gently guided her down until her back was against the floor. Instead of unclasping her bra, he reached inside of it and pulled her breasts out. He took one turgid tip into his mouth and sucked greedily. Noelle moaned, feeling like she'd burst any second. How many nights had she lain in bed touching herself while imagining it was James's hands? This was so much better than a dream. The circumstances weren't ideal but she'd deal with the consequences later.

James covered to her other nipple with the same voraciousness, nipping and licking as Noelle sobbed his name. "Oh, James, what are you doing to me?"

"Something that has only been in my fantasies for the past several months."

Her hand, still wrapped around his cock, gently pumped his hard shaft for several strokes. James grabbed her wrist, stopping her. "I need you now, Noelle. Please don't say no."

He eased her hand away from his dick; with a moan James then undid her pants and worked them down her hips.

Noelle lay on the floor, helpless to do anything other than shiver with need for him. He made short order of yanking her panties off and tossing them aside. He pushed his pants and boxers down, releasing his cock to her hungry gaze. It was just as magnificent as she remembered, long, thick hard and ready for her.

He pushed her thighs apart and guided his cock to her slick entrance in hurried movements. James slid the tip of his cock along her slit before pushing past her labia just enough to tease her clit.

Noelle bucked her hips against him eager to be filled. "Stop playing."

A ghost of a smile crossed his face before he surged forward, pushing so deeply inside of her, their bodies fused into one harmonious being. "Ah, so tight," he groaned with his eyes squeezed shut. "I missed this so much, missed you."

Noelle didn't want to hear that because it would turn this moment into something else entirely, something she couldn't handle. So instead Noelle concentrated on her baser needs and the way his cock felt deliciously stretching her walls until she didn't think they could give anymore.

James lay still on top of her. "Give me a second. I just want to savor this moment." His warm breath brushed the side of her face. James planted his hands on either side of her head and braced his arms to support his body as he began to move inside of her, slowly at first and then gradually picked up speed. "So damn good. So wet and tight." His eyes were still closed as he seemed to delight in this stolen moment the two of them shared.

Noelle ran her hands down his chest and lifted her hips to meet his thrusts. They moved in time with each other as a trail of fire scorched its way throughout her body. It felt so right even though her mind screamed this was so wrong.

Apparently not getting what he needed, James let out a growl, grabbed one of her legs and raised it over his hip before thrusting mercilessly into her channel. His cock went so deep it almost hurt, but it was the kind of pain that made Noelle want more of it. James was like a berserker, taking all she had to give. She could barely keep up with him but somehow she managed to until her climax hit her so hard. Noelle screamed at the top of her lungs. "James!" Stars danced before her eyes after the intensity of her orgasm but James kept going almost as if he couldn't stop.

Noelle braced herself for another ride on the James rollercoaster. He took her to heights she didn't think imaginable. James was insatiable but finally, after releasing a primal yell of his own, he shot his seed deep inside of Noelle. She opened her arms to him as he collapsed on top of her.

She hugged him tightly, holding him close and not wanting the moment to end because when it did she'd have to remember the bad. Things were so damaged between them, Noelle didn't think they could be fixed. So she needed to pretend, if only for a little while.

But that was not to be, because a knock on the door interrupted the comfortable silence that had fallen. "Noelle, are you okay? I thought I heard you yelling." It was Pamela, one of her helpers.

"Uh, yeah, I'm good. I'll be out in a bit." She silently congratulated herself for managing to sound semi-normal.

"Okay…if you're sure." Pamela seemed hesitant.

"I'm fine, really," she called out, completely embarrassed now because she was positive her employees had figured out what she was doing in her office. It was a good thing Paul wasn't in today or else she'd get an earful from him.

"James, get off."

She thought he would argue with her but he complied. James stood and pulled up his pants. He then retrieved her clothes, handed them to her and held out is hand to help her up.

Noelle took the offered hand warily, then turned her back to him as she redressed and tried to get herself in a decent enough order to face her employees and any other customers that came through.

"For the record, I didn't come here for that, Noelle. I promise you I didn't."

Remembering how torn up he'd been on his arrival, she decided not to call his bluff. After all, he could have very well been telling the truth. "Oh? Then why did you come?"

"I needed to see you."

She squeezed the bridge of her nose as she gathered her thoughts. "James, I understand that you're having a tough time at whatever it is you're going through, but I hope you don't make it a habit of coming over to see me just because you feel like it." Taking a deep breath she turned to face him. When she turned around, she gasped at the sight of his face. He looked like he'd aged ten years, his eyes were still bloodshot from crying and he was a general mess, not the put-together man he usually projected. She wished she hadn't been so harsh in her delivery but it had to be said. With the state he'd left her heart in, she couldn't risk letting him in again.

"I know. You're far more generous than most people would have been under the circumstances. You were the one good thing in my life but I was too busy tilting at windmills to see it. Noelle, up until a few days I set out on a quest to win you back not taking into consideration how you might feel. Even with all that happened in the last several months, I was selfish where you were concerned. I know you're involved with Paul and I promise, I won't say anything to him about this, but I believed you were mine and I felt I was entitled to you. But that was me still being an asshole."

Noelle felt kind of guilty that James still believed something was going on between her and Paul besides friendship. "But Paul and I—"

"No, you don't have to explain. I'm not owed an explanation but I owe you one. You see, I loved—I love you and I was too proud and arrogant to realize it when I had you. I should have told you when I had the chance to make you mine for real, not just as a mistress but as my friend, my lover and my partner. But I blew it and now I have to accept we'll probably never be together. I don't deserve you after the way I treated you. I can't apologize enough for my behavior but I just want to clear something up for the record. I was never ashamed to be seen in public with you, Noelle. I was ashamed of myself." He walked across the office until he stood in front of her. "I'm proud of what you've accomplished, Noelle. And if you ever need me, you call me anytime, morning, noon or night." James leaned forward and gave gentle peck on her cheek before walking out the door and also, as she suspected, out of her life.

This was what she'd wanted, but she never expected it to hurt this bad.

Chapter Twenty-Three

"I'm so glad to see you here, James. I didn't think you'd come. Word is you've been lying low lately. Eleanor greeted him with a kiss on both sides of his cheek.

"It's hard to turn down an invitation for the children's hospital. This is one of the charities I donate to and actually care about. Besides, you're now on the board so I'm also here to support a friend."

Eleanor beamed. "Well, I'm glad you've decided to come. What's with the dark suit? You look like you're dressed for a funeral."

"Actually, I'm heading to one after I leave, so I can't stay long."

"Oh, I'm so sorry. Was it someone close to you?"

"No actually. I'm not going to pay respects. Basically, I'll be laying some demons to rest."

Eleanor raised a brow. "Care to elaborate?"

"I could but we'd be here all day. Besides, I don't want to take the focus away from your event."

"Well if you need to talk about it, you know I'm here for you."

"I appreciate it, Eleanor. But I'd much rather hear about how things are going with the restructuring."

"Oh, you know how it is. Daddy had employed all these stodgy old men who have been with the companies for years.

They don't like taking orders from a woman, nor do they like the idea of me trying to take the business into the twenty-first century. And by the way, I've been meaning to call you so we can set up an appointment to go over some business propositions I thought you'd be interested in." She seemed to thrive in her new role at Harrington's and they were both proud of what she'd accomplished in such a short period. Her company was by no means out of trouble, but James believed Eleanor was full of sound and innovative ideas that would eventually turn the company around for the better.

"No problem. Set something up through my EA and we'll make it happen."

She raised a dark red brow. "So you've finally found a competent assistant?"

James chuckled, taking no offense in her question. "Yes, I finally found someone. Sally is as efficient as they come. As for me lying low, I've been out of the country quite a bit for the last few months. I was in Japan for two weeks and in Australia for a month. From there I went to Germany and then finished up in Brazil. It's a lot of traveling but the distraction has been welcome."

She touched his hand. "And how have you been doing besides working yourself into an early grave?"

"I'm getting by." Four months had passed since his last visit to Noelle's bakery. To keep himself from breaking his promise to Noelle, James had immersed himself into his work, going into the office shortly after dawn and leaving close to midnight. The only time he wasn't working was when he was at the gym or the rare occasions he'd have lunch with Eleanor.

While many of their meet-ups entailed him consulting her on her business ventures, most times they got together simply because they enjoyed each other's company. He could talk to her without feeling judged, she made him laugh and she was easy to be around. James never would have imagined he and Eleanor would turn out to be such good friends.

James had done a lot of soul-searching and reevaluating his life lately. He was thirty-nine and had more money than he'd be able to spend in several lifetimes, but had no one to share it with. He was deeply regretful about how focused he'd been on his quest for the perfect life, he'd had little time to cultivate real friendships. He couldn't count on the business associates and country club acquaintances to be there for him if he ever truly needed help. And he only had himself to blame. Hurt by his past, James refused to let anyone in and now all he had were material things.

Running a large conglomerate and traveling around the world no longer held the glamour he once imagined it did. And at the end of the night when he lied in bed, he was lonely. The thought of taking another mistress was distasteful to him. He'd sold the penthouse, unable to bear the memories of Noelle. James couldn't imagine being with anyone else after experiencing real love.

More and more, he considered taking a page out of his brother's book and walking away from it all. The old man was dead. Sheldon Beaumont Alexander was someone he'd likened to the boogeyman as a child, and someone far worse when he was older. Now that he was gone, James wasn't sure how he felt. The news of Sheldon's death was in the papers, where it was also announced the family would have a small private ceremony, so he was surprised when David had called and invited him. It was the first time he'd heard from his brother since their confrontation four months ago. James didn't read more into the invite than what it really was: a chance to say his last "fuck you" to a man who was hopefully now roasting in Hell.

"Well, I hope you realize there's more to life than work," Eleanor patted him on the arm.

"Says the lady who's been burning the candle on both ends lately."

"Harrington's requires every hour of my devotion I can give it, or else those stodgy old fogies will run it to the ground. Your organization, however, is thriving; therefore it wouldn't hurt if you took a little time off."

"To be frank, I've been thinking about that a lot lately. I may consider going on vacation, a real one with no laptop or cell phone. Just me, the ocean and a strong drink."

"That sounds delightful. But don't just consider it, do it. Oh, there it is. If you'll excuse me for a moment James, it looks like the cupcake tower is here. Since some of the kids will be here for this event, I thought it would be a nice touch. I ordered it from that place that did the art gallery event." Eleanor breezed away without realizing the effect her last words had on him.

Hearing Noelle might possibly be at this event sent his heart racing. He'd vowed to stay away but he wasn't sure how he'd react if he came face to face with her again.

Suddenly, needing air, James headed outside. All he could think of was Noelle. She might be here and he couldn't trust himself not to do something foolish around her. Once outside, he leaned against the wall and took a deep breath. Just the mere thought of her sent his body into overdrive. He remembered the last time they were together, how beautiful she'd looked, her scent and her taste. His cock stirred and his arms ached to hold her within them again.

When James felt he'd gotten himself under control, he headed back inside and nearly ran into Noelle. She was heading outside flanked by two teenagers, whom he assumed worked at the bakery. When she spotted him, her steps faltered but she continued walking. For a second, he thought she'd walk past him but instead, she stopped when she was next to him.

"You two can go to the van. I'll be there in a second. And if you turn on the radio, make sure it's not too loud." She handed keys to the closest kid and waited for them to leave before turning to James. "Hi."

She looked incredible. Even with the barest amount of makeup she had the type of fresh-faced beauty that came naturally, which no amount of money could replicate. "How are you, Noelle?"

"I can't complain. Business has been ridiculous lately. I never would have thought the bakery would take off the way it has. How have you been?"

"Existing." He realized it was a vague answer but he didn't know of any other way to put it. Without her, he couldn't really call what he was doing living. But he wouldn't tell her that. It would more than likely cause her embarrassment.

She shuffled from side to side and bit her bottom lip before speaking. "James, um. I'm actually glad I ran into you."

"You are?" He couldn't hide his surprise even if he tried.

"Yeah, I've been thinking a lot lately and I've been so angry with you, holding on to the hurt of that year we had together. I've come to a few realizations and yes, you were a jerk, but I played a big part in that."

"What are you saying, Noelle? How could you possibly be responsible for my asshole behavior? None of it was your fault. And I can apologize to you to a million times but it will never be sufficient for what I did to you."

She shrugged. "But sorry isn't going to change anything. I can accept your apology and move on with my life but it doesn't absolve me of my role in the entire debacle. I went into that whole arrangement thinking I could change you, fooling myself that we could have something more. You see, I…I think I fell in love with you almost immediately, James. And I used that love as an excuse for allowing you to treat me so shabbily."

It was the first time she admitted she was in love with him. James had suspected she had feelings for him when he'd made the biggest mistake of his life and made her his mistress, but he'd ignored them, telling himself she loved his money and lifestyle. He didn't dare ask how she felt about him now because he feared he had killed any good feeling she had left for him. "I'm sor—"

She held up her hand, stopping him mid-sentence. "Don't apologize anymore, James. It's okay, because you see, I forgive you. I have to in order to forgive myself. The very first instance I realized you didn't feel the same for me, I should have walked away. Even when I knew you were seeing someone and was eventually engaged to her, I kept lying to myself."

"That's over Noelle. Eleanor and I are no longer engaged."

She raised her eyebrows and opened her mouth but she remained mute.

"I didn't love her. I couldn't go through with marrying her when I had feelings for someone else. You."

"James…"

"I know it's probably too late Noelle but—"

"James, there you are. I was looking for you." Eleanor walked over to them and touched his arm lightly. To the outside observer, that touch might have appeared like an intimate gesture, but Eleanor was just the touchy-feely type with people she was comfortable with.

Noelle, who had only moments before seemed like she was willing to finally listen to him, visibly shut down. Her mouth clenched and her eyes narrowed as she shot him an accusatory glare.

"Ah, Noelle," Eleanor turned to her. "I'm so glad I got to see you before you ran off. The cupcake tower looks amazing, the children will love it. Why don't you stick around for a while to enjoy the event? I'm sure a lot of people will want to know where we ordered that wonderful display from."

Noelle, whose angry stare was still focused on James, shook her head. "No. I have other deliveries to make. But thank you. I've left some cards by the display in case anyone wants to contact the bakery, although my business partner usually handles all the details."

"Oh, yes, Paul. I talked to him at length. I'm very pleased to see the order is even better than I envisioned it would be. You do excellent work."

Noelle turned to Eleanor. "Thank you. Well, I have to get going. Good luck with your event and glad you liked the cupcake tower." She was about to leave but James couldn't let her go like this, not with her thinking he was a liar.

"Noelle, wait!" He reached out and caught her hand. "Eleanor and I—"

She ripped her hand away from his. "Stop it. Fool me once, shame on you. Fool me twice, shame on me." Noelle practically ran out the building.

"Shit."

"I really messed this one up, didn't I? That's what I get for interfering." Eleanor said, her voice heavy with regret.

James was torn between going after Noelle and finding out what Eleanor meant. He finally turned to Eleanor because he knew Noelle wouldn't be receptive to him. "What do you mean? You didn't do anything wrong by coming over here."

"That's not what I meant. I've really stuck my nose in it. Remember when we were at the gallery?"

"Yes," he answered slowly.

"It was my assistant who suggested I order cupcakes for the kids at this event and the wheels started spinning in my head. Shortly after the gallery event, I learned the woman you couldn't take your eyes off of was the same person who'd done those fantastic cakes at the gallery. So I thought I'd hire her bakery to do the job in hopes of the two of you seeing each other. It's why I stressed how much I wanted you to come today. It was none of my business to interfere, but you've looked so miserable lately and I wanted to help you in some way for all the help you've given me. Call me a hopeless romantic, but please don't be mad at me, James."

James wished she hadn't interfered but Eleanor had meant well, so there was no point in taking out his frustration on her. He sighed. "Don't worry about it. I appreciate your good intentions but I'm beginning to think that ship has sailed."

"Don't say that. I can see you still care for her. If it weren't for my lousy timing, you two would still be talking. I should have let the two of you be."

"It's all right. Look, I really need to get going. I have the funeral."

"James, don't give up on love. Okay? You know about my issues. Because I'm not brave enough to live my truth yet, I let someone really special get away. Don't ever stop fighting if there's even a smidgeon of a chance the two of you can find happiness together."

This was the first time he'd heard Eleanor mention someone else in her life. He'd been so wrapped up in his own misery he didn't notice hers.

"And it's too late for you, Eleanor?"

"Yes. She's moved on and is happy. Me on the other hand, I'm paying my penance. I see a lot of me in you, James. I think that's why we've become fast friends."

"I think at this point, I may have to give her as much space as she needs."

"Hmm, if you think so." She didn't seem satisfied with his answer but thankfully didn't elaborate.

"I'm heading out now but I'll be in touch." He leaned over and gave her a kiss on the cheek.

"Sure."

James believed his pain had dulled, but seeing Noelle again had brought it back in full force.

By the time Noelle returned to the bakery, Donna and Lisa were closing down everything. The shop closed earlier on the weekends and she was grateful for the reprieve. After unloading the van and locking up, Noelle headed to her office, and fell in her chair with a heavy sigh.

Paul stuck his head inside. "How'd it go?"

"On a business level, we did great. Quite a few people asked for a card."

"But…?"

"But James was there. With his fiancée. I talked to him and he told me he was no longer engaged. And then guess who shows up? It was her event actually. Did you know this, Paul?"

"I arranged everything with a Harriet Smith, I'm assuming that must have been her assistant. I might have talked to her once but I honestly didn't make the connection. If I would have known, I wouldn't have taken the job."

Noelle shook her head. "Don't be silly. Business is business. I just wish I would have been better prepared for the confrontation. Actually I'm kind of glad I ran into James. It's reinforced my resolve to stay away from him. He almost had me convinced."

"What do you mean?"

"James was here a few months ago and things got a little out of hand. I didn't tell you or Simone because I didn't want the two of you to judge me."

"Besides the time he came when I was here?"

"Yes."

"I have a confession of my own. I already know."

"How?"

"I overheard the girls talking about a "hottie" going to your office where they heard some moaning and groaning."

Noelle's face grew hot from her embarrassment. When the girls hadn't said anything to her about it, she assumed they might not have known what was going on, but this was confirmation they did. "Oh no," she groaned.

"Don't worry. I had a long conversation with them about spreading gossip in the workplace and I made it abundantly clear their jobs depend on it. But I'm sure you'll be more discreet next time."

"It was just a one-time thing. If you knew about it, why haven't you ever said anything?"

"Because I figured you'd tell me when you were ready. So what happened? I'm sure there's more to the story than just you two bumping uglies."

"He was a mess."

"A mess in what way?"

"He was disheveled. I'd never seen him look like that before. And then he broke down and cried like he lost everything he had in world. It was really awkward at first because I didn't know how to react. But I could tell he was in a lot of pain. So I gave him comfort and that led to more."

Paul raised a brow in apparent disbelief. "Are we talking about James?'

"Yes."

"James Rothschild?"

"Yes."

"James Rothschild, my former boss, billionaire, CEO James Rothschild?"

"Yes! There's only one James we both know. Look, I was just as surprised as you are right now and I was there."

"It just seems so out of character for him. Did he ever say what had upset him?"

"No, we never got that far. That's when Donna and Lisa knocked on the door to see if everything was okay. I haven't seen him again since today."

"I see."

"That's all you have to say, Paul?" Usually her friend was quite outspoken when it came to James. He had never been shy in telling her to cut him off completely so his silence now, baffled her.

"I'm not sure if there's anything I can say. I know he hurt you and I saw how devastated you were over him. I wouldn't wish that pain on my worst enemy, let alone someone I've come to care about as much as you. But you're not over him, are you?"

She wasn't but she was loath to admit it to someone other than herself. "What makes you think that?"

"That was a yes or no question, Noelle. But I guess I have my answer. Maybe the two of you need to have a talk in order for you to move on. You won't be able to close that chapter of your life unless you finish writing it."

That made more sense than she was willing to admit, but seeing James with his fiancée again had opened old wounds. When he'd declared his love for her, a brief second she was ready to admit she still loved him too. Almost. Noelle wasn't sure she had the strength to see him again without shattering the little bit of self-confidence she'd managed to build. She wanted to believe she'd hold firm with him but James Rothschild was the Kryptonite to her Superman.

"You may be right but I don't trust myself around him. What if I do something stupid again?"

"And what if you don't? You'll never know. To be quite honest, I never thought James was a terrible person, I just didn't like how he treated you. I am by no means advocating you give him another chance but you two need to hash out your issues, otherwise you'll be stuck in limbo. You owe it to yourself."

"You're right, but I'm scared I'll make a fool of myself again."

"Don't be so down on yourself, babe. I know you'll do what's best for you."

"Thanks for the vote of confidence, Paul."

"That's what friends are for. You don't have to make any decisions now. Just think about it, okay?"

"Sure."

"Good."

"And now that we have that established, how is it going on the Simone front?"

Paul rolled his eyes. "That cousin of yours is more stubborn than a mule. But I think I'm wearing her down. She doesn't run the other way when she sees me coming at least."

"That's a positive sign. She asks for you sometimes."

Paul perked up, a grin spreading across his handsome face. "Really? What does she ask?"

"Just how you're doing and general questions involving the business."

"That woman is going to be my future wife whether she realizes it or not."

Noelle chuckled, happy to get her mind off her immediate problems. "So I guess that will make us cousins if you succeed."

"Bite your tongue, woman. It's not if I succeed. It's *when* I succeed."

Noelle shook her head at her friend, wishing she had his ability to be sure so of things.

Chapter Twenty-Four

"*For dust thou art, and unto dust thou shalt return.*" The priest threw a handful of dirt on the coffin as he recited several more bible verses. James had stopped paying attention as soon as the casket containing the old bastard was placed on the casket-lowering device.

"If the family will now come forward to pay one last tribute to their loved one," the priest directed.

Gillian sniffed delicately, a single tear slid down her cheek as she placed an armful of roses on the casket. James knew it was all a show because she was heartless. David's mother, Cassandra, placed an equally large floral arrangement on the coffin before returning to her chair. David remained seated, his expression stony and unreadable, although James could imagine what the other man was thinking.

Some people James recognized from the business world placed small tokens on the casket before the groundskeepers assisted the funeral director in lowering the casket into the ground. James was particularly keen on this part of the service. This was the symbolic end of a painful past that had caused him nothing but shame and anger that he'd carried with him until very recently.

David had surprisingly offered him a seat up front with the family, a concession that Cassandra had obviously disapproved of. James, however, had declined and preferred to remain standing in the back. He stood in the same spot when most of the attendees had scattered.

"I still don't see why you had to invite *him*. Your poor grandfather is probably rolling in his grave at this very second knowing you have that...him here." Cassandra said just loud enough for James to hear.

"Grandfather is right there. Why don't you jump in the grave and open the casket to see if he's rolling around. James is family after all. Why shouldn't he be here to pay his respects to dear departed Grandfather?" His brother's voice dripped with sarcasm over those last words.

"Lower your voice. What if someone hears?" Cassandra shushed him.

"You weren't interested in lowering your voice when you wanted to call him a bastard. That's what you were going to say about him, weren't you? But you don't want anyone to know your late husband fathered another child while he was still married to you because that would mean he found you lacking in some way."

Cassandra turned bright red as she stood up abruptly. "Well, David. I don't know what's gotten into you, but I'm heading back to my hotel room. I won't ask you to apologize even though you really should. I'll just mark this down as grief over your grandfather's death."

"You do that, mother. You end up doing what you want to anyway."

"I will not stay here and be talked to like that. Vincenzo, let's go," she barked at her husband who looked young enough to be her son as well. Cassandra marched off with a hapless Vincenzo in tow.

Gillian chose that moment to chime in. "David, was it really necessary for you to talk to your mother like that? It's not like she was wrong. This was a touchy issue for your grandfather. I understand why you did invite James but maybe out of respect for your grandfather—"

David threw his head back and laughed. "That's rich. You actually think I respected that degenerate. Good one, Gillian. And do me a favor. Don't sit here and pretend like you give a damn other than sticking around long enough to hear the reading of the will."

Gillian's face turned bright red. "David, like your mother said, I'll put this down as grief. I suppose I'll give you a little time alone to say your last goodbyes." Gillian stood and walked away, but not before smiling at James in the way she used to that would have him eating out of her hand. When they were younger that smile worked on him, now it left him cold. He nodded abruptly as his only acknowledgement.

With David and him as the only ones at the grave, James moved around to the front and took a seat next to his brother. Neither man talked as they both stared at the tombstone that headed the plot. *Sheldon R. Alexander. Loving Husband, Father, Grandfather and Friend.*

"I'm wondering if that's the same Sheldon Alexander I knew, otherwise the tombstone is lying," James said to break the ice.

David chuckled softly. "If it were up to me, I would have simply put his name and be done with it. And I wouldn't have bothered with a tombstone except I need to know which grave to piss on when I come to visit it again. Mother and Gillian insisted on the inscription, for the sake of appearance."

"Of course. How are you holding up?"

David shrugged. "You'd think I'd be doing back flips. Ding-dong the asshole's dead. But I just feel kind of empty. I feel absolutely nothing, no anger, no sadness, no happiness. I just can't wait to dump all my stocks and just take off. I've got it all planned out. I'm in discussion with my lawyers to liquidate all my assets and serve Gillian with divorce papers. After the will's read, I'm going to travel a bit and try to figure out my life."

"Did Gillian ask for a divorce?"

"She's been frolicking all over the globe with a man older than grandfather. My guess is she's waiting until after the will is read to tell me she wants a divorce but I plan on beating her to it. I'll at least get to salvage the little pride I have left."

"I'm sorry, David."

"Don't be. Finally, I'm going to do something I want to do with my life and I'll have no else to answer to."

"Where do you plan on going?"

"I'll figure it out when I book my flight. Look, uh, James…about what you said before. I'm not sure how this brother thing works. I'm not even sure how to be a good friend, but whenever I'm done traveling, I wouldn't mind maintaining contact."

It wasn't much, but James figured that was all David was willing to concede at the moment. The two of them had been through too much and the acrimonious nature of their relationship had lasted way longer than it should have for them to suddenly to become bosom buddies, so James understood. "Yes, I'd like that." James stood. "You probably want to be alone right now, but I look forward to hearing from you."

David nodded.

James took one last look at the grave where the man who caused so much pain laid in his final resting place. And like David, he felt nothing.

As he headed to his vehicle, he was waylaid by a frantic Gillian. She practically threw herself in his arms. "Oh James, I'm so glad you were able to come. I'll miss Grandfather so much." Those crocodile tears plopped from her eyes.

James looked pointedly at her hands clinging to his suit. "Gillian, you're crying like you actually care." He shook her off of him.

She sniffed. "Why are you being so cold?"

"Only minutes ago you were questioning my appearance here."

"Because I didn't want David to think I still cared for you. He's terribly jealous of you."

"And I wonder why?"

She blinked innocently. "I'm not sure what you're getting at."

"It's like you gave him a reason to be jealous, but I have a feeling David will be just fine."

She frowned. "And since when have the two of you become so chummy?"

"I wouldn't call us that but we've reached an understanding."

"It seems pointless to acknowledge the connection now. He's run the business into the ground and the Alexander name has basically become a laughingstock in our circles. But it's not too late for us, James."

Was she high? He could think of no other reason why she'd be under the delusion he actually still gave a fuck about her. "You're kidding, right?"

"I know you might still be cross with me for choosing David over you, but my parents were pressuring me to marry well. And you know they depended on me to make a good connection. I wish I hadn't chosen convenience over love."

"You do realize your husband is only a few hundred feet away from us."

"He won't be my husband for long. I plan on divorcing him. We can finally be together." She clutched his suit once again.

"Gillian, remove your hands or else I'll forget you're a woman."

She gasped, letting go. "Why are you being so cruel? I refuse to believe your feelings have changed for me."

"That's because you have an ego the size of New York. I just didn't see it then. Do you see your husband over there?" James pointed in David's direction. "You could have made the most out of what you had with him but it wasn't enough for you. I will admit that I did care for you. Once. But not anymore. But, you never loved me. Love means putting the other person first, something you're clearly incapable of."

"That's not true! I did love you. I mean I do love you."

"You loved the idea of fooling around with the boy born on the other side of the sheet but you never had any intention of being with me on a permanent basis, did you?"

"I want to be with you now," she whined. She seemed to do that a lot, a quality he hadn't noticed until now. The longer he talked to her, the more grateful he was he'd got a lucky and escaped from her.

She was a self-centered narcissist, but he could only feel pity for her and mild disgust. "Sometimes, Gillian, we can't have what we want." As he walked away, he found the irony that he'd once had those words said to him. He was determined in that moment that no matter what he would no longer let his yesterday dictate his tomorrow.

Noelle debated contacting James for the next few days but wasn't sure what to do. She waffled back and forth from just letting things be to picking up the phone and calling him. That following Tuesday after her run-in with James, Noelle received a surprise visitor.

She was at the front of the bakery helping with the morning rush, when she spotted a familiar redhead in line. Noelle planned to tell the woman to fuck off if she wanted to warn her off of James. To Noelle's surprise, when it was the redhead's turn, she smiled at Noelle. "Hi. I don't think we were formally introduced at the hospital event. I'm Eleanor."

"Yes," Noelle said not returning the smile.

"Well, I was wondering if I might have a minute of your time."

Noelle gestured to the people in shop. "As you can see, we're a little busy right now."

"I can wait. In the meantime, I'd like one of your key lime cupcakes."

Without taking her eyes off the elegantly dressed redhead, Noelle retrieved the cupcake from its case and placed in it on a disposable plate. "That will be two-fifty."

"Do you take cards?"

"Sure." Noelle took the card and swiped it on the register.

Once the transaction was complete, Eleanor smiled at her again. "I'll just have a seat at one of these tables and wait for you if you don't mind."

Noelle shrugged. "Suit yourself. I need to take care of all my customers first."

"No worries. I have some time to kill." And that's exactly what she did. As Noelle helped the customers, Eleanor sat at one of the tables nibbling her cupcake.

Once the shop cleared out, Noelle reluctantly joined her at the table. "Look, if you're here to warn me off of James, you're wasting your time. There's nothing between us."

Eleanor raised one finely arched brow. "I see." She took another bite from her cupcake.

Noelle grew impatient. "Look, as you can see, things can get a little hectic around here, so please, just say your peace and leave."

Eleanor put her cupcake down. "This is delicious by the way. Of course, I'll probably have to run an extra two miles on the treadmill and take an extra Pilates class to burn this off."

Noelle barely stopped herself from rolling her eyes but she didn't respond.

"Noelle, we don't know each other but I came here about James."

"I figured."

"I believe you've got the wrong impression about us. James and I are just friends. He's helped me through a really difficult time and I don't think I'll ever be able to repay him for what he's done."

"What about your engagement?" Noelle asked cautiously.

"We called it off. We don't love each other. Honestly, we were only engaged as a matter of convenience."

This news shouldn't have mattered but it did. She stubbornly dug in her heels, however. "I'm not sure why you're telling me this. James and I are nothing to each other."

"I'm telling you because James still loves you and what's more, I think you still love him too."

Noelle was rendered speechless for a few moments before she found her voice. "Is that what he told you, that he still loved me?"

"It wasn't something he volunteered at first but I managed to get it out of him. Besides, I was there at the art gallery and saw the way he looked at you. I put two and two together. So I kind of interfered a bit."

"By coming here?"

"That and hiring you to provide the cupcake tower at my event this past Saturday. I was kind of hoping you and James would run into each other but it didn't quite work out the way I expected. You saw me and assumed James and I were still together. We haven't been for months. Every now and then he escorts me to some events and he's been helping me save my family business, but there's nothing between us beyond that."

The cynic in Noelle wouldn't allow her to let her guard down just yet. "And you're telling me this all out of the kindness of your heart?"

"I see you still don't believe me."

"Eleanor, I'm sure you mean well but telling me this won't make much difference."

Eleanor's smile faltered. "Why not? I saw the way you looked at him, too. You still have feelings for him. Why don't you go to him?"

"Because it's too late. And there's a lot that's happened between us that you're not aware of. I'm not sure how James was with you but he wasn't always nice."

"I won't presume to know what happened, but I can tell when two people care about each other and you two obviously still do. Please talk to him. If the two of you can't work something out, at least you'll be able to move on with your life, and so can he."

Paul had basically told her the same thing. This had to be some kind of sign. Maybe it was time she and James had a talk.

Noelle blew out a long breath. "This is something I'll need to think about."

"I understand." She gathered her purse. "Thank you for sitting with me Noelle. I need to get back to my office, but it was really nice finally talking to you."

"Likewise." Noelle stood up with her.

"Hopefully, we'll see more of each other soon."

Long after the shop was closed Noelle still remained in the bakery, telling herself she wanted to work on some new recipes, but she couldn't get the conversation with Eleanor out of her mind. Finally, she gave up pretending to work and searched through her desk. After rooting around a few drawers, she retrieved the card James had given her months ago.

She studied the number before picking up the phone and dialing the number.

"Mr. Rothschild's phone, Stella speaking, how may I assist you?"

Noelle almost hung up, quickly losing nerve. "Uh, may I speak to him please?"

"May I tell him who's calling?"

"Noelle."

"One moment please." The woman was back in less than a minute. "I'm putting you through to him now."

"Hello?" James asked with uncertainty. "Noelle?"

Chapter Twenty-Five

James couldn't make it out of his office fast enough. After a long day, the last thing he'd expected was a call from Noelle. When he was informed the person calling his personal line was Noelle, he thought he'd misheard his secretary at first. He was pretty sure it was his imagination until he actually answered the phone and heard her voice. Noelle wanted to meet him in one hour and suggested the deli that they'd gone to on the night they had met.

He eagerly agreed and wasted no time shutting down his computer and rushing to his destination. He made it to the deli within a half hour of her call and waited anxiously for her to arrive. James wasn't sure why she wanted to see him, but he was just happy to see her in any capacity.

James eyed his watch impatiently and shifted in his seat several times as he waited for Noelle to arrive. Relief assailed him when she walked into the deli. She wore a pair of jeans and a t-shirt that displayed the logo of her bakery. It was apparent that she'd just left work. Her tight curls clung to her head like a halo, and her eyes were large and luminous.

As she approached, she neither smiled nor frowned, keeping her expression neutral. She slid into the seat across from him. "Hi, James. Thanks for meeting me on such short notice." Her voice was hesitant.

"When I said I was just a call away if you needed me, I meant it. I'm glad to see you again." He balled his fists in his lap to keep himself from reaching across the booth and touching her. "So what can I help you with?"

She cleared her throat as she broke eye contact with him. She twiddled her thumbs in a nervous gesture. "Actually, it's how we can help each other."

"I'm not sure if I follow."

"I think it's time for us to have the talk we should have had a long time ago. I started telling you at the hospital but I guess I kind of made a fool of myself jumping to conclusions like that."

"If I had been in your shoes, I probably would have made the same mistake. But I swear, Eleanor is just a friend."

"Apparently a good one. She came to the bakery and spoke on your behalf."

He groaned out loud. The last impression he wanted to give to Noelle was that he needed someone else to fight his battles. "Believe it or not I didn't send her."

"I know. She made it quite clear you didn't. She's nice. She probably would have made you a good wife."

"She would have made me a great wife, actually. But there's just one problem. She's not you."

Noelle's eyes widened. "James…"

"It's true, Noelle. The problem is I only wish I'd had the courage to tell you when I had the chance instead of hurting you the way I did."

She bit her bottom lip and looked away again. "I'm not really sure what to say to that. Last year, it would have been everything to hear you say that to me but I'm not the same person I was. I like who I've become and I don't want to go back but it's important for me to tell you why I was the way I was, that is if you have the time to listen."

"For you, I have all the time in the world."

A slight smile tilted her luscious lips; he so badly wanted to kiss them. James managed to get his body under control so that he could listen to what she had to say.

The silence between them lengthened as Noelle fidgeted in her seat. He imagined she was trying to find the right words to say. Finally, she began. "I'm still a work in progress, but when I look back on myself from when we were in the middle of our arrangement, and way before then, I can see how pathetic I was."

He wouldn't stand for anyone talking bad about her, not even Noelle herself. "Noelle, you were far from pathetic. I saw a sweet, gentle woman who was probably a little unsure of herself but you had a warmth about you that a guy like me wants to bask in. As I got to know you better, I found you to be compassionate and genuine, a rare commodity these days, it seems."

"That's nice of you to say, James."

"It's the truth. Sorry for the interruption but I needed to get that out in the open."

"Thanks. I'm not really sure where to start, and I don't want to bore you with all the details that are probably better left in the past, but when we first met my self-esteem was fragile. I was so starved for love, I latched on to the first person who made me feel…wanted." She broke off. "I'm not doing a good job of explaining myself." She laughed nervously.

James threw caution to the wind and reached across the table and captured her hand in his. He saw it as a positive sign when she didn't pull her hand away. "You're doing a fine job so far." He rubbed the back of her hand with his thumb, unable to resist the temptation.

"I wasn't always like this in case you wondered. When my mom was alive, she always managed to make me feel loved and special. I'm not sure if it was because my father died before I was born and she tried extra hard, but whatever reason, I always knew my mom loved me. But then she died. That's who Paul and I named the bakery after, by the way. Her name was Dorothy Bea but most people called her Dot. You would have liked her. There wasn't a person my mom couldn't charm." A smile flitted across Noelle's lips.

"If she was anything like you, I'm sure I would have."

Noelle lowered her eyelids, hiding her thoughts from him. "As you can imagine, it was devastating for me to lose her. One day we were making cupcakes in the kitchen and the next day she was gone. She was my best friend and I still miss her so much."

James could feel her sorrow. He felt the same way when his grandfather had died, his one and only champion. "It was like no one else would ever love you the way that person did, right?"

"Yes. How did you know?"

"We're not as different as you think, but go ahead. Tell me more about your mom."

Noelle smile seeming to find joy in her mother's memory. "She was such a beautiful person inside and out. She was really smart and always had something nice to say. We'd do a lot of fun stuff together, like going to the beach or the library or the park. My favorite moments though were on Sundays, when we'd bake. She'd create the most amazing things. Most of the recipes I use now came from her.

"So when she died, her death shattered me. I was hustled off to live with an aunt I barely knew. She was my mom's older sister. Mom never mentioned Aunt Frieda much except to say they didn't always see eye to eye. I remember the first thing my aunt said to me on the day I went to live with her. She said, she was only doing her Christian duty and hopefully, I don't turn out to be a heathen like my mother."

James wished she was exaggerating but he knew firsthand how vicious people could be. "That's pretty awful."

Noelle shrugged. "That's not the worst thing she's ever said to me. My aunt lived with her husband, Sylvester, who was quite a bit older than her, and her two sons from her second marriage, and Simone from her first."

"So Sylvester was her third husband?"

"According to Simone, Sylvester was her fifth and they're still together. Sylvester is a pastor and I think my aunt likes the allure of being the First Lady of a church. She put on a front as being a holy Christian woman, but to me and Simone she was horrible. Not a day went by when she didn't she call me a burden, useless, stupid, or ugly. It didn't help that my cousins, Derrick and Damon, took their cue from her, tormenting me at home and at school. They were popular so they basically turned the entire student body turned against me. I had no friends. After hearing how worthless I was over and over again, I started accepting it." Noelle sounded sad as she relayed her story to him. James wanted to track her aunt down and wring her neck.

How could anyone say such things to a child, and call themselves a Christian, no less. He was never big on religion but he understood the basic Judeo-Christian principles. Noelle's aunt didn't sound like a true follower of her faith.

"She was wrong, Noelle."

"I didn't know that then. I just took her word as gospel. I doubt I would have survived living there had it not been for Simone. But when she left I used art as my escape, but Aunt Frieda tried to destroy that too. I once had a notebook full of drawings but Aunt Frieda found them in my room and tossed it into the fireplace. She told me it was garbage and I guess that's why I had a hard time believing in my own talent. It crushed me and made me hopeless.

"But the mental games and verbal abuse weren't as bad as the things she'd say about my mother. She'd used to say to things about Mom to get under my skin and it worked. I never knew why she hated me so much."

"Do you think the bad blood between her and your mom spilled over to you?"

"I think so. It wasn't until very recently I realized Aunt Frieda was jealous of my mother. My mom was resourceful. She put herself through school, took care of me and never relied on anyone for help. My mom had it together and people liked her. And Aunt Frieda resented her for it."

The more he heard about Noelle's aunt, the more his disgust grew. "Do you think she took you in solely for the purpose of tormenting you in a warped way to get back at your mother?"

"That could be part of it, but the main reason was the money. My mom was struck by a drunk driver, but she could have survived her wound. She died from malpractice. The hospital made a significant settlement in my mom's name which was put in a trust for me. Only a guardian would be able to draw funds from it for my care until I turned eighteen. My aunt knew this but she never used any of that money on me. My clothes were hand-me-downs from the church's donation bin and I was rarely allowed any extras unless my aunt felt like showing off her benevolence to her church friends. She spent most of that money on herself and her sons."

James flinched as he listened to Noelle's tale of torment. "How could that woman live with herself?"

Noelle laughed without humor. "She seemed to do it quite well, actually. The icing on the cake is, when I was seventeen she pushed me into a relationship with one of the church deacons. She told me I'd have to marry him because I wouldn't do better for myself since I was too stupid to be on my own. I didn't even like Walter but I felt I had no choice. He made my skin crawl, not to mention he was a disgusting pervert. But I was so programmed I believed he was all I deserved." She looked down as if she was ashamed of herself. In James's opinion, the only person who should be ashamed was her aunt.

"Thank goodness Simone came for me when I turned eighteen. She helped me get control of my trust. Simone wanted me to live with her but I didn't want to be a burden, so I lived on my own for a couple of years, working a dead end job. But it was a small town and I ran into my aunt more than a few times. Let's just say they weren't pleasant encounters. Finally Simone convinced me to move away and live with her. Living with Simone was different. She was supportive and loving and she encouraged me to apply to art school. To my surprise I made it in, but I was so damaged from living with my aunt, I lacked the confidence to finish. I felt like such a loser no matter how much Simone tried to prop me up. And that's where you came in. You were this handsome, self-assured man, and I was awestruck by you. I couldn't believe someone like you would want me, but your good looks and charm weren't the real reasons I fell for you."

She stopped, finally pulling her hand away as she began to fidget again.

"Why Noelle?"

"I felt this connection between us because you were broken, too. You hide it well but it takes a person who's suffered to notice it in someone else. I took it as a sign that we were meant to be. But we were disastrous together because we were both damaged goods, and we acted out to mask that pain we silently suffered. You felt the need to treat me the way you did and I let you because I didn't know any better. I thought I had to suffer for our love and that you'd eventually change. But you didn't and I finally realized you wouldn't…not until you admitted you were damaged, too."

A damp trail traced his cheek before James realized, several tears had fallen. Her story broke his heart. He ached for the little girl who felt unloved and the woman she'd become who was so desperate for that love that she took anything given to her. The fact that he played a role in it added to his guilt. He'd never doubted Noelle's intelligence but her insight surprised him nonetheless.

James had told himself that he no longer cared about the people that hurt him for so long that he'd began to believe the lie.

Noelle slid out of the booth and joined him on his side. She wiped the tears from his face. "If you want to let go of whatever it is you're holding on to, you can, but if you're not ready, that's okay too. Whoever hurt you or made you the way you are or were, it wasn't your fault. It was them," she said softly. She was so close if he leaned over just a little more, their lips would touch. He suddenly noticed a few other patrons at the deli were staring at them. He wasn't used to making himself vulnerable and wasn't comfortable enough to give anyone a show. But he did owe it to Noelle to tell her his side of things.

"Do you mind if we get out of here? Go for a drive? I promise I'll talk in the car."

"I drove the van here."

"It's okay, I can drop you off."

"Okay."

Chapter Twenty-Six

Noelle felt like a weight had been lifted off her shoulders after telling James about her past. It was cathartic in the way that for the first time she acknowledged how her aunt, cousins, the school bullies, and Walter had treated her wasn't her fault. Letting go of that was a freeing experience and she hoped it would do the same for James.

Noelle could no longer lie to herself anymore. She still loved him. That didn't necessarily mean the two of them would end up together and have the happy ending that was in the movies, but at least this night would set them both on a path of much needed healing.

As they rode in silence, Noelle took that time to reflect. Occasionally, she'd wipe away a tear, feeling relieved that she'd finally been able to talk about her past. Not even Simone had known the full depths of Noelle's pain. She felt as if she could really breathe again.

When James pulled his car up to a large gate surrounding a mansion, he gave a verbal command to his vehicle's dashboard computer and the gate opened.

"Is this your house?"

"Do you mind? I promise I won't try anything. I thought we'd get more privacy here. And this may be my only chance to show you my home. I should have done this a long time ago."

"James..."

"I know. This will change nothing."

She didn't disagree with him and instead focused on the huge structure in front of her.

"You live in this house all by yourself?"

"I have a live in housekeeper but she's off for the next couple weeks to handle a family emergency."

"It's huge. It must have a lot of amenities."

"This house has a home theater, a gym and a bowling alley. I'll give you the tour if you'd like."

"That's okay. If you have your own private gym, why do you have a gym membership?"

"I use my home gym when I wake up in the morning and since the gym membership is a perk for all the executives at my company, I usually go there when I get off work."

"That makes sense."

They fell silent again as he pulled into a garage. He led her through a side door. "Wow, this place is nice." It was something right out of *Dynasty*. And she thought her penthouse was pretty fancy. She was aware of his wealth but it still amazed her that people actually lived like this. "It's pretty big for one person."

"Yes, but I'd always intended to marry and start a family."

"The average family can do quite well with a house one-tenth of this size. Not that I'm knocking it. It's a beautiful home."

"It's not a home; this place is just somewhere to rest my head. It's really just a status symbol that appealed to my ego at the time I bought it."

"You make it sound so bad. You have the money to purchase it. It's not like you're living beyond your means."

"I guess, but I'm just telling you this place doesn't really hold much meaning for me. Can I get you something to drink?"

"What? No butler to take care of that?" she teased him.

He smiled but shook his head. "I'm not home enough to appreciate a butler and I never really figured out what their purpose was. How about that drink?"

"No thanks." He led her to a sitting room that was elegantly decorated.

She chose a seat on the edge of a leather arm chair, and James took the seat at the end of the couch catty-cornered from her. Their knees almost touched and she quickly repositioned herself. The man affected her in ways she couldn't control. She was just here to talk. "So," she prompted him to start as he continued to stare at her with that impenetrable gaze.

"I'm sorry. I can't help staring because you're so beautiful." It had only been recently when Noelle was able to view herself as an attractive woman, but it was still difficult to take a compliment at face value. When James said it, however, she knew he meant it. She could feel it.

"You're stalling."

"Sorry," James said again with a grin. "But I'm sure you understand how difficult it is opening up about a difficult past."

"Of course."

"My childhood wasn't pretty either. My mother was a drug addict and I didn't know who my father was until I was nine."

Noelle gasped. "Oh, James, I'm sorry."

"It's not as bad as you think. She was more neglectful than abusive, even though she had her moments. I had her father, my Grandpa Lou. Like your mother, my grandfather was my best friend. He took care of me and looked out for me. He was my hero."

"He must have been very special."

"He was. But he worked a job that involved hard, back-breaking labor which eventually debilitated him. He was wheelchair bound after an accident on the job, probably when I was around eight. At that point, the line was kind of blurred on who was taking care of whom. My mom would disappear for weeks, sometimes months at a time, mostly on drug binges or because she found some new man to fund her habit. But getting back to when I learned who my father was, I learned his name was Stephen Alexander of AlCore. I'm not sure if you've heard of it but it was a pretty big deal. They were industrial suppliers. The Alexanders had money, status and the whole nine yards. I found out about Stephen at his funeral."

"That's awful, James."

"I couldn't feel something for a man I'd never met but I was always curious about him, of course. What kid wouldn't wonder about his father? My mother would mention him from time to time but it was never kind words. So one day she takes me to a funeral and tells me that man is in the casket is my father. It's the day I meet Sheldon Alexander, excuse me but I refuse to call that evil son of a bitch my grandfather. Anyway, there was no denying I was an Alexander, I looked just like a younger version of Stephen. Anyway, when Sheldon and I first met, he looked at me and called me a bastard."

"That's so cruel. You were just a child."

"I guess in his opinion, it was never too early to put his inferiors in their place. I would later learn when I got a little older that my grandfather had been the Alexanders' gardener and that's how my mother and father had met. My father was already married and his wife fell pregnant around the same time my mother did. From my understanding, she was told to abort me and when she didn't my grandfather lost his job. My mother wasn't the maternal type so I can only assume she thought she'd get a steady stream of funds if she kept me. But it didn't quite turn out that way for her. I think my father may have given her money from time to time but Sheldon controlled the purse strings in that family. He also made sure my grandfather wouldn't find decent work around town. He had to resort to taking menial jobs, under-the-table jobs, until he hurt himself. And even though we struggled, my grandfather made it seem like we were the richest family in the world. I never considered us poor until I attended the Goodwell Academy. That's a private academy for the children of the very wealthy. Turns out after my father died, he'd left money for my education to go the academy he'd attended as a boy. That's when I realized we weren't rich at all. Not only weren't we wealthy, I was a nobody. From the time I attended that school, I was made aware that my shoes weren't designer-made. I didn't have a two thousand dollar back pack and I couldn't afford to go on the expensive field trips. And David, my half-brother who also attended the school, led the charge."

Noelle raised her brows in surprise. "The David you'd told me about before was your brother?"

"Yes. I suppose tormenting me was his way of distancing himself from me. I got the nickname 'Welfare' because the other kids saw me as a charity case. There wasn't a day that didn't go by when I wasn't taunted or beat up in the adolescent years. The headmaster looked the other way because he was essentially an employee of these kids' parents. Once I hit my growth spurt and learned to defend myself, the physical bullying ceased but the social torment continued. I tried to fit in by excelling in class and joining sports teams, and though I did well, the kids still talked about my drug addict mother and called me white trash, most of the time when they knew I was within hearing distance. They'd pretend they didn't mean for me to hear it but I knew that wasn't the case."

Noelle closed her eyes as she listened to his story. Hearing how badly he'd been tormented in school brought back some of the meaner pranks the kids had pulled on her. The one she remembered most vividly was when she'd worn a pair of light-colored pants to school. One of the girls who happened to be dating her cousin, Derrick, had poured some chocolate pudding on a seat, knowing Noelle would inadvertently sit in it. The kids laughed at her and said she crapped her pants. It was a joke to them but she'd cried herself to sleep that night. It saddened her to know James had suffered a similar torment among his peers. "I'm so sorry, James."

"Thanks, but I'm not telling you this to gain sympathy, it's just how things were. Despite all that, I still tried to fit in and get those people to like me and they never did, but one day I got partnered with Gillian Jamison in chemistry. She was probably one of the more popular girls in school. She was gorgeous and sweet, or at least I believed she was. And the best part was, she liked me too. She didn't care about my background. I fell head over heels. We dated most of our senior year. She made school bearable. I thought things were looking up but they took a turn for the worst. My mom, who had been missing for almost a year, was found dead in an alley from an apparent overdose. The kids were ruthless. I didn't really love her as much as a son should but she was still my mother. We didn't have much money to bury her but my grandfather borrowed against his whole life policy to give her a proper burial. I think the only reason her death affected me was because it was so hard on Grandpa Lou. To shorten this already long story, one of David's cronies kept pushing my buttons until I snapped. I beat the shit out of him and broke his nose. I was expelled with only had a semester to go."

"Didn't they understand the other guy started it?" Noelle asked, outraged at the injustice.

James smirked. "You forget, I was a nobody and this kid's family was old money. I was actually quite lucky not to end up in jail. I'd had a scholarship lined up at Yale but I lost it because of my expulsion. I had to take the test for my GED instead of getting that prestigious Goodwell diploma. It broke my grandfather's heart because I know he was looking forward to seeing me walk across that stage."

"That's terrible."

He grimaced. "It actually worked out the way it was supposed to. My grandfather became really ill with an aggressive form of cancer. The cost of treatment alone exceeded his Medicare coverage and while I'd picked up a few jobs to help us make ends meet it wasn't enough. Now mind you, I'd never asked the Alexanders for anything but for my grandfather, I was willing to swallow my pride. So I made an appointment with Sheldon. I was actually kind of surprised that he agreed to see me. I found it odd that he wanted the meeting to be at one of the apartments he kept and not at his office. I didn't think too much of it because I was focused on asking for financial help for Grandpa Lou."

James gulped and his hand began to shake.

"Do you need a moment?" Noelle asked softly.

"No, I have to get this out or I never will." He hesitated for a few more seconds before continuing. "I made it clear to Sheldon I'd pay back every penny and then...he told me nothing in life was free. Before I knew what he meant, he grabbed me by the neck and slammed me against the wall. I was surprised at first because I didn't expect it. He took my arm and twisted it behind my back until I thought it would snap. He was so strong and the more I struggled the tighter he held on. Next thing I know he bent me over a table and he's calling me these names, vile names, variations of what my school tormenters called me but more sexual. But I'm not even sure if it was about the sex or more about humiliating me. He wanted to show me he had the power and I was nothing. He said as much to me."

"He raped you?" Noelle whispered in shock. What kind of person would do something like this to his own flesh and blood?

"He didn't penetrate me if that's what you're asking but it wasn't from lack of trying. He almost did. I still have nightmares about his cold hands on my body and his old shriveled dick on my back. I fought harder than I ever had and broke away from him. I got out of there as quick as I could but not before belting him in the face. And as I ran, I hear him chuckling because he knows my grandfather will die without the care he needed. I also think he laughed because at the end of the day he knew there was nothing I could do about it. A few months later Grandpa Lou died. On the night I sat in the hospital with him, as he took his last breath, Gillian called me to break up. She ended up with my brother subsequently. I think when I buried my grandfather a part of me died. That's when I set my goal to never beg. I wouldn't beg acceptance, I'd demand, I'd have the best of everything: money, power, women, and the perfect trophy wife."

"Everything was going according to plan and then I met you and I was confronted with that boy I was and it angered me because I didn't want to feel that helpless again. You made me feel vulnerable, and I fought and raged against it. I was nasty to you because I didn't want to be weak for anyone. But the truth is, I was already weak because I wasn't really in charge of life like I believed I was. I used my past as an excuse for becoming a dick. And, truth be told, all the material things I thought would make me happy don't mean much to me. And now that Sheldon is gone, I hope he's roasting for what he's done, to all the people he tormented, but it doesn't change anything. There comes a point in a person's life when they have to stop blaming other people for their life choices and start taking responsibility for themselves. I'm halfway there I think, but like you said earlier, healing takes time."

There was so much pain and heartache in his story she couldn't imagine how he felt. Though she didn't excuse his treatment of her, she now had a different perspective. She reached out and touched his knee.

He placed his hand over hers and their eyes met.

"Noelle….no matter what happens between us, I'll always love you."

"I love you, too, James."

"What happens now?" he asked tentatively.

"We heal."

Epilogue

"James, you're messing up my kitchen. What the hell are you doing?" Noelle exclaimed after seeing the various dishes and ingredients laying everywhere.

He grinned when he looked up from what he was doing. "I'm making dinner for, my lady."

Noelle shook her head as she walked into room and gave him a quick peck on the lips. "You're going to make me regret giving you the keys to my house. I'm grateful for you taking the initiative to paint and work on all the little projects that need to be done around the place, but I draw the line at you messing up my kitchen. You know how anal I am about it."

"Well, I was hoping I'd have the meal ready and the kitchen cleaned before you got home. Speaking of which, what are you doing home so early? I thought it was your turn to close the bakery today."

"Paul's taking care of it. I wanted to come home and take a long soak. I've been in the bakery since five this morning."

"Why don't you go ahead and take that bath and by the time you're finished, everything will be ready."

"I'm kind of scared to see what you've whipped up considering your culinary experience is limited to grilled cheese sandwiches, frozen dinners and peanut butter and jelly."

He flinched in mock pain. "I'm hurt you have little faith in me but I forgive you. Go ahead and have your bath."

Noelle was reluctant to leave him alone in the kitchen to wreak more havoc, but a warm bubble bath was calling her. She gave him one more quick peck on the cheek before heading upstairs to her room. Noelle drew a bath for herself and poured in a capful of scented bubble mix.

She let out a long sigh as she sunk into the bubbles in her bathtub. In her bathroom. In her house. She'd bought her three-bedroom colonial for a steal. It needed some work but she was looking forward to fixing it up. She was a homeowner and every time she walked through the door, she felt a sense of pride. This past year had bought many changes. The bakery was doing so well, Noelle and Paul decided to hire a few more people to do the bulk of the baking and handling non-specialty cake orders, while Noelle focused on what they labeled the designer cakes. She was in charge of training and teaching new techniques. She still helped out where it was needed and came up with new recipes to introduce. Noelle and Paul were thinking of expanding their operation to open a second location and decided to take a cautious approach. Instead of opening a new store, they decided to find a bigger space and make one side a bakery and the other side a café. If business continued to do well, in a couple years they intended to open that second bakery.

Paul was so much more than a business partner to her but a close friend and confidant. Though it was clear to her he still had a crush on Simone, he had recently started dating. Noelle was sure if her cousin gave him even the slightest indication she was interested in him, he'd drop anyone he was dating for her. As for Simone, Noelle worried about her cousin. Her boutique was doing well but it had become her life. Noelle could see the signs that something was going on with her cousin, but Simone would shut down whenever Noelle inquired if anything was the matter. Noelle hoped in time Simone would open up to her.

After admitting they still loved each other, Noelle and James decided they needed to start over again and get to know each other as friends while they both sought the professional help they needed to better fight their demons. In the beginning, they hung out platonically, deciding to leave the sex out of the relationship as they got to know each other. It was an unofficial trial to see how compatible they actually were. Their time together changed how Noelle felt about James. Her love grew deeper. It was no longer a love she felt for a man she believed him to be but a love for the man he actually was. James was considerate, made time for her, complimented her frequently, listened when she had a tough day at the bakery and found ways to make her smile. He let his guard down, was open and had no problem telling her how he felt. Finally after a few months, they decided to make things official, although they decided to go slow.

The year had been amazing. Therapy had taught her how to love herself, her business was successful and she was especially proud to be a first time homeowner. She and James did discuss her moving in with him but she liked the idea of living on her own for a while. It filled her with a sense of accomplishment. James spent most nights at her place anyway. She'd even made room in her closet for his things. She was truly grateful to have James, not because he completed her life but because he enhanced it.

Noelle didn't realize she'd dozed off in the tub until James entered the bathroom with a glass of wine in hand.

"Sweetheart, you have to be careful not to fall asleep in the tub."

Noelle sat up and took the glass of wine he handed to her. "I didn't realize I was so tired." She took a sip. "Mmm, you spoil me."

"You deserve to be pampered. You're a queen."

"Aww, you're so sweet, James."

"No, you are." He leaned over and brushed his lips against hers. Her nipples puckered and her pussy tingled. The man drove her wild.

"Hmm, anymore of that and I think I might join you in the tub. Besides, dinner will get cold."

She raised a brow. "Since when did you care about the temperature of dinner? As a matter of fact the last time I cooked for you, we never got around to eating."

"Oh I ate plenty."

She giggled. "I'm not talking about my pussy you perv."

"I didn't hear you complain. Okay, enough chit chat, let me help you out of the tub." He took her glass of wine and set it aside before lifting her out of the tub. When he placed her gently on her feet, James grabbed a towel, took a seat on the toilet and pulled her between his legs. Slowly he began to towel her dry, letting his fingers slip over her bare skin as he went about his task. His thumb grazed each nipple and he gently cupped her buttocks and gave them a gentle squeeze. By the time he finished, her body was dry but her pussy was completely wet. Her body practically vibrated with need.

James then grabbed a bottle of her scented lotion from the sink and slowly rubbed it into her body. He took his time massaging the liquid into her skin. "James, you're doing this on purpose," she groaned.

"I'm just taking care of you, baby."

"If you really wanted to take care of me, you wouldn't tease me this way."

Her knees were weak and she didn't think she'd be able to stand any longer. As though sensing her need, James stood up and lifted her on to the sink and then sank down in front of her until he was eye level to her pussy. He spread her knees apart. He grinned. "I guess I can make room for an appetizer." He pushed his middle finger between her slick folds and slid it into her hot core.

Noelle threw her head back and moaned in ecstasy. Every time the man touched her, her body went up in flames. No matter how many times they made love, touched or kissed, it was magic. She spread herself wider, silently signaling him to taste her. James needed no further encouragement. He leaned forward and flicked her clit with the tip of his tongue. He added another finger into her pussy as he latched on to her sensitive bud and sucked in earnest.

She dug her fingers through his hair and held his head close, mashing her pussy against his face. "Oh James, that feels so good."

James gently bit her clit sending her over the edge to her climax, but even as she convulsed and shook from her orgasm, he continued to lick the juices from her pussy and inner thighs. More than anything, Noelle wanted his cock.

"Make love to me, James."

He gave her pussy one last lick before pulling away from her. That's dessert. Remember, dinner's waiting."

"You can't be serious. You can't leave me here like this. I need you, baby." She reached out for him but he backed away from her.

"Later sweetheart. Get dressed and I'll meet you downstairs in ten minutes." She wanted to protest but he was already on his feet and heading out the bathroom.

Noelle was still pouting by the time she joined him. "That was so mean James," she took a seat across the table from him.

"I promise I'll make it up to you sweetheart. Why don't you eat dinner? If it's not as warm as you like, I can heat it up for you."

Noelle noticed for the first time that James had set the table with the nice table setting she reserved for when she had company. He also used her good china. On her plate was a large juicy-looking steak, roasted potatoes and string beans. "Wow, James. This all looks great. This is the nicest meal you've ever cooked for me. What's the occasion?"

He smiled. "Does there have to be an occasion? Sometimes we should do things just because."

"Well this is very nice. And I appreciate you cooking dinner for me, but I'm still mad at you for teasing me like that."

"Hopefully, by the end of the night you'll forgive me."

"I'll think about," she grumbled as she cut into her steak.

The conversation remained light as they finished their meals. They each shared how their day went and told each other funny anecdotes. Once she was finished with dinner, Noelle pushed her plate away. "That was delicious. Thank you for dinner, honey."

"How about dessert now?"

"I couldn't eat another bite."

"How about another glass of wine?"

Noelle giggled. "You don't have to get me drunk. I'm an easy date."

"I insist."

There was something in his tone that made her hesitate for a second. "Uh, okay."

"I'll be right back."

She wondered why he was being so secretive all of a sudden but didn't have time to dwell on it long because he was quick to return but instead of two glasses of wine, he had champagne in hand.

"Wow, you're being really fancy tonight. What are we celebrating?"

He handed her a glass. "Us." He took a seat and held out his glass for a toast. "You've made me very happy, Noelle, and I just wanted to let you know how much I love you."

Her heart swelled with love for him. "I love you too, James."

"To us."

"To us." They clinked their glasses together and she brought the glass to her lips. She took a generous gulp until she felt something hard against her lips. She looked into the glass and gasped. She looked at him for confirmation. "James?"

He made his way to her side and dropped to one knee as he took the glass from her hand. He slipped his fingers into her glass and retrieved a diamond engagement ring. "I know we said we'd wait a while before we took this step, but I don't want to go another day without making a pledge to love and cherish you for the rest of your life. I vow to do everything in my power to make you happy."

Tears welled in her eyes. She nodded eagerly, accepting his proposal. When she thought of all they'd been through; the pain, the tears, the heartache, and finally the healing, the love and the laughter, Noelle knew there was no one she'd rather spend the rest of her life with than James.

They would have the rest of their lives together, loving and giving each other whatever they wanted.

About the Author

USA Today Bestselling Author Eve has always enjoyed creating characters and stories from an early age. As a child she was always getting into mischief, so when she lost her television privileges (which was often), writing was her outlet. Her stories have gotten quite a bit spicier since then! When she's not writing or spending time with her family, Eve is reading, baking, traveling or kicking butt in 80's trivia. She loves hearing from her readers. She can be contacted through her website at: www.evevaughn.com.

More Books From Eve Vaughn:

Finding Divine

The Kyriakis Curse:
Book One of the Kyriakis Series

GianMarco:
Book One of the Blood Brothers Series

Niccolo:
Book Two of the Blood Brothers Series

Romeo:
Book Three of the Blood Brothers Series

Jagger:
Book Four of the Blood Brothers Series